THE KITTY PARTY MURDER

THE KITTY PARTY MURDER

KIRAN MANRAL

HarperCollins *Publishers* India

First published by HarperCollins *Publishers* in 2020
A-75, Sector 57, Noida, Uttar Pradesh 201301, India
www.harpercollins.co.in

2 4 6 8 10 9 7 5 3 1

P-ISBN: 978-93-9032-762-1
E-ISBN: 978-93-9032-763-8

Typeset in 11/13.7 Minion Pro at
Manipal Technologies Limited, Manipal

Printed and bound at
Thomson Press (India) Ltd

MIX
Paper
FSC FSC™ C010615

This book is produced from independently certified FSC™ paper to ensure responsible forest management.

To Krish.
May you find your dreams as I found mine.
May they all come true.
And someday, I hope you will forgive me for all the times I've shooed you off because I was working.

1

In Which Life Is Measured Out in Spoonfuls of Sugar

THURSDAY

Monsoon is not the greatest time to have a hectic social life in a city like Mumbai. For one, you have to pack away all your good shoes, you dare not risk them getting soggy, and muck-encrusted. Which leaves you with the only option of – horrified gasp – wearing rainy shoes or galoshes. Or gumboots if you please. You do get such adorable gumboots these days. But the problem is getting into a restaurant or a coffee shop with your feet in these gumboots, and no chance of showing off your lovely pearlescent pinked toes, and the fantastic pedicure you got the other day. I tell you, the monsoon is a vile season. The vilest of vile. The kind of vile that has you pack away all your good footwear and clothes, even though the maximum you could get them wet is while running to where the car is parked on the off-chance that the spouse is driving, and ergo won't be convinced to bring the car right up to where you are.

And then there is the hair. It flops. Its refuses to be springy and bouncy and act like well-behaved hair should, no matter what volumizing shampoo and conditioner you switch to or which fancy many-fingered attachment you use on your hair dryer. I have often been reduced to scraping all my hair back into a small bun at the nape of my neck, flattening out the strays with serum, just to look human. I combine this with a slash of crimson lipstick and smoky eyes and kid myself I look Mediterranean.

Hello, Im Kanan. Or Kay, as my friends call me. I'm thirty-five, almost thirty-six, but don't tell anyone that. I prefer staying thirty-five. It is a decent age to be at when anything over thirty is considered fodder for the graveyard – or the stuff those chappies dig out from rocks, dust off and place in museums. What are they called? Fossils, yes.

Also, I'm married to my college sweetheart. He will be referred to as the spouse in the rest of this work. Then there's our offspring, aka 'the brat', also known in school and on official papers as Kabir Mehra. Or as he would like to be known, as Kabir Khan, or Kabir Kapoor. Or occasionally Bruce Kapoor. Depending on whether he has just watched *Batman* or *The Incredible Hulk* for the zillionth time. Bruce is a cool name for cool dudes in his lexicon. Bruce Banner. Bruce Wayne. Bruce Weber. He should have been a Bruce, he's told me often enough. I suspect as he grows he might try to get his name changed legally to Bruce. Bruce Mehra. I've even caught him trying out the new, improved name on his rough notebooks to get a feel of it.

He is a child who knows what he will do when he grows up and the Hindi film industry should gird its loins and ready itself for such talent, good looks and dancing skills about to hit it twenty-odd years from now. Already, he knows when he goes on stage for performances organized by his school and his Bollywood class that he needs to position himself right up front, in full view of the audience, never mind if he has to do some hectic fist-fighting in the green room before the show to get his chosen position. It speaks volumes of his passion to excel in show business, and who am I to discourage burgeoning ambition?

So here I was, sitting in my living room, stuck indoors thanks to the torrents of rain washing the entire cityscape stretched out before me in a slate greyness, while dipping pakoras into a mug of steaming adrak-waali chai and feeling all is well with the world as the sun shone out of my not-quite-reticent behind. Metaphorically speaking, of course.

Ah yes, dipping pakoras into chai was not exactly the prescribed way of chucking them fried missiles of diabolical calories from the devil into one's system, but it was how I had eaten pakoras ever since I was a child, despite the mater's protestations about the residual oil rendering my beverage undrinkable.

Thankfully, I had no such qualms and could glug the oily tea down with zero hesitation. I could almost see the oil molecules charging through my intestine and zapping into my bloodstream, from where they rushed helter-skelter into nooks and crevices, settle down and put up paintings on the wall before applying for ration cards, Aadhar cards and electricity connection for proof of residence.

You get my drift. Illegal squatting of such calories in my once-smooth-as-a-gazelle limbs had made the surface of my thighs resemble the kind of road one takes through the hinterlands. Some day I would get down to reclaiming my gazelle limbs, but till then I called myself 'statuesque'. I could ignore the accusing glances thrown my way when I attempted to squeeze myself into an almost packed elevator only to have the overfull alarm begin beeping wildly.

The child, the light of my life and the apple of my eye, and the tenor in my yell, bounded up to me, having just returned from school a couple of minutes ago and been shag dried in manner of large dog by means of very absorbent towel. 'Mamma!' He ran up and hugged me, and I was quick to place the cup of tea at a spot where it couldn't be overturned by a misdirected limb. Becoming a mother sharpens your reflexes to levels that could bag you a role in one of the Matrix movies. I should have known there was a request coming.

'Can I eat oney smileys fer lunch?'

This being his lunchtime – and him being the spawn of two individuals who lived on what scientists and dieticians decry as food unhealthy enough to fell woolly mammoths and other such gargantuan creatures – he needed unhealthy, deep-fried food like he needed air. I, being paranoid mamma of the first order, tried hard to rein this in. There were enough articles in them newspapers blazing terrifying headlines about childhood obesity leading to adult obesity, which could strike you dead from a heart attack just from the shock of reading them.

'Four smileys,' I bargained, 'and some dal-chawal.'

'Six smileys an two chikkin sosages,' the brat counter-offered. 'An wen I finis I'm going to watch *Doraemon*,' he stated in a tone that brooked no argument.

Like all good mothers, I caved in and retreated, tail tucked between my legs. When the UN peace negotiators failed to do their bit to negotiate for world peace between warring nations, I could send him in on deputation to do the needful. Provided, of course, that he was paid in smileys and chicken sausages.

I deduced he was getting both protein and carbohydrates in a single meal, along with fat which was direly needed on his frame –which was so skinny that elderly relatives meeting us after a while would stare at me in an evil, accusatory manner, suspecting me of wolfing down the child's food quota, leaving him to subsist on crumbs, while I expanded so terribly that the weighing scale quivered when I approached.

I even threw in ketchup and hoped the tomatoes in it would count as yet another food group of processed phytochemicals, and suchlike, and that all these put together would constitute a balanced diet, and therefore let me off the hook from the good Lord above who was probably keeping a little diary noting down all the instances when I slacked off, and caved in to the temptation of convenience foods and zero argument.

In repentance, I returned a pakora, en route to my lips, to the plate it had travelled from. 'Jamuna,' I called out to my girl Friday cum live-in help cum grim voice of conscience on all things dietary. My voice was tremulous in the way it becomes when I have to force myself to resist all temptation, especially of the deep-fried variety. 'Bas. Take these back to the kitchen, and hide them somewhere I can't see them. And even if I beg and plead for them, be firm and don't waver and bring them back. Better still, eat them all up before I change my mind. I will not have dinner tonight.'

She looked back at me placidly. 'Should I keep the Nutella bottle and the bread up front in the refrigerator for when you come into the kitchen in the middle of the night?' I shot her a glance that could turn any mortal to stone, but she stayed firm, her skin having adapted to being perfectly gorgon-proof. You get my point.

'That's all for now, Jamuna,' I felt compelled to say, just to get her back to the kitchen. She stomped off, popping an errant pakora into her mouth.

I put my head down in my hands and marinated in self-loathing for a bit. I resolved to walk an extra hour every day the next week.

I could already see the effect of such surreptitious gluttony on her – she who had been a skinny wraith when she entered my service was now bursting at the seams, literally and figuratively, the picture of good health and youth, but unfortunately not beauty.

Jamuna is not a beauty. When the list of women who have been blessed with a visage strong enough to scare off intruders at night is made, Jamuna will top the list. She has the kind of face that defines square and bovine simultaneously. What the good Lord held back in terms of appearance, he scattered generously on her in terms of a pleasant temperament and a complete lack of slothfulness. Jamuna was the kind of maid I had been gifted thanks to some good karma I had earned in my previous life, and I guarded her fiercely from the seductive poaching overtures made by other residents in the complex by plying her with cosmetics, fairness creams and salwar suits with embroidery down the yoke. That was also why I overlooked the inexplicable disappearance of cookies from a jar that had been filled a day previous to my reaching out for it, keeping in mind that the resident pint-size could not hope to reach it even with the help of a chair and vaulting ambition.

The monsoons were a dreary affair in Mumbai. The rains poured down with a smarmy sense of self-importance, knowing that the residents of this city would probably be down on their knees and thanking the rain gods, given that the authorities had been threatening them with horrific water cuts. Some places in the city were already getting water for only one measly hour at unearthly hours like 1.00 a.m., when sane people would be in bed, asleep and doing the kind of things unmentionable in a book which is meant for U-rated audiences. It terrified me, the prospect of spending the wee hours of the morning getting up to fill water in every available receptacle rather than catching up on my beauty sleep. A week of that and I could get a walk-on part in the next Resident Evil movie as one of the undead. No audition required.

The monsoon sky in Mumbai was a slate grey of uniformed despondency that made one want to sit under the bright halogen lights of a sunbed to feel one's spirits lift as one's skin prunes itself to carcinogenic levels. The sunbed was a largely alien concept to us, although my aunt by marriage who lived in Sweden swore by the beneficial effects of ensconcing herself within it and frying her skin (Caucasian white) to a leathery brown once every few weeks.

The child was seated placidly on his table and chair and was busy in his two-handed wolfing down of the fried food I secretly coveted. He looked up at me and accurately read the hunger in my expression.

'Mamma,' he said, 'yu wan one?' holding out a smiley generously. I had a generous child. At his age, and with this spread before me, I would have gathered my fodder to myself and squealed murder had anyone suggested I share. Abashed, I shook my head furiously and went into the bedroom to pull on my sneakers. I was wearing my exercise clothes that I hadn't exercised in all day: a pair of trackpants with the obligatory white stripe down the side, and a T-shirt that was slim-fit enough to give slim-fits a bad name, given that I was neither in the slim nor the fit. I would pound the stairs today, I decided, if it was the last thing I did. They could put a wreath of white lilies on my corpse and put out an ad saying, 'She died on her feet, size six.'

The stairway in our complex, thankfully, did not open out on to the doors of every flat, and was secluded behind a door that allowed you to stop for a while, breathe deep, pull in your gut and start the long, winding trek up. The stairway is where the refuge area access is located every eight floors and midway between two floors, we have the servant bathrooms. No one ever takes the stairs. Ever. It also means that if you were struck by a heart attack midway between the tenth and the eleventh floors, no one would hear you scream, and the cleaning staff would discover your stiffened body the next morning. I'd had my stint with discovering corpses on deserted roads a few months ago, and trust me, it was not an experience I would wish upon anyone else. For one, it is heave inducing. For another, the police eventually swarm around and ask you a zillion questions in a manner that makes you want to confess all your sins, including eating all of the offspring's chocolate stash and telling him they went bad. Coming back to the stairway, the deserted bit of it suited me just fine. I didn't want any witnesses to me going purple in the face, and bending over in agony when the effort became too much.

I was likely to huff and puff more heavily than the big bad wolf by the time I reached floor three. Climbing up to floor twenty was going to be an achievement I would need to tom-tom about by posting status updates on Facebook and Twitter and suchlike. I clicked the mandatory selfie and Instagrammed the beginning of my stairway workouts for the day. I hashtagged it to death.

My fingers were more buffed and worked out than the rest of my body, given how many updates I posted across social media about my intent to work out. I would do anything except go to a gym. I have a gym membership, annual and for a couple, at discounted rate, which is utilized only by the spouse who lifts all the weights and works out at the elliptical on alternate days from his squash sessions so his biceps are now of the variant that cause grown women to swoon when flexed. Not that he did. Not in my presence at least. He was better behaved than that. He merely wore fitted T-shirts so they could swoon around him in synchronized formation and part, sighing, like the Red Sea as commanded by Moses as he walked past. It was terribly unfair, I declared, for him to be super buff while I draped myself in tents, kidding myself that they camouflaged the avoirdupois in the manner avoirdupois was meant to be camouflaged.

Working out at a gym was the stuff of nightmares for me, nightmares so terrible that when I did, I would wake in the middle of the night, sweating in panic that my Dri-FITS had split at the back and my old, unravelling underwear was on full public display. It was the terror of sharing a mirrored wall with a room populated by glamazons wearing clothes so clingy, they would need a surgical procedure to get them off their bodies.

Then the need to make oneself as inconspicuous as possible in a remote corner of the gym – where one could do one's weights or freehand exercises or whatever one needed to do to get the fat dissolving – without being acutely conscious. Not drawing attention to oneself was the key in a gym populated by TV-actor types, who checked angles and best sides while they bench-pressed. And there was the added ignominy of fencing off them supercilious glances of them super-fit ones, who did not know that sag could sometimes become a permanent state of being for breasts after a year-long course of being milch cow to spawn of the womb, given that bottle feeds were verboten with new-age paediatricians.

I hated gyms. If I could be a member of a gym where it was guaranteed that only similar-sized and cellulite-afflicted individuals would congregate to shed their fat, I would be the first person to sign up; after all, misery loves company. We would all drape ourselves across the handles of the treadmills and elliptical trainers and discuss ways to cheat on our diet, while chomping on the chocolate doughnuts dusted with sugar we need to get our sugar levels back to normal after all that hectic exercising of our tongues.

Anyway. There I was climbing valiantly up the stairs, feeling the thigh muscles contract and release and thus push the cellulite sitting happily on their sides to get up and get going, when I heard a sudden loud scream. A rather startling scream. The kind of scream that, when heard in horror movies, is promptly followed by the onscreen presence of a vile, supernatural force intent on extracting entrails from whichever unlucky human happens to be in the immediate periphery and ingesting them, for starters. I jumped out of my skin. If that were technically possible. I jumped anyway. True to form, I then knocked my shin in the most violent manner against the landing of the next stairway which made me yowl in a most unpleasant and unladylike manner, more in the category of cats serenading their partners over knocked-over bins in the middle of the night. Silence greeted my yowling. The screaming had stopped.

Where had it come from, I wondered. And in the manner of the typical dumb blonde in horror films who sets out to investigate said source of screams, I retraced my footsteps. Then it came again. And again. The hair on my arms stood on end, which reminded me, a trip for defoliation was overdue.

I so should go laser off the entire surplus foliage on the body, rather than this piecemeal business of the monthly waxing.

I was between the seventh and eighth floors and knew almost all the residents of the four flats on each floor of the building. I sprang out of the doorway ready and alert to offer my assistance in any way possible. But I had no clue where the screams had emanated from. I waited a while on floor seven but saw no hectic activity from any flat. I then retraced my steps up to the stairs to the eighth floor, where I accosted a solitary maid waiting impatiently for the lift. I bore down on her like a press reporter chasing an FIR in the making. '*Kahan se aayee woh cheekh?*' I asked.

She looked at me, blank-eyed, and edged away suspiciously. '*Kaunsi cheekh? Maine to kuch nahi suna,* madam!'

Surely I could not be hearing voices. Surely someone would know the source of the awful screams. Despite my misgivings, of which there were many, I rang the doorbell to old Mrs Kapur's home, which promptly set off a series of intensely threatening yappings from her Pomeranian Silky, who was obviously elated at the prospect of new ankles to nip at. I could hear the shuffling of tired feet as Mrs Kapur lumbered up to the door and put a questioning eye to the keyhole. All the chains and bolts were undone slowly, and the door opened wide and welcoming.

'*Arey, Kanan beta,* what a pleasant surprise, *kaise aana hua? Aao aao.*'

She was beaming too grandly for me to not step inside, and so I did. We are a very hospitable race of people. The height of rudeness is to have folks standing on your doorstep and not invite them in. I thanked the Lord for the thick material of the trackpants I had on which was effectively resisting all of Silky's attempts to access my ankle bone for gnawing-off purposes. 'Err …' I looked down at said furball dancing around my ankles, letting out intermittent yips of frustration. 'Could you please …'

'Siiilllkyyy!' yelled a voice from within one of the bedrooms. It was stentorian enough to get the infernal canine off my legs and bounding into the room, tail tucked obediently between hind legs. Mr Kapur was at home on this rainy day. A retired civil servant, he spent most of his day normally out on official-looking work, which involved a hard-shell briefcase which I was sure contained an assortment of weapons and their parts. Mrs Kapur insisted it was a consultancy for cooperative housing societies that he ran, being well versed in administration, but the whole thing sounded rather mysterious.

'Actually,' I began, 'I was climbing up the stairs …'

'*Arey* kya *hua,* stairs *se kyun aayi*? The lift wasn't working? I tell you, these lift-maintenance contractors are really the pits. I've been yelling at every AGM that we need to replace them, but you think anyone would listen to me?'

'No, no, I was climbing them for exercise.' She cast a censorial eye over my slim-fit and nodded approvingly at the mention of exercise. 'Anyway,' I interrupted hastily before the flow of conversation could take a completely different direction, 'I heard a loud scream while I was on the stairs, now. It was a woman's voice …'

Mrs Kapur looked surprised, but then she looked surprised most of the time given that her eyebrows had been plucked to such levels.

'I didn't hear anything,' she said, shaking her head in aforementioned perennially surprised manner.

That surprised me. Maybe I was hearing things after all. Maybe the cook had unknowingly mixed in some ground bhang in the chutney I'd downed with the pakoras and I was hallucinating. The maid on the seventh floor hadn't heard anything either. It was just me hearing strange screams. I was already done with the 'I see dead people' part of the deal. Some months ago, I'd imagined I'd seen the ghost of the dear departed Sheetal Jaiswal, but that's another story for another book. Any more dead people and ghostly encounters, and the spouse would just have me hauled straitjacketed into the place where they put away the cuckoo folk so the regular folk can go about being regular.

I smiled and murmured vague things about maybe having misheard, and that perhaps it was an echo of someone yelling at their recalcitrant kid to buckle up on some godforsaken task – which the kid was dawdling over, as kids are wont to do – and gently began backing out of the house. Silky growled mutedly from the bedroom where she could no doubt sniff the aphrodisiacal scent of my deodorant and was being held back from taking action on my perceived escape. I could picture her straining at the leash. I wondered if she was a changeling dog, a dog who should have been given the body of an attack dog and had been, by some cruel quirk of fate, mercilessly shoved into the body of an unintimidating white-furred Pomeranian.

'How can you go without having anything to eat or drink?' said Mrs Kapur, moving with an alarming swiftness to physically block my escape and erase this perceived blot on her hostess skills. I looked around, in mounting alarm, for a gracious way to dodge her, without actually needing to do a mini audition for a player role in the Kabaddi Premier League. 'You must have some tea! Some biscuits! Shall I make some pakoras?' I shuddered at the thought of pakoras. I had barely just escaped them, and here they were confronting me again. What is a woman to do with temptation but to give in?

I gave up the unequal battle. In the manner of all the ladies from the land of the five rivers, Mrs Kapur was a sturdy, tall creature and it would take skills beyond my ken to escape from her when she was determined to make me stay. Putting her hands on my shoulders in the kind of friendly manner that thugs in the Bronx must use when they spy a stranger in the parts, she steered me adeptly to a sofa chair and plonked me down. Her maid came in with an instantness that was truly terrifying, bearing a tray with two cups of tea and an assortment of biscuits and cookies, which were just calling out my name at subsonic decibel levels audible only to my ears.

Chocolate-chip cookies. I could see the chunks of chocolate embedded in the cookies, and though mass produced, the chocolate was still capable of doing vile things to my state of mind, and viler things to the state of my thighs. I desisted. I moved back. I made apologetic sounds about how I had to leave immediately, having left some pot on the stove, which would have boiled over by now. Mrs Kapur firmly brushed aside my protestations with the air of a woman who has presided over many luncheons and tea parties.

'I really mustn't!' I protested in vain, as Mrs Kapur sat poised with the spoon to ladle sugar into my tea. 'One spoon or two? Or Sugar Free – you must be having Sugar Free, no. *Beta* …' she yelled in the general direction of the kitchen, '*zara woh* Sugar Free *ki dibiya le aana.*'

'Sugar will do, thank you,' I said, and had the cup handed to me with one spoon of sugar, stirred briskly. I had no choice but to accept it graciously, sip delicately, and settle back for a few minutes of casual conversation, which took off from the maintenance and upkeep of the staircase area – which was according to common consensus, a couple of days away from being a vertical municipal waste dump, with alien life forms growing out of the detritus – and gained momentum with the character assassination of a lady from the next wing, who was Mrs Kapur's marked enemy on the premises, given that both had Pomeranians of similar shape and size. The two dogs competed in the cute-dog stakes amongst the pint-sizes playing in the park.

All thoughts of further exercise having been scrapped unceremoniously, I downed the tea in unladylike haste, took my leave with much exchange of arbitrary pleasantries and made my way towards my floor, via the lift, all pretence of exercising being dropped now that I was down by two chocolate-chip cookies. I found the offspring scootying down the passageway in typical six-year-old manner, in that he didn't see fit to negotiate corners and dead ends in any way other than by crashing into them with impact levels that rattled the unwary onlooker's teeth.

I dodged narrowly out of the way, escaping with life and limbs intact, while he crashed into the wall chortling. 'I frightened yu!' he claimed with much glee, delighting in seeing me quivering from limb to limb.

I could just see him at eighteen, driver's licence freshly glinting in his wallet, behind the wheel of the car scraping past unsuspecting pedestrians with his hair blowing in the wind and a police car in hot pursuit. And I was going to be the mom signing on the jail bond, and berating him in a fishmonger-like harangue about the lack of responsibility and how he had shamed us parents and how we were washing our hands off him, ad infinitum ad nauseam, to which of course, he would be unresponsive like any self-respecting young person, who post-adolescence decides that parents are to be ignored except when money is to be demanded for his fruitless pursuit of hedonism.

Right now, though, I plucked him off his three-wheeling inferno from Dante's Hell and frogmarched him right back into the house.

The heavens were still pouring outside and the skies were supernaturally dark. Some jagged streaks of lightning cut through the air in the distance and landed on spots far towards the beach, and some, as far as the eye could see, landed over open sea. This was the perfect kind of weather, if one was so inclined, to decide to camp out in a haunted house and spend some pleasant time with spooks and ghouls. I, of course, had no such inclination. Ever. I was terrified of anything remotely paranormal.

I sat down on the sofa, my limbs leaden with extra tea and lack of adequate exercise. The child draped himself limply over furniture, disgusted with the lack of playing options on such a day. 'I is very bored. Eveything is boreding. What I'll do now?'

It was a very valid question. One that I should have, in the ideal-parenting magazine, answered with an enthusiastic, 'Let Us Play the Spelling Game' or 'Let Us Do Fingerpainting'. Or let us make this 3D jigsaw with a million pieces, most of which will end up behind the sofa cushions and in the plant holders. In truth though, I was most uninspired to be that kind of a parent right now.

I looked at him and sighed. And pulled him onto my lap. 'Let us watch television together,' I replied in the exact manner parenting experts tell you not to. And we slipped into a television-induced haze of somnolence, induced by flickering images of cartoons, switching between reality shows and music channels, from whence we rose, bleary-eyed, only to greet the surly spouse and pater when he entered the premises dripping more rain onto the carpet than was necessary and cursing the traffic in language which had me clamp my palms around the child's ears.

We gulped down a hurried dinner and took ourselves to sweet sleep, to the hiss of the wind battering our windows and the steady pattering of rain down on the balconies. Through the howling wind, I thought I heard some screaming riding on the air, and drifted off into a deep sleep where I dreamt of being locked within a stairway, without an exit, and where ear-piercing screams kept echoing. I woke up in a cold sweat, with the sudden uneasy premonition that something terrible was going to happen right here in this building. On the stairway.

2

Of Domestic Violence Shattering the Peace of the Gossips

FRIDAY

The alarm ringing the next morning laid forth the bleak prospect of it being another dull rainy day as I peeled open my reluctant eyelids. I pulled the covers back over my head, and let the sound of the grey pitter-patter wash over me. The spouse opened one questioning eye and wondered why I was not up and about and getting dressed, to go forth and carpe the cellulite.

'I'd like to sleep for one hour without your snoring drilling my eardrums,' he muttered, trying unsuccessfully to muffle his voice under the covers. When they indict me for murder, my defence attorneys might get me out on a plea of temporary insanity brought about by unsolicited snarky comments about my snoring and cellulite.

I, unfortunately, had no immediate retort to this so I let it pass this once, just muttering that it was too rainy to go running and he was doomed to have me drill his eardrums. The right retort would come to me, even if it took a few weeks, and then would I let him have it. I snored volubly for an additional hour, rising and shining just moments before I was due to get my hands dirty in the morning routine of supervising lunch and tiffin boxes and suchlike. The child was sprawled like a starfish across his bed. In a recent and very upsetting development, he had weaned himself off the parental bed and decided he would henceforth only sleep in his bed, ghosties under the bed notwithstanding. While inwardly I lauded him for his courage, a small part of me was very offended that he was growing up without me having given him express permission to do so.

I went into his room and snuggled up to him. I missed his baby smell and his baby snores next to me every night. He turned his body towards me and held me tight. I let him, for five minutes, until he just had to get up or miss his school bus.

'Get up Kabir,' I said lovingly, and kissed his cheeks and forehead. Not a microsecond of a pause in the snoring and breathing pattern. I tickled him a bit, and for a few seconds, he squirmed uncomfortably and chortled, swatting my hands with his eyes closed.

'Lemme sleep, lemme sleep,' he squeaked between bouts of laughter. The spouse walked into the room and unceremoniously doused the child with half a bottle of water. The child sat up and gasped for breath, looking like a newly hatched duckling. He sputtered angrily and, in the way of six-year-olds, made said sputtering look cute.

The glass of milk was at his bedside and his uniform was ironed and placed at the foot of the bed with his shoes on the floor in front. He was hauled to the bathroom to be tooth-brushed and bathed with much squawking of vociferous protestation, which would have done a striking worker being frogmarched off to jail by the police proud.

The intercom buzzed just as I grabbed the child by the hand and was about to take him down to the gate to have him clamber onto the bus, greeting assorted friends and adversaries with whoops of delight or punches as appropriate, dependent on current levels of friendship, best friendship or enmity.

'Hello?' I answered, handing over charge of the child to Jamuna, gesticulating wildly at her to take him down to the gate. 'Raincoat *pehnao*, raincoat *pehnao*,' I yelled at them, as they both ignored me, true to form. The boy promptly shrugged off his bag from his back and handed it to her in true manner of sloth he had undoubtedly got in genetic inheritance from his mother. I gestured frantically to her that he was to bear his own bag, at which he ran off into the lift leaving Jamuna scrambling behind him to get into the next lift that stopped on our floor.

'Did you hear …' It was Raji, bearing news. And Raji bearing news at 7.30 a.m. in the morning on the intercom without the usual ping on WhatsApp could only mean it was news of such tremendous importance that it couldn't even be put on defer till the husbands had been fed breakfast and shovelled out of the house with mandatory peck on the cheek. 'What?' I breathed, scared to even begin hazarding a guess as to what it could possibly be. Death, divorce, suicide, or – gasp – her husband leaving her for that pretty young thing in his office he seemed to be a trifle too fond of. Thankfully, it was none of the above.

'The lady from the fifth floor, the one in 504? The one who always wears those huge salwar-kameezes, in those loud colours with the floral prints?' Her voice dropped a notch from the descriptive to the scathing. 'In synthetics, with the maroon lipstick and nail polish?' I got the image, vividly. The mind's eye virulently demanded soothing eye drops.

'Yes, yes,' I hissed. 'Whatever happened to her?'

Raji is not one to beat around the bush. She gets to the point. Directly. I dreaded meeting her in clothes that had seen better days, because she would open the conversation by telling me I needed to convert them into kitchen rags. She would even offer a handy pair of scissors to do the needful, if I showed a smidgen of hesitation. That is to say nothing of what she has said about the hair on my head when I've missed a protein treatment or two – she had once stated that even a starving horse might refuse it, had it been offered as fodder.

'Her neighbour says she was probably being beaten up last evening at around 6 p.m. There were screams, and sometime later she was running down the road in her nightgown with her husband chasing after her. And this morning, she came into the building, the watchman tells me, with a bandage around her head and her husband helping her walk. In the *same* nightgown.'

We could go *HAWWWW*! over the being seen in the same nightgown in public twice a bit later.

But this was domestic violence we had on our hands. On the premises!

I had heard screams the previous evening, at approximately the same time as mentioned. And yes, they could have been the screams of someone being beaten up. My blood froze in my veins, arteries and other internal organs. The kind of cold freeze that in the normal course of events occurs when you are stuck in the tundras with the sledge dogs deserting you, and the winter chill causing your digits to freeze and fall off, and making you die of hypothermia unless of course, this was an eighties' Bollywood film, and you would have the 'hero' thaw you out with body heat, which would involve the meeting of Mr Sperm with Miss Egg, followed by a song with 100 background dancers performing callisthenics. Or if it was a producer on a tight budget, two flowers being jammed up against each other in implied orgasmic coitus.

Coming back to screams, when I had heard them last evening, I'd confused myself by imagining they had come from up higher, when in fact, they had come from a couple of floors lower. I had been on the stairway at 6 p.m. It could have been her. She could have been calling for help and I had been right there, and hadn't responded. I needed to find a spoonful of water and jump right in and drown myself with the shame.

'I heard a scream,' I said, thinking aloud. 'Raji, you know I heard a scream at around that time, I went up to find out. I went to Mrs Kapur's and ended up having tea ...'

She snorted. 'Poor you. How are the ankles?' Silky's predilection for nipping unwary exposed ankles was well known and folks gave her and her belligerent owner a wide berth especially in enclosed spaces like elevators, with some wary 'once bitten twice shy' folk being known to cantilever themselves over the handrails in record time. The monthly society meetings were a battleground for frayed tempers, with Silky being the moot question in the debate around separate lifts for dogs and domestic servants which had yet to be resolved.

'No, thankfully, I had one of those thick trackpants on, you know the ones that were 50 per cent off last week, remember, I picked them up, the black with the pink waistband and the hoodie jacket with flowers ...' She squeaked to indicate she had placed it and proceeded to tell me all about how she had picked the twin version in the purple. We planned to alert each other the next time we went running together, in the event we ended up looking like a girl band on the loose. A few moments later, we came back to reality and dogs that needed to be kept under lock and key.

'That dog,' she said, her tone indicating she had an unpleasant memory to share, 'once ripped to shreds a pair of linen trousers I'd just picked up the previous day from Cottonworld. It's a public menace.' A pleasant moment of silence elapsed where we both paid our respects to the dear departed linen trousers and fantasized about how this yapping menace to ankles could be herded into the dog van and sent off to the pound. 'Anyway,' she continued, 'we think we should go visit, just to check on her and express neighbourly sympathy and such. Are you in?'

'Of course,' I replied. I could never resist being on scene at a controversy and getting first-hand information. 'Do we need to take anyone else?' I asked, always ready to make an entire Broadway production out of anything that could be done perfectly well with just a couple of people.

Thankfully, Raji was both older and wiser, though we chose to ignore the 'older' most times, even when she was diagnosed as perimenopausal by her gynae after bouts of extreme sweating when we assumed she was heart-attacking and would make an attractive corpse. She swiftly dismissed the idea. 'Of course not, you ninny,' she said not so politely. 'Why do you think I called and didn't even put it on the group.' (The Group being the WhatsApp group of the ladies living in the complex – a thriving hotbed of allegiances, enmities and tasteless forwards, and the graveyard of awful political jokes – was the Matrix that controlled the inner workings of the activities of the complex.)

We agreed upon a mutually convenient time we would assemble on the floor concerned and take ourselves to see the afflicted woman.

I ended the conversation to find the spouse, bathed, dressed and freshly perfumed, standing in front of me, scowling and pawing the ground, little puffs of smoke emitting from his nostrils. Breakfast had not yet been served, and the clock had clicked past departure-for-office time. I scampered into the kitchen to scoop up the brekkers made into a convenient plate and deposited it on the dining table. Have I ever mentioned that the spouse is an easy-going man, only when fed appropriately from time to time? But the 'time to time' is the key here. If the food items are delayed by even a nanosecond when hunger strikes, the spouse will channel the bull from his birth sign and start snorting.

Occasionally he bellows, and when he does we all run for cover. He paws at the ground too. Thus far, he hasn't reached levels where he has actually gored anyone to a bloody death, but I came close one fine day when he had parked himself at the dinner table and I was oblivious to all need to get the dinner served, being engrossed in an absolutely delicious discussion about the sudden changed appearance of the lady from the eighth floor, post what was supposed to be a vacation but seemed to be one which combined a visit to a plastic surgeon for what seemed like new, firmer and bigger breasts. Let's just say the plaster fell from the ceiling for a good couple of days after that outburst.

The spouse ate in grumpy silence as I sat across from him and contemplated his visage. A perma-line had creased itself into his handsome forehead and his eyes seemed constantly narrowed in thought. 'You need to take a holiday,' I declared grandly. He continued to jab into his phone, with the earnest concentration of someone who would cause the world markets to collapse if he took his eyes off the screen.

'Did you hear me?' I asked, with the involuntary increase in volume that happens when spouses don't register what one is saying.

He looked at me, his full spoon poised mid-flight, en route to his mouth. 'What? Why? We just went on holiday.'

'That wasn't a holiday, that was a chaos of trying to pack in sightseeing and shopping between flights. You need a holiday. One of those where you chill on the beach and bake beneath the sun and drink all the beer you want, and eat all the fish you want, and then come back to take on the city and its stress with a vengeance.'

I noticed a thunderstorm darkening his face. The man used to have a sense of humour and a funny bone. Unfortunately, the years and the stress that comes from a mistaken notion that global business would come to a complete halt should he not show up at the office had completely buried the funny bone, and an entire force of starving pack hounds wouldn't be able to dig it up if they tried.

'Don't you know that this is an extremely busy time for me?' The spouse was perennially on busy time. It made him feel good, though. If he wasn't busy he would have nothing to scowl about. He scowled even when watching TV, busily. He even made his non-busy time busy – weekends were packed with a spreadsheet detailing the minutiae of how he planned to spend it.

I directed the conversation gently to the hot topic of the suspected domestic-violence case on the fifth floor yesterday.

'You know the lady from the fifth floor?' Which in retrospect was a stupid question because there were multiple ladies living on the fifth floor.

'Why would I know any lady from the fifth floor, Kay?' he replied, his hand movements uninterrupted as he ferried fork from plate to mouth in smooth movements, pausing occasionally to sip his juice – orange, calcium, iron and Vitamin D fortified, with real pulp, if you must know.

I kicked myself on the mental ankle and continued bravely, while the frown on the spousal forehead deepened, 'The lady from 504, who refused to move from the front of the lift panel the other day to let us press eighteen? The one who was really huge and with the really dark panda eyes and the shiny red salwar-kameez with the yellow flowers and the double mangalsutras and the chipped nail polish?'

Recognition dawned bright and clear in the man's eyes and mingled with a look that could only be explained as unmitigated horror. 'What about her?' he asked with the clear conscience of a man who knows that nothing accusatory could be hurled at him regarding said woman from the fifth floor, who stood valiantly in front of the lift panel.

'Her husband beat her up …'

He raised an eyebrow.

'Horrible, isn't it?' I continued bravely. 'He beat her up.' I repeated for added emphasis given the lack of more appropriate horrified reaction.

'Oh, that's terrible,' the spouse replied, shovelling more of the calorific stuff into his mouth, and going back for seconds. 'I hope she wasn't hurt.' He looked down into his beeping phone and began scrolling through the messages that demanded urgent responses, not doing which would risk upsetting the turtle that held the earth up on its back.

'We are going to visit her today.' I looked firm because I anticipated the coming dissuasion. You do not stay married to a man for well over a decade without knowing what will come next. The spouse was a man who kept his rather attractive nose out of other people's business. I was the one who would make it my own, poke my rather substantial nose well and truly in, and get out with my little nose hairs singed. There was a reason we were together: yin and yang, opposites and suchlike.

'Did you even know her? I didn't see you smile at her or vice versa, the other day in the lift!'

I quailed a bit under his stern gaze. Only for a second. I had the kind of impervious hide that had been developed through years and years of having barbs bounce off me on a return trajectory that took them straight back to their point of origin, in this case, the spouse.

'It's the decent thing to do,' I replied firmly. 'She is a neighbour after all.' I could feel my halo on helicopter-spin speed around my head, which was getting increasingly swollen with all the good deeds I planned to pack into the course of a single day.

'Seriously, Kay, find something to do. Get back to work.'

'I already promised Raji I'd come with her,' I said, staying firm on my predestined path to uninvited neighbourly concern spreading happiness and light in the society complex.

'Raji,' he said, in the tone that you would expect from a person who has just been shown an educational film on the health effects of tobacco smoking and is reeling from the visuals. He then did the slight head shake and eye-roll that meant he was not going to take the conversation further and that he knew that nothing he said would dissuade me from being Good Samaritan with Pril-level of sparkle halo around my cranium, blinding in its intensity. He shovelled some nutrition into his mouth with the kind of grace that comes from not caring about the cumulative calories being ingested in a single forkful.

I stared at him in envy while pronging a deprived forkful at my bowl of watermelon. My eyes followed his hand as it lifted fork from plate to mouth and I sighed as he deposited the contents into his mouth. 'Stop staring at my plate like a dog eyeing a bone, Kay. Ask Jamuna to make you some proper breakfast instead of this fruit business, if you're hungry.'

I declined haughtily. I had to diet. I was already at the weight I had been at full term during my only pregnancy, and could no longer pretend it was the baby fat, given that folks kept asking me whether I'd had a second baby recently.

The newly acquired touchscreen Android with slots for two SIMs-one of which was currently languishing unutilized – and which is never more than ten centimetres away from my person, buzzed. I had the kind of ringtone guaranteed to wake the dead, deemed essential because I often zoned out in a public situation like shopping or eating, and the poor phone would be left to ring interminably as search parties were sent out to locate me before it even occurred to me to check for missed calls. Therefore, an appropriate catchy dance track had been set on full volume as my ringtone by the concerned and loving spouse, who had suffered the most, having developed calluses on his thumb from redailing.

Runa, the screen screamed, in flashing all-caps letters. I winced. I debated furiously whether to answer the call or not. Runa was that kind of a friend. One had to be in a very brave mood to speak with her.

One would be a coward to not answer. It guaranteed one's ear getting bitten off when one deigned to next answer a call from her. Cowardice won. Would be easier to answer the call now than to gather the courage to return the call later. Runa, a school friend, was a private detective. And a woman who needed no man. Which was great because she didn't need to spend her life worrying about defoliating and being feminine and delicate and suchlike, which would have been difficult to start with, given there was nothing feminine and delicate and ladylike about Runa, except, perhaps her name.

Runa was also perhaps the only person in the world who could make me squirm in my size-six shoes, and feel all of ten years old. I had been known to develop an acute case of frog-in-the-throat when in her presence, thanks to her ability to inflict a stare, which could crack open a walnut at ten paces, upon any helpless soul she took a displeasure to. This ability proved quite an advantage in her line of work and she was able to extract a full written confession in triplicate even from those who hadn't committed any crime.

I plastered a smile on my face for Dutch courage and swiped the green icon, quite an anomaly given that handsets these days look nothing like the icon on the call-receive button. 'Hi, Runa, what's up?' I said in a tone so upbeat and cheery, the only logical explanation for it would be that I was sniffing illegal substances with the help of credit cards to align them into thin lines the first thing in the morning. The spouse mopped his lips with his napkin, and indicated through abbreviated sign language that he was leaving.

People normally left the room when Runa entered, even if it was over the sound waves.

'I need your help,' she said.

I gulped. The last time round I had called Runa up and asked for her help had resulted in an intrepid adventure. It had me rambling on the backstreets of my neighbourhood in my kitten heels, ferreting out hair scrunchies and diamanté-edged pendants, carefully avoiding spots on the road that had seen innocent blood being shed. To be precise, the blood of the hapless Sheetal Jaiswal, resident of the apartment complex I lived in, done away with by her philandering husband, known as The Hairball. He had been named so because of the abundant facial foliage which probably had his food needing a map in order to reach his foodpipe. That was my first encounter with a true-to-life murder and I'd coasted along on the vicarious thrills of being that close to crime without having mucked up my manicure for quite a few months.

'I have a case, and I need someone like you to help me solve it.'

For a moment, the head swelled to hot-air-balloon levels and gently floated to the upper regions of the stratosphere. Runa needed me, little old me, me whom they called a nice person but not too sharp, to help her solve it. 'Someone like you.' she had said. What would the spouse say when I told him about this? He would see me in a different light: a grim, no-nonsense, case-solving private detective. He would look at me with new-found respect, now that I was actually doing something with a purpose, and potentially an income.

'Will you pay me?'

'What!' she squawked in tones so piercing, the dead in the neighbourhood cemetery would have sat up in their graves, rubbing their skeletal eye sockets in confusion.

'Did I take a single rupee from you when I agreed to work on that case of yours last December? Did I? Did I, Kay?' she said with a huge sigh that rolled across into my ears, dangerously threatening the internal and external air-pressure balance level that held my eardrum in place. 'I expected better from you. Here I give you an opportunity to be my assistant, something youngsters, fitter and sharper than you, are willing to pay *me* for and you ask me for payment?'

'Petrol money?' I could drive a hard bargain when I wanted to. It wasn't for nothing that I was the designated resident haggler when the gang went rasta shopping.

'Okay, okay, now meet me at Café Coffee Day down your road in two hours. Make that noon, sharp. When I say sharp I mean when the hands join together at the zenith of the clock, not when you finish incidental shopping on your way.' I winced. My eardrums protested. 'Okay. Bring a notepad, you'll want to take notes. Bring a pen, a pen that works. Eyeliner and lip liner won't do to write all I want you to write.' She was damned if she thought I would sacrifice precious cosmetics for writing purposes. The blasphemy. Before I could correct her on this moot point, she clicked off with the assurance that I would be there, hair in a braid, at the appointed hour, ready to throw myself into the apprenticeship with a fervour that would put the younger and the fitter and the sharper of the species to shame.

At the appointed hour, having ordered myself coffee and a classic chicken sandwich, breakfast menu as it was billed (what? surely I had been good at breakfast with only a bowlful of watermelon so I could reward myself with this. And I could have lunch at dinner time to make up), I settled myself comfortably into the armchair I had grabbed, which sank so low that I just knew I would have to request assistance to haul self out once the chicken sandwich had been ingested. The coffee shop was relatively deserted. An earnest couple sat somewhere at the back talking in low voices, two women and one man, dressed in the uniform pinstriped shirt tucked into slim-fit trousers, with thin belt and pointed heels (for the women) and made earnest hand gestures in the course of a conversation I couldn't overhear. That was when Runa breezed in and dumped her backpack into the adjoining armchair, bringing with her a sudden hush in the air.

Runa had that kind of impact. She was solid, she was Runa, built like one of those tanks that lumbered along down Janpath in the Republic Day parade. She had short hair, a no-fuss hairstyle she had cut once every three months at the neighbourhood men's salon, a square face, small sharp eyes that missed nothing, and could be narrowed to deadly effect when she was not pleased. She used to carry a khukri in her backpack but had now graduated to a gun, she told me, making a small quiver of fear do a chilled fingered Macarena up and down my spine.

'Have you ordered something?' she asked, and seeing that I was midway through the bread-and-animal-protein combination, 'You have ordered,' she stated flatly. She placed her order and her deal for me on the table in quick succession.

Runa was the kind of friend you loved to hate, who always made you feel two feet tall and back in grade one, where the most shameful thing you could do was to wet your pants in fear and then get ribbed about it till you passed out of class ten and hoped everyone had forgotten about it until one day, in a fancy cafe, you heard a rude voice behind you yell out 'Aeee Susuinthepant!' And you dove head first under the table pretending your contact lenses had fallen out and needed immediate retrieval. Anyway, that was Runa. The one person who always reduced me to Squealie.

'I have a case I need you to come in on. A lady is dead. Suicide. Her husband wants me to find out why.'

She quickly filled me in on the details. I took notes in handwriting so crazy any self-respecting doctor would have been proud of it. The gist was as follows: one nos dead body found with slit wrists at home, and a half-written suicide note with three names of the ladies from a Tuesday kitty group that the deceased was part of found in handbag. Name of deceased: Jaya Bhatia. Photograph of deceased showed her to be the prototype of the Lokhandwala mommy brigade with perma-straightened highlighted, hair that was far removed from what nature had gifted her on her nativity, a strappy top she was bursting out of in a manner that would have any outfielder put his hands together for a catch, and enough warpaint on the face so one would have no idea of what she really looked like once the cleanser had been duly plied. There was also a photograph of said note duly WhatsApped to me by Runa. To my trained eye, it looked like the list folks begin making when they expect to be hosting soirees at home with select friends, but I reserved my opinion until it was asked for.

'He suspects the reason has to do with her kitty group of friends. I need you to infiltrate that group. It could be because of the note, it could also be because her phone showed the last few calls as having been received from these two women mentioned on the note in her handbag. He says there was no reason for her to commit suicide. She wasn't in any depression, they had a happy marriage and she was looking forward to a cruise they'd been booked on for the Diwali vacation. If she'd wanted to commit suicide, he said, she would have done so after going on the cruise and after having uploaded the pictures of the cruise on Facebook.'

One more kitty group. I was drowning in kitty groups. The home-pot-luck-lunch kitty group. The once-a-month restaurant-lunch-and-housie kitty group. The school-mom kitty group. The old-society-complex kitty group I hadn't been able to gently extricate myself from and at the meetings of which I now found myself snoring gently while the others bitched gladly about newcomers I had no clue about. 'Is it a ladies-only kitty? Is there food involved?' I asked, getting to the point in keeping with the style Runa employed, and which she would undoubtedly appreciate. She gave me the look she would have normally kept on reserve for rodents dead for an indeterminate period of time and being brought in and displayed on the carpet by proud family pet. 'Of course, to both questions,' she replied.

Maternal guilt reared its ugly head as I looked at the watch on the wrist. The child would have arrived home, hot faced and irritable straight off the school bus and demanding cholesterol-laden foods like Happy Meal 'Chikkabuggawidxtracheez' rather than what good, sensible children ingrained with good, healthy food habits would choose, namely dal, chawal, roti and sabzi: the four pillars of the quintessentially healthy Indian meal. My stomach growled in an alarmingly loud manner at the thought. I looked around guiltily to see if heads had turned at the sound.

'Then fill me in on the details and watch me in action,' I replied, raising my hand to grab the attention of a passing waiter in order to replenish the carbs and proteins on my now depleted plate. Detectives in training needed fortification.

3

In Which Kay Makes Bodily Contact with Unknown Women

FRIDAY CONTINUES

When I returned home that afternoon, swinging bags of newly acquired purchases, and with my handbag containing the hastily scribbled notes and numbers, the sun was moving across the midpoint of the sky towards the western horizon, the day having done a volte-face and morphed into one of those damning bright and sunny kinds, which did not bode well for the piles of rotting, uncollected garbage round the block, marinated by three days of incessant rain. I held a handkerchief to my nose to prevent any unforeseen swooning – couldn't risk breaking a tile in the hallway again – and instructed Jamuna to close all the sliding doors to the balcony.

'What on earth is that foul smell?' I asked, hurrying to spray the premises with room freshener, wondering if the offspring had once again picked up a maggot-infested stray off the compound and brought it home as a pet, and whether I would have to deal with the song and dance and rolling-on-the-floor tantrums followed by the weeping incessantly until the nose turned red enough to challenge Rudolph in the red-nose sweepstakes when I declared that this was a no-pet household and that included fish. 'Jamunaaa,' I called, and she emerged, wiping her hands clean on what was a not-so-clean kitchen napkin, which I immediately confiscated in order to marinate it in bleach and detergent before it was deemed safe for kitchen use again. 'Are you sure no pigeon has died on top of the air conditioner?'

'They're dredging the canal at the back, Bhabhi. Apparently it was to be pre-monsoon desilting work, the maid from next door tells me, but it was delayed,' Jamuna filled me in with the breathlessness that was her trademark whenever she had information to dispense.

The offspring, having been deposited at the gate by the school bus, had been picked up, cleaned up and fed, and was now conducting curious experiments with action figures involving the ice tray and water and the freezer compartment. This was probably in response to the recent viewing of *The Avengers* where Captain America emerges from permafrost incarceration and takes on the baddies with redoubled vigour. He waved to me in an offhand manner and asked if I had bought him a toy, a packet of Lays or at least an iPod. I regretted that I only had on my person a T-shirt I'd picked for him at the mall. 'Is a Never Give Up John Cena tshird?' I shook my head sadly. He turned a scathing shoulder away in disgust and resumed his experiments.

The intercom buzzed again. In that shrill, tinny, infernal way that intercoms do when you have no desire to answer them.

'Yes,' I barked into it, in most ungracious manner.

'Kanan.' It was Raji, her voice the kind of calm that didn't sound too good. She was just about to resolve my dilemma, but I didn't know it yet. 'The lady from the fifth floor? The one we were to visit?' I smote my forehead. In the excitement of Runa summoning me to be 'On a Case', I had clean forgotten about courtesy visits to women who have supposedly been assaulted by spouses.

'Do you think we should go visit? After all, we barely know her? This can be embarrassing, if she doesn't want it out in the open. It isn't like she was ill and got operated on or something?'

I hemmed. I hawed. It went against my grain of curiosity to ignore something as momentous as this. I agreed. 'Maybe we can go visit her casually after a few days?'

'Maybe,' Raji conceded. 'But we must. Can't let this sort of thing continue in the society. Sets a bad example.' Not that I could imagine soft-spoken Vivek, Raji's husband, ever being brave enough to learn from said bad example. Raji would chase him out of the marital home with the roti belan and a few well-aimed whacks thrown in for good measure.

It upset me though. This bashing up of women set my teeth on edge, it made me want to go out and swing cudgels and do some slogan shouting and some painting faces black and putting in a garland of shoes, and bringing in a donkey on the premises for express purposes of parading around said wife beater on it, but these things don't get resolved with such measures. But we needed to show solidarity with the lady from 504 and I was going to make sure I did. Even if it meant spitting in the face of her husband when I bumped into him in the lift. For that, I would need someone to point him out to me. Wouldn't do to go around spitting at total innocents.

It was tiring business, this assistant detective position, even if I hadn't quite got round to investigating how I could inveigle myself into this group of kitty ladies, one of whom, Runa had kindly informed me, lived in my apartment complex, albeit in the next wing. I had but a nodding acquaintance with her, but was determined to better said nodding acquaintance into something firmer and more lasting, which included an invite to join her kitty group that operated on the modus of a cash handout of 10,000 per month, and a party at any suburban restaurant at the time of the draw and the handout. I would read up my copious and rather haphazard notes on the recently deceased by her own hand in a bit. Right now, I needed a bath of the 'lazing for an hour in the tub' variety. Sunny days in the midst of the Mumbai monsoon did send the perspiratory glands into overdrive – and if there was anything I had a horror of, it was leaving behind an olfactory trail that would have unwary souls keeling over in my wake.

I loved my bath time. Bath time for women is what the first god of advertising in India, Alyque Padamsee, commercially exploited by getting Karen Lunel to dive into chilly mountain waterfalls in a lime green bikini for Liril – without getting arrested for cruelty and intention to cause death through pneumonia and suchlike.

I am not a shower person. I am a balti-bath person on a regular day. It comes from guilt about there being a water shortage in the city, and showering I am told wastes water. In a city like Mumbai, the act of drawing out a bathtub seems sinful. This was a city where people wake up at ungodly hours to fill every container they have in the house with the drops of water that dribble in from unyielding taps, and manage to trickle off before noses have been washed, and utensils still lie sulking in basins waiting to be scrubbed. I can't have people moping around unwashed and unbathed on my conscience.

And on days when I have the time, the energy and the assurance that all phone calls will be dealt with without me needing to emerge, dripping, like Daryl Hannah of mermaid fame onto the carpet, I draw myself a bath. In the tub. A long, warm bath-oil- and bubble-bath-soaked one. I even light some aromatic candles in the bathroom. Today was one of those days. The child was occupied with figuring out how the Captain America action figure survived under permafrost, aka the ice tray in the freezer compartment. Jamuna was around to handle emergency phone calls. And I hadn't seen a horror movie involving long strands of hair emerging from bathtub drains, strangling innocent bathers into mummified corpses, in a while. I poured in some aromatic stuff which they said was guaranteed to make my skin look and feel like velvet. I set the timer by the side of the bathtub to ensure I didn't fall asleep and spend the entire afternoon lolling in the water, and ending up with skin the texture of wizened prunes. *Aarrrggh!* The thought. It reminded me of one wonderful time when I was drained out with typhoid and in a moment of misplaced vanity applied a kaolin pack on my face and fell asleep. When I washed it off a couple of hours later, I was a wrinkled old crone with skin crumpled to crêpe paper. It took intensive dosing of Nivea from the blue tub to bring it back to some semblance of normality and to let myself speak without fear of my face cracking on me. Thank God for timers. Cannot trust self not to fall asleep and drown myself unwittingly in the bathtub.

I always climbed into a tub with the uncomfortable feeling that someone from the water police was about to burst into the bathroom, and march me off for grand larceny of precious resources. Or a pair of hands with terribly unmanicured nails, or were those knives, would grab me around the midsection and drag me down into the tub which would suddenly morph into bottomlessness and dankness, all the result, of course, of watching too many horror movies for my own good.

Maybe there was a Freddy Krueger lurking within the bottomless waters just waiting to slit me into strips of veal. Or whatever human flesh is called. I gritted my teeth and settled in, luxuriating in bubbles in true filmi style when I heard the mobile ring. Thanks to bad planning, there was no spot next to the bath that I considered safe enough to keep the phone on, given I'd dropped two phones into the bathtub already and had had to consign them to the wastepaper bin. I listened to it ring, wondering whether I should let it continue ringing, and then the horrible thoughts began flooding my mind.

What if it was a call to let me know I had won a random contest with a prize that involved a holiday for two – all expenses paid – to a luxury resort, and since I didn't respond it would go to the next person who would answer their call, and would agree to bring their chequebooks along. Or it could be someone calling to inform me that I had won diamond jewellery worth some not-so-obscene amount in the shoppers' sweepstakes, which had made me skitter around feverishly last month buying things I so didn't need. Maybe the prize would be an all-you-can-buy-within-an-hour deal. Maybe they were giving me a lifetime's worth of free credit on clothes. Maybe it was a call from Runa.

I got up in a hurry. Or rather, as much of a hurry that I would allow myself – given that the water in the tub was still lusciously bubbled and could conceal a small army of gremlins within – and grabbed the towel, positioned conveniently within reach. I then quickly wiped self, dragged on my

Mandarin-print bathrobe, a gift from beloved sister-in-law from her last trip to Bangkok, which refused to complete wrap over like a decent bathrobe should but instead gaped enticingly to reveal flashes of cellulite to by now unshockable Jamuna, and emerged blinking into the dry light of the bedroom to grab the phone, which annoyingly went silent in my hand.

And it was an unfamiliar number. Is there anything more irritating than getting out of a nice warm bath to answer a call from an unknown number? Perhaps reaching the sale you had been waiting for all year and finding out what you had earmarked was not available in your size could top this, but little else.

I called back. A polite female voice replied.

'Could I speak with Mrs Mehra, please?' it asked. I frowned, puzzled, before I realized it was me who was being asked for and replied in the affirmative. No one I knew called me Mrs Mehra. It was always Kanan or Kay.

'This is Mrs Mehra,' I replied in my gracious, deep-from-the-throat phone voice, which was as posh as I could get without bringing out the Noritake and the cutwork table napkins.

'Good evening, Mrs Mehra,' she replied, her voice being of the chirpy variant that would have me looking into her pupils to check for telltale signs of ingestion of mood enhancers.

'Yaars,' I prodded along the conversation, aware that I was dripping inelegantly onto the little runner along the bed and it would probably not dry out if the sun did not deign to continue its brilliant run in the skies tomorrow.

'I'm calling from Romulus.'

I had a sinking sensation in the pit of my stomach. I had shopped, rather unwisely, at the store the previous month for a credit card swipe worthy of receiving an instant and rather annoyed call from the spouse who thankfully was in another country at the time, else he would have driven home that instant and done a replay of the Spanish Inquisition with me. And not in the euphemistic way, as made popular by a book with fifty shades of black and white in duotone combination.

'You had entered the lucky draw when you shopped?' Yes, yes of course, that was the only reason I had overplayed my hand and shopped for more clothes than my bursting-at-the-seams wardrobe could manage. The jackpot was an all-expenses-paid vacation for two to Bali.

'I am pleased to inform you that you have won the lucky draw.'

The world swum around me gently, and I held onto the wall in drowning-man-clutching-at-straw manner, trying to step away from the centrifuge.

'I won?'

'You won,' she repeated, calmly.

'The all-expenses-paid vacation for two to Bali?' I needed to clarify. I repeated my statement.

'The all-expenses-paid vacation for two to Bali, yes,' she repeated back to me. I did a quick fist pump in the air, never mind the damn runner, now wet enough to conduct swimming lessons for beginners on.

'Our executive will be in touch with you regarding further details on this number. We need to know which dates would be suitable for you to take the vacation. You have the option of choosing any five days between now and the end of next month.' A vision of the husband channelling the Grinch who stole Christmas when I mentioned the need for him to take a vacation flashed before the mind's eye, in full technicolour.

'Errm. Can I discuss this with my husband and get back to you?'

The bath abandoned, I hastily poured myself and my avoirdupois into respectable clothing. I dialled the spouse to convey the good news. 'I'm in a meeting, I'll call you later,' he said, sotto voce, as I began squeaking merrily into the phone when he answered after the umpteenth ring.

The husband's 'call you later's never materialized, and knowing this, I took myself to the task at hand: namely, that of Runa's decree that I befriend the lady I had but nodding acquaintance with from Tower C and extend my friendship by leaps and bounds so that she would invite me instantly into her kitty circuit so I could begin extracting information about the recently deceased.

I went through my hastily scrawled notes. The child wandered in, fresh from a bout of energetic cycling in the passage, where much crashing into walls signified that some sort of racing was under way with the boy from the flat at the end of the corridor. Much dramatic yelling and falling indicated further that this was not a friendly race, and much competitive spirit was being displayed, which augured well for a future in which he would probably have to take competitive exams as a hobby if he was to get anywhere in life. He wandered in and, seeing me with brow furrowed and pen poised in hand, rushed in where angels feared to tread.

'Are yu doing yer homevurk or oney pretending?' When I assured him that I was really working, he looked sceptical and said, 'Okay, wen yu'll finis? I wantu go down to the park.'

The park was where I could meet the Tower C resident who was my target, or at the least, I could make discreet enquiries about her with other residents of Tower C. Devyani Sharma she was, as my notes went, thirty-four, mother to a six-year-old male child, married to Shivdutt Sharma, who was something-something in finance with a multinational firm that had its office a short walk away from where our apartment complex was, but he was currently posted abroad. Devyani had chosen not to accompany him, I had learnt, for reasons unknown. It was a sensible decision, according to me. Husbands are best dealt with from a distance.

I peered at the photograph Runa had kindly supplied me of the happy family, filched from her Facebook profile, left unguarded with lax privacy settings, most likely. 'Dat's Divyam,' the offspring squawked. 'How yu got his pichshur?'

'Is he your friend?'

'Yus, he'z my fren. We play WWE together, he be's Randy Orton, I be Jon Cena and we have coffin match in the sandpit.'

This explained why he often returned home with sand pouring out of his ears and his nose, and needed to be vacuum-cleaned and hung out on the clothesline before being deemed fit for public consumption again. 'What is his flat number?' I asked.

'I don know.'

I was not one to give up so easily. I took the child's hand, looked out at the cloudless horizon and pulled on my walking shoes. 'Come, child, we're going down to the park to play. And I want to meet your friend, Divyam.'

'Okay, bud if he tellz yu I beat him don shaoud ad me in front of him.'

The sky was a nice mottled grey-yellow that comes from a thin cloud that one hopes blocks out the UVA and B radiation, but actually doesn't, and one thanked the good Lord that one had had the prescience to apply sunblock – Neutrogena Ultra Sheer Dry Touch SPF 50+, if you insist on knowing, the only one that doesn't have me break out in pimples the size of Vesuvius in full flow – lavishly on all exposed parts of self before stepping out of the hallowed portal of home. The child tripped alongside, yelling kiddie-level invective to passing mates cycling or footballing their weekend away. They yelled back in camaraderie, passing pertinent encouraging comments on how his pants were falling off and how his hair was styled to look like a sick animal's mangy pelt.

I ruffled said mangy pelt in pride, not regretting the moment at the men's salon when I asked the man bearing an electric razor to go as close to the scalp as he could in order to save me another visit in the immediate future, given how quickly the nutrients in the food the spawn took in went straight to his hair, bypassing all other body parts. 'See, I tole yu,' he hissed angrily. 'Don cut my hair so shord nex time. I tole yu nod to do zero cut.'

The park is where the flotsam jetsam of the colony gathered in the eventide to discuss maids, water supply woes, the irregular hours and visitors of the television actress in Tower A, with whispers of cricketing heroes being spotted ringing the doorbell in the wee hours, and the fight that Mr and Mrs Khosla had the other day that almost saw knives drawn at dusk, and other such minutiae of living in a gated community. The child let go of my hand as we approached the play area, which comprised a sandpit, a jungle gym, a slide, a merry-go-round, a see-saw and suchlike, divided in two age-appropriate locations, with the equipment for the smaller kids being located a good distance away from what was of use for the bigger kids. On one of the swings, the pint-size I knew now as Divyam was chortling as a girl I took to be the maid in charge of him swung him up and down, while being primarily engaged in giggly conversation on her phone. The two boys made bodily contact with a high five as the swing passed Kabir, followed by Divyam gesturing imperiously for the swinging to be brought to an immediate halt, and then dismounting, and rushing smack dab into Kabir and two seconds later both of them ending up in what could only be politely described as the Lilliputian version of a regular football scrimmage.

'Stop it, Kabir,' I squealed, terrified that in their enthusiasm, they would end up needing a cast on a limb each. Rushing in from the other end of the park was a lady I did not notice in my panic, who also yelled, 'Stop it, Divyam.' And when the two of us collided, the impact was such that I felt myself crash onto the cold, unwelcoming tiling of the jogging track and the world around me went black. A pure pitch-black, with none of the stars and fireworks the comic books and cartoon serials assure you happen in the mind's eye when one blacks out.

The last thing I heard was Kabir's voice, right at my ear: 'Mamma, yu is died?'

4

In Which Kay Makes Inroads into Her Investigation

SATURDAY

The morning came upon us swiftly, the kind of swiftness that has sleep still lingering on in one's eyes and one's brain. The sky was grey, but not in the I Plan to Rain on Your Parade Now grey, so I took a chance and tugged on velour grey tracks and tee and took myself and my cellulite down for a run, risking the very likely chance that a passing stray might mistake me for a pachyderm AWOL from the zoo. I had been consistently exercising in the vain hope that the regular run around the neighbourhood was the Holy Grail to losing the love handles. But, obviously, the cellulite and I hadn't come to any sort of arrangement over the procedure for giving up possession of said thighs.

I had long contemplated liposuction, given friend's talk about going in for a spot of lipo like they were going in to get their nails done, but the coward in me shuddered at the thought of having a pipe stuck into me and living parts of my tissue prodded to get fat deposits sucked out. Promises of having thighs that could fit into socks couldn't tempt me to lie down on a cold plastic sheet and have my fat vacuumed out from me. I would rather go about it the legitimate way, and one day, surely, my patience and my worn shoes would be rewarded. One could always live in hope.

As I walked and ran alternately on the unyielding grey asphalt and the interlocking tiles that made up the pavement on our reclaimed marshland, I thought back to the previous evening. After I had been splashed on the face with copious amounts of water obtained from kiddie water-bottles that had accompanied them to the park, and had been helped to my feet, and placed gently on a sturdy concrete bench, the woman in motion I had collided with had placed herself in my line of vision and apologized profusely. Devyani Sharma.

'I hope you aren't hurt, are you feeling okay? It was such a shock to see you just fall down and go unconscious …' She placed an immaculately manicured hand, a square-nailed French manicure if you must know, dramatically on her chest and squeezed her eyes shut. 'I thought you had died.'

'So did I.' I laughed, to show that I was in fact alive and well and could crack a joke at my expense.

Mrs Kapur's dog spotted me from a distance and strained merrily at her leash at the cheering prospect of a familiar ankle to nip at and I, with a spryness that belied my momentary indisposition, leapt to my feet and began the quick getaway.

'Are you sure you're okay?' she insisted. 'Sit down a while longer.' Luckily, Silky's rather distractible attention was taken up by a pug being carried around like an infant in his owner's arms and she was now yipping energetically at the offending party, letting me off the hook for the moment.

I assured Devyani that all my parts were in working condition and the brain hadn't been rattled in the cranium. She was a ferociously fit woman of medium height, with cheekbones that could cut butter. She had perma-straightened and highlighted hair that she held off the face with a luridly coloured scrunchy and was wearing gym wear that clung to her, revealing a body that had been put through the personal-trainer wringer at least four times a week and had not seen vile carbohydrates pass through her lips for what I would bet was many years now.

Introductions were made by the children who remembered their manners, when the adults had forgotten theirs. As the crowd around me dispersed when it was clear I was perfectly lucid, I asked her where she worked out and where she had had her hair done.

'Kabir and Divyam are great pals,' she said. 'We've just moved here a couple of weeks ago from Andheri and he's just making friends. Kabir is one of the few kids he gets along with. They're both, err, very spirited.' We looked on fondly at the respective spawns of our wombs who were now hurtling themselves down the slide at limb-dislocating speeds, which would require onlookers with nervous dispositions to be led away to calmer spots and administered their nerve-strengthening tonics.

I patted the bench by my side. 'And what about you? Have you made any friends here yet?'

She sighed, deeply. The leaves of the bush next to us rustled. 'People here have been nice and friendly, but everyone already has their own groups. I think it will take some time.'

I was the proverbial 'friendly golden retriever in human form' of the complex: I befriended everyone from the elderly retired, and doddering around on their evening constitutionals, to the younger and fitter lot, who burnt rubber running circles round the jogging track – some of whom were currently doing their daily five-kilometre count, and swaying me with their breeze as they whizzed past.

The evening ended with me inviting her over to tea the next day, so the kids could enjoy a play date at home, allowing us to chat comfortably without needing to rush off to check on them.

I had informed Runa of the breakthrough. 'Step on it, Kay, get into that kitty group even if it means you have to sell your grandmother's soul.'

Considering my grandmother, God rest her soul, was a pretty nasty piece of work and had been permanently disapproving of me, whom she considered a blot on the family record of only civil servants, doctors and engineers, this seemed like a fairly good bargain.

I dragged my panting self back to the house, and had just about downed a pitcherful of the Carbo Plus to replenish lost salts and such, when the doorbell rang.

Jamuna, she of the ear-piercing pitch when doorbell answering, answered said doorbell. 'Bhabhhhhiiiii ...' she began. I trotted off at a fast pace to ensure that a second call was not required and I was well within her line of sight, which I did suspect of veering towards the myopic.

A scrawny head poked itself around the door jamb – was the dog walker from next door. The kind of dog walker who had to be lauded heartily for the courage in taking on a dog twice his own height down onto roads where he was bound to find other interesting dogs to attack and therefore would run off at a pace that would put firing rockets speeding into space to shame. It was to his credit that he could rein in such a dog with a simple call, while, err, healthier folks would have had the soles of their feet scraped off by being dragged behind 'speeding faster than a bullet' dog the size of a slightly stunted horse.

'Madam, madam,' he began in that infernal way some people have when they assume you have your ears clogged up with waxy secretions not cleaned out at regular intervals with appropriate earbuds.

'*Haan bhaiya, kya hai*?' I said to reassure him that his voice was reaching my brain, without encountering any obstacles en route. '*Bolo*,' I added encouragingly, though reticence was not a word written in the dictionary with relevance to him.

'*Panch male par kuch ho raha hai! Ek* lady *chillaa rahi hai,* 504 *waali* madam!' He paused to add emphasis. '*Zor se. Jaise* torture *ho raha hai. Aur* stairs *par bhaag rahi thi*.'

All thoughts of play dates and investigations into suicides by kitty-partying ladies flew out of the exhaust vent along with the smoke being raised by the cook who was concocting breakfast with the concentration of Hermione in Potions class at Hogwarts. It did not strike me to ask him what he had been doing on the stairway on the fifth floor at this point to have seen running ladies and heard torture-levels of screaming. Such questions become irrelevant when immediate action is required.

In the true manner of folk who drop all their immediate tasks at hand and stand open-mouthed in bunches on the fringes of busy roads, in order to watch with concentrated effort a road crew digging a hole in the road to lay pipes in, I immediately dropped all thoughts of getting myself bathed and deodorized, and instead scooted off in the direction of the lift, making a mandatory call to Raji to arrive at said floor for backup if required. If there was a wife beater hard at work, we were about to roll our sleeves up and do some thrashing ourselves.

We landed on the fifth floor within an interval of five seconds during which there was no screaming to be heard, barring the disembodied mid-western-Japanese accented voice, which insisted we stay clear of the doors, and pin-drop silence elsewhere. We stood confused in the passage and looked at each other. There was peace and quiet. A listless moth fluttered at a doorway, then gave up all hopes of entering, found itself a corner and went into deep, immediate sleep.

The bullet had to be bitten; I stomped up to 504 and rang the doorbell. More silence ensued. I rang it again. We waited for five minutes wherein we discussed the price of onions and why the local greengrocers were supplying such stale and overpriced broccoli and coloured bell peppers, and how we were so overdue on our beauty treatments that we could feel our pores converting themselves into oil geysers. Then the door opened on us. The suddenness left us gaping mid-sentence, which wasn't the best look.

'Yes,' said a bulky figure, dressed in a nightgown, looking as though she had been in a deep, dreamless sleep, induced by sleeping aids that had been ingested the previous night.

She was a familiar face, a face one had nodded to or smiled at in the uncomfortable elevator proximity moments, but had never had deep or meaningful conversations with ever. We had never bonded over intense discussions about how muggy it had suddenly become or how the rains were being a bitch on newly acquired stilettos.

'Err,' I began uncomfortably, since she seemed to be far from any screaming and running-on-stairways mode, 'Actually, we thought we heard some screaming, we just came to check if everything was okay.'

She looked at me with the surliest Who Died and Made You Good Cop expression. 'I didn't hear any screams. Of any kind. Thank you for your concern, but as you can see, everything is fine here.'

'Actually, someone told us you were running on the stairs.'

She fastened her beady eyes on me, and I felt my innards being crushed. She had probably taken a correspondence course from Jane the Volturi and had graduated with an A+.

'As is obvious' – she looked at me defiantly – 'I am not in the physical condition to go running on the stairs. I also have dislocated kneecaps, which makes walking difficult ... and which is why I've piled on all this weight.'

I tucked my metaphorical tail between my legs, smiled apologetically and made a dash for the lift, with Raji hot on my heels – faces red enough to send any self-respecting tomato into a sulk – making a mental note to slam-dunk the dog walker's head into the commode. And press flush.

Raji sidled into the lift with me. We went down in tacit understanding to her floor, where we stepped out on the landing to discuss the strange screams folks were hearing on the stairway, and specifically from this flat, given the other flats on the floor were unoccupied save one on the far end. After fifteen minutes of hectic discussion, which included three missed calls from home, summarily ignored because they would most likely be from Jamuna hyperventilating because she couldn't find the spare supply of toilet detergent, we went off to our respective homes, the case of the screaming lady running on stairways unsolved and niggling at the back of the cranium.

Devyani Sharma presented herself at the door at 4.30 p.m. on the dot, accompanied by Divyam, who had been scrubbed clean with his hair combed and parted to the side for the occasion. The respective pint-sizes took themselves into Kabir's room, where the agenda *du* play date was pillow fight, more pillow fight, then WWE cage match with the action figures and the arena the spouse had been arm-twisted into purchasing on the last weekend spent at the mall, in true modern-family-fun manner.

Around an hour and a half and three coffees and two glasses of wine later, I had been inducted into her kitty group, there having been an unfortunate dropout as she informed me, without going into the gory details. Gory details, I could do without. I was of the genus who could drop into a dead faint at the sight of blood from a fresh-cut chicken and tiptoed into the kitchen to check on what was cooking only when I was assured with Mother Die promises from my cook that all stray drops of red corpuscles in plasma had been dealt with.

'It was quite a shock,' she said, hand fluttering dramatically. 'One day she was fine and the next she was dead. Suicide. Slit her wrists and bled all over the bed, I'm told. Her husband found her, with blue nails and lips.' Her voice dropped to a whisper in the manner mothers adopt when there is scary news to be conveyed within a two-kilometre radius of offspring under ten. The stomach did a delicate heave at the sound of a person marinating herself in all that blood gushing from her wrists. How did she do it, I wondered, covered in gooseflesh. How did she know just how deep to cut so that she bled adequately? Did she take a kitchen knife and run it across her wrists? What was the pain like? Did the blood gush or trickle? I began to feel faint with all the thinking. I was not used to too much unwarranted thinking, I needed to cool down the old brain before it overheated itself with all the exertion and exploded. I took huge, inelegant sips of the wine, contrary to all that they tell you about sipping gently and savouring the taste on your palate before swallowing.

'Any idea why she did it?' I asked gently. After all, there was no harm in getting to work right away, even though I was not officially in the group.

'Some financial problems, I hear,' she said. 'And she had some health issues. But I don't really know for sure, this is all gossip I hear.'

'What about her husband?' I persisted. 'Any problems there? An affair, a potential divorce?'

She shook her head blankly. 'I wouldn't know. As I said, I barely met them all once a month now that I'd moved out of the apartment complex. We basically communicated over the WhatsApp group.'

I had already made polite and discreet enquiries about the rest of the members of said kitty group on the very valid premise that I needed to know the kind of crowd I was signing up to spend time with. There were twelve of them, as is mandatory with every kitty that lasts for a year, with each getting their turn to host the group for lunch at a restaurant once a year. This time, the chit had been drawn in favour of a Lokhandwala resident, who was to host the group at a newly opened restaurant in her part of the suburb, which claimed to serve cuisine from all the South East Asian countries. My salivary glands were already on over-drool at the prospect of all those glistening rows of overflowing dishes calling my name in dulcet tones. But I had a task at hand, one that involved unearthing why a lady with everything going for her would slit her wrists. The thought made me briskly responsible and I got to ferreting out as much as I could about the recently deceased from the unwary Devyani.

'We have this month's lunch scheduled for Tuesday. I'll tell the rest of the group I've found us a new member,' she said, beaming in 'cat who'd devoured unwary canary, feathers and all' manner. I nodded graciously to indicate it was I who was doing them a favour by coming in mid-year, when half the kitty had been done with, and I was not getting the woman's kitty because the money she had paid up would be returned honourably to her spouse when the chit came up with her name on it. With phone numbers exchanged and some polite air-kissing, and promises to meet up in the lobby of my building on the mentioned date and go to the lunch together, we parted.

I had signed up to be member of yet another kitty. I counted them off on my fingers, with a growing sense of horror. The metamorphosis was complete. I was now officially what my parent's generation called a housewife and what this generation termed a homemaker. I felt my marsupial pouched stomach drop to my toes. My heart had quickened up to levels that could have echoed through the V-necked T-shirt I had dragged on. Just why had I decided to hang up my power suits without shoulder pads, in favour of getting burped and spat at all over by this mewling ball of flesh, who had now morphed into a WWE action figure collector who didn't want mamma to even hold his hand in public for fear of 'peepul will laff at me', I asked myself.

The phone rang, and Runa yelled at me in all caps from the screen. I winced and put the instrument gently to my ear. 'So,' she demanded, her voice gravelly from probably chewing pebbles and broken bottles for her midday meal, 'are you in the kitty group yet or not?'

'I'm in,' I conveyed. 'It wasn't too difficult. After all, it is difficult to find someone who is willing to take on someone else's kitty in the middle of the year. They were only too happy for me to come on board, I mean I am sort of a kitty veteran ...'

She cut me short in the insufferably abrupt manner she has, which will probably get her shot one day when she tries to cut into the sales pitch the counter chap at the coffee shop gives when he lists out the coffee variants and sizes available because she'll make him lose track and he'll have to start from scratch all over again, at which point the folk behind in the line who have been growing beards and applying for senior-citizen benefits will lose their patience, and pull out their handguns.

'I don't want to know about your social life, Kay, I consider these kitty parties a criminal waste of time and money and don't see how you can be happy whiling away time and energy and not to mention money on such frivolous activities when people are dying in ...'

She thought for a while, and then continued, 'Syria.'

I tried hard to think of who was dying in Syria and gave up. I am not, as they say, informed about world affairs, never mind that I am fully informed about affairs in the society complex. Affairs and extramarital affairs and all such which was grist for the daily gossip mills.

'Anyway, what time will you be there on Tuesday? I'll be on the next table listening in.' It was difficult to imagine Runa – in kurti and jeans and backpack and hair cut straight from a neighbourhood gents' salon to ensure that a simple comb was rendered redundant – seated at the next table, in a restaurant filled to the brim with Botoxed and liposuctioned peroxide blondes who lunched. 'Try and get closer to the ladies mentioned in the note. Make friends.'

Her hissing demand reminded me of the mater in the days when I was in the Girl See Boy phase and every coffee shop meetup mandated the 'Be friendly' talk from the mom who had realized that my stance of sitting with legs crossed, arms crossed and chin tilted upwards in defiance was not proving to be helpful.

'It doesn't work that way, Runa,' I said, trying to explain the dynamics of kitty lunches gently to Runa, she never having been part of the process and thus unaware of how the friendships in these progressed. 'First there will be the introductions. And then there is the question of the seating placement. Then there will be the interrogation.' I dreaded this specific bit of the process of joining already-in-place kitty groups. The interrogation was de rigeur, the very thought of it had my ganglions and neurons aquiver.

'Interrogation?' she barked. 'Why will they interrogate you, Squealie? You've got to interrogate them.'

I drew a deep breath and sighed. 'Runa, I'm the new member of the kitty. I will have to answer questions. Many questions. They will investigate me down to my playschool and the beauty salon I visit. And my husband's annual take-home, and the number of foreign vacations I have stamped on my passport.'

'Tcheh!' she spat with disdain into the phone. 'I thought at kitty parties all they did was play housie and then gossip and eat, making it impossible for anyone else on the premises to have a civil conversation.'

'Oh, that too. But it's my first time with the group tomorrow, so they'll want to get to know me. Hence.'

I have known women of nervous dispositions who have had to be led away sobbing into their handkerchiefs when they've been the focus of inquisitions by the leading lights of kitty groups, who wish to be reassured that they are worthy enough of being included in the hallowed ranks of those who meet once a month and party together. I would have to fortify myself with a shot of the spirit that cheers before I ventured forth into the dimly lit confines of the restaurant where the lunch was to be held.

When the spouse returned home in the evening, I gently divested him of briefcase and jacket, led him gently into the bedroom, shut the door, and while he was still recovering from wondering what had brought on this spate of unanticipated good luck, hit him for the cash-down component for the kitty to be joined, after sweetening the deal by telling him about the all-expenses-paid-for vacation for two to Bali we were to go on, which I had completely forgotten to tell him about the previous day. Needless to say, he didn't quite approve of either, but like most well-meaning husbands, who want a bit of calm and tranquillity in their lives, coughed up the requisite amount, or the promise of, and nodded vaguely to the demand of taking a week off from work to vacation, with me alone, in Bali. I calmly ignored the sudden look of unbridled panic in his eyes, as I spoke about wearing my new bikini on the beach.

5

Of a Wedding to Be Attended

SUNDAY

Like all Sundays in suburbia, this one was lazy and late. We stirred and opened each eye carefully as the straggling rays of the sun pierced through the undecided clouds and curtains and prodded us, lying slothful and supine, while the rest of the world was getting set to carpe-diem their day of rest with back-to-back activities. The hands on the wall clock indicated it was 8 a.m., an hour that no sane person should wake on, given it was Sunday. I pulled the blanket over self and ignored said clock. The spouse sprang up with an unseemly jolt and prodded me awake in investigative manner, much like one would prod a piece of fish on a fishmonger's slab to check freshness quotient.

'I forgot to tell you, we have a wedding to attend this evening. Mr Bhalla's daughter is getting married, I received the invite at the office and forgot it there.'

Mr Bhalla, being Mr Pushpinder Bhalla, he of the multiple businesses and multiple chins and stomachs, and a personage of such importance that even if you were hospitalized for dengue you would grab your platelet transfusion stand and hotfoot it to the reception rather than risk being in his bad books. One did not *not* turn up at a Bhalla wedding, if one valued one's existence as part of the plankton of the social sea. One cleaned up, donned one's best spats and scurried to the venue, showing all of one's dental improvement work and setting the metal detectors at the entrance off. Of how the spouse had personal acquaintance with Mr Bhalla, I didn't know, but in some mysterious way, they had connected when the spouse and a friend had visited him for some deal regarding property that the spouse's friend was redeveloping, and they had got chatting, and occasionally met over drinks at the club. Mr Bhalla's, not the spouse's.

I sat bolt upright in a way that would have done Linda Blair of the demonic possession state proud. 'Now you tell me? I haven't even been to the parlour, I'm overdue for my peel, and I missed my tummy-tuck session this week ...'

He gave me one of those looks that the dictionary would put down as scathing. 'You're perfectly fine, Kay.'

Fine? *Fine?* I needed to take him to get his eyes checked, the man obviously had not looked at me closely for a while. My eyebrows were caterpillars crawling around unrestrained all over my forehead, making their way into my hairline, the hair roots needed to be touched up, the blonde highlights having migrated to cooler climes away from the scalp, the grey along the hairline winking at me cheekily, the jowls had migrated to lower hemispheres, passports in hand, and the limbs were begging for strips of wax to get them back to smoothness or, failing that, a set of ribbons for braiding of foliage. I needed to gather my nerve and laser it all off, but the irrational fear of getting fried to a crisp had been keeping me from it.

The phone was switched on before the teeth were brushed, and I wondered if any parlours opened before breakfast as I began scrolling through my speed dial with a ferocity that would put an Olympic-level sprinter to shame.

Sure enough, as soon as the phone was switched on, the inbox beeped frantically like an army of shoplifters were about to make their escape. 'Where are you?' hissed Runa, via WhatsApp, which looked as unpleasant as I was sure her mood was. The call followed seconds later, as I knew it would. When patience was being distributed by the good Lord, Runa had probably taken off for a loo break or her nicotine fix and missed her handout.

Sure enough, 'Runa,' screamed the capital letters on the display screen as the phone trilled infernally with the spouse raising a curious eye at me as to these early-morning summons on a Sunday. I still had to break the news of the detective internship to him and this was news breaking that needed to be done gently, preferably post a good meal and plenty of running hand through hair. My hand. His hair.

'Yes, Runa,' I whispered, aware that the spouse had one ear cocked wondering about 'first thing in the morning phone calls' which never brought good news.

'Speak clearly, Squealie, did your tongue get entangled in your teeth?' Ah. You could trust Runa to be polite. She also had full and detailed recollection of elocution competitions where I went on, did the deer-in-headlights act, forgot lines, and was called back behind curtains, and began volubly to remind me of a certain incident in class four where I was to recite *Lochinvar* but compromised happily with whatever came first to the blank mind, which unfortunately happened to be Jack and Jill as of the up-the-hill version of trekkers, and the more prurient version of coming back down with a daughter. I winced. It was not an episode in my early history that I was particularly proud of or cared to recollect the first thing in the morning.

'And that too we couldn't understand, because as usual you were speaking with pebbles in your mouth,' she continued blithely, chortling at her own wisecracks. The sheer decibel level of her voice had pierced the tympanum and got the cranks and cogs in my brain whirring in full-alert mode, all the residual sleepiness dissipated.

'That was Demosthenes, not me, you have the history of the world confused,' I replied, in a rare show of spirit. Runa changed tack.

'Where are you, Kay, been calling you since morning … and one important thing, you can't have your phone switched off when you're on a case, okay?' Runa spoke in a manner that did not brook dissent. No one dared contradict Runa.

'I want to give you a small voice-recording device. You need to record every conversation between yourself and Devyani Sharma, and the conversation at the table during the lunch on Tuesday and even conversations that happen when you go to the restroom.'

'I'll call you later,' I hissed in reply as the spouse emerged from the bathroom, teeth brushed to a blinding sparkle, and bellowing for his morning cuppa to the domestic staff.

The child emerged from his room, blinking and whining, and was gathered up by his father. 'Who was it?' the spouse asked, while doing a version of the Tickle Him Silly with the offspring, who was chortling so much I could time the start of the hiccups.

'Runa,' I muttered, in non-committal manner, and stomped off to the relative security of the closed bathroom, hoping all would be forgotten by the time I emerged and a cup of tea had provided adequate distraction, along with the Sunday newspapers, which would ensure I saw only his knuckles until breakfast was served.

Unfortunately, in a dramatic development, which almost had me check his forehead for signs of oncoming high fever, the spouse put the child down and held the bathroom door ajar, asking me, 'Why did Runa call on a Sunday morning?'

Thus cornered, and with a George Washington sense of truthfulness and honesty, I explained, in broad strokes, the internship as a sleuth. The spouse expressed his displeasure by rolling his eyes and warning me in his deceptively mild manner – which always meant that he was on slow boil – to stay out of things that didn't concern me, and to start sending out my résumé if I really needed something to occupy myself. Blasphemy. Get back to the nine-to-five grind, and be a corporate slave again when I could do exciting things like intern with a detective and go under cover as a kitty group member at all-you-can-eat buffets? Why, there was no competition at all in my mind. Never mind that I actually had to pay to have this job. I brushed the teeth with a ferocity that almost took off all my caps, and emerged seething with determination to speak my piece on me doing what interested me and how I needed something more challenging than a corporate nine-to-five, and God help me, this was flexitime.

The spawn of the womb, in the interim, had discovered DayGlo markers made a pleasing if eye-popping design on the cedar-hued veneer and was going at it with a fervour that would have made Michelangelo develop performance anxiety while working his brush on the ceiling of that little chapel.

'No, Kabir, no!' I yelled, dragging him away from creating further damage and he demanded mango-flavoured drinks and various packaged edibles which were well known for increasing obesity and providing empty calories, and then whined a bit wanting 'chikkin lollipoks' on the menu for breakfast.

That was when the doorbell rang, and I answered it to find no one there. But I was so not letting a random person ring my doorbell and run off, especially if it turned out to be the twelve-year-old from upstairs – he was going to get hauled up by his ear and have it tweaked for him as well.

I picked up my pace and darted into the corridor that lay behind the door to our lobby which led to the stairwell. Which, incidentally, was all the things a stairwell should not be this early in the morning, namely dark and grey and musty – all things not helped by the rain that had started pouring down outside. The tube lights in the stairway flickered eerily, in true slasher-film mode. 'Hello, hello …' I ran out. 'Who rang the doorbell, come back or I'm going to tell your mom.'

Ermm, yes, I was convinced it was the pint-sized one from upstairs who strangely enough looked like a right delinquent, the kind who would be catching butterflies in the garden only to pull their wings right off, or the sort who gathers together waste paper and starts fires in deserted parking lots. In short, the kind of kid you would never want your angel of a child to socialize with, and who by the true determination of the universe and the cosmos becomes your child's 'bestest friend in the whole wide world' and you need pliers to keep them apart.

I trotted lightly up the stairs, confident of finding the critter, only to be stopped in my tracks by a horrific scream. This was no ordinary scream. This was the kind of scream that

I had heard before, and had had to endure a cup of tea and conversation with Mrs Kapur and also deal with holes in my new trackpants from the yapping Silky for.

I froze. I couldn't figure out where the scream had come from. Up or down. I stood uncertainly, waiting for it to come again.

And it did.

It was from the floors below. I trotted down as quickly as my lumbering form would allow me and poked my head through the doorway on each floor, wondering where exactly the sound had come from. Yet another scream rent the air, like a soul was being torn from a body. I was on the seventh floor now and it felt like it was right next to me. I popped out on to the landing and looked around. All the doors of the homes were shut, and by all appearances everything was peaceful. I rang the doorbell of a friend who lived on the seventh floor.

I wasn't exactly dressed for social visits in my PJs and my face was still to see a splash of water to brighten its countenance. At least the teeth thankfully had said their good-morning how-are-yous to the toothbrush.

'Prita,' I gasped, as a confused-looking woman opened the door to me. 'Did you hear the screams?'

Her pretty face furrowed into a confused frown. 'What screams? I didn't hear any screams!'

Now it was my turn to furrow my face. 'Arey, how could you not hear it, there were three loud screams, right now. Really. Cross my heart.' I clutched the turkey skin on my neck in delineation of the veracity of what I was saying. I bobbed my head up and down in an attempt to convince her, and the door in front of hers opened and a man bundled off towards the lift, his tennis bag flung over his shoulder. His wife stood at the door wanting to be let into the conversation.

'Whatever happened, Prita?' she asked. Prita looked at her and sought to validate what I was asking her. 'Did you hear any screaming, Vineeta?' The Dogras, said the nameplate: ceramic tiles with a simple font, pasted inside a wooden frame, the kind one could pick up at any mall on a limited budget, placed next to a door which was still in the original framing and wood finish as had been supplied by the builder. I concluded said Dogras were residents who were here on rent, and ergo had not invested in altering the premises to add their own personal touch.

Prita's door, just the opposite, was an interior decorator's wet dream. It boasted plaster-of-Paris arches flanked by two Roman columns and studiedly dilapidated brickwork down the passage with planters filled with real, dilapidated plants, which went nicely with the air of ruin that was meant to conjure up splendour. Prita so didn't have the green thumb, or maybe she had not made her acquaintance with Magic Grow, the miracle fertilizer I chucked into all my pots every week to make them thrive. I made a mental note to pass her some to try. Anyway, Vineeta was shaking her head vigorously in the negative to indicate that she had not heard any screaming of any decibel level. I wanted to clunk my head to check whether it was pure aural ringing which was causing auditory hallucinations.

And now they both were staring at me suspiciously, wondering if they needed to call in the security to frogmarch me to the loony bin. 'It's the second time I've heard screams on the staircase.'

'Err, Kay, why are you on the staircase?'

It was a perfectly valid question, one to which I had no answer. Except the truth. 'The first time, actually, I was climbing the stairs for some exercise, and now, someone rang my doorbell and disappeared into the stairwell and I was trying to chase them to yell at them.'

They looked at each other. 'Kay, darling,' Prita began, 'why don't you go home and rest a while and take something to calm your nerves, you're obviously under some sort of stress.'

Hmm. Of course, I was. I hadn't been shopping at sales in over a month now. This by itself was enough to make me go down on my knees and sob. I needed to shop. Mindlessly. I needed to max out a credit card so bad that all these auditory hallucinations of people screaming when they were not supposed to would disappear.

'Errm. Yes,' I replied. 'Yes, I will.' I turned around and walked towards the lift but could feel them making cuckoo gestures by twirling their forefingers beside their temples.

The screams still resonated in my head. Why could no one else hear them?

I knew what it was, I was sugar deprived and ergo hallucinating. I needed to get a kilo of some mithai delivered home, or maybe I could send the driver out for it. Or perhaps macarons from Le 15. Maybe he could be instructed to bring along some ras malai while he was there. Maybe that ras malai could be concealed in the vegetable tray of the refrigerator, where no one looked, only to be taken out when I really, really needed something sweet and would die if I didn't get it.

Stop it, Kay! I was stern and unrelenting. I would order sugar-free ras malai. I had quite enough of the tyres threatening to burst the seams of my clothing and have me revealed as a green-skinned, grunting, oversized oaf who couldn't get through a parking lot without uprooting the cars on either side because of the wide berth her hips needed to get through.

'Why did you go running off, Kay?' the spouse asked as I entered. 'It was just the newspaper chappie delivering the papers as usual.'

I smote my forehead with my palm. All these screams on the staircase had got me quite crazed up.

The landline rang. It could only mean it was 8.30 a.m. and time for the pater and mater to make their weekly Sunday morning call to speak to their only begotten grandchild. I exchanged basic pleasantries and handed the instrument to the offspring, and listened in as he listed a litany of complaints about how vilely he was being tortured and deprived of toys and treats by his cruel mother. Whenever he returned from any amount of time spent with the grandparents on the maternal side, it usually took a snake whip and time out in the naughty corner for a week before I could get him back to a tolerable modicum of good behaviour.

The pater came on line as the sprog handed the instrument back to me with glee twinkling in his eyes about the tongue-lashing he'd put me in for. 'What is this, beta?' the aged parent began with no preamble, and continued in the same vein for around ten minutes about how I was not being the perfect parent their grandchild deserved. 'Your brother might be giving us a grandchild too,' he added.

The brother, settled in London and married a few months ago, had been quick on the job, I added impolitely. He harrumphed embarrassedly and ignored my statement.

'Did he specifically tell you that they're expecting a baby?'

He had the grace to sound embarrassed. 'Not really, but we have suggested to him that we will be very delighted if they do.'

'*Gah!* Pappa, really ...'

The mater came on the line, her voice crisp and determined like the starched cotton saree she had no doubt draped herself in that morning, as she did every morning, the starching of sarees being a weekly ritual that saw the backyard of their bungalow in Pune converted into a modified dhobi ghat. 'Why have we not seen our grandchild since your brother's wedding reception?'

Had it really been so long? Over half the year had passed without proper permission given in writing, in triplicate. 'Ma, you could always come down whenever you want to, you don't need an invitation to visit us, do you?'

The mater audibly bristled on the phone. 'Of course, one does not visit a married daughter in her married home just like that. It is not done.'

There was a brief pause and the sound of something terrific crashing in the background. 'This man, your father,' she specified in the event that I got the mistaken notion that there was another man on the premises. 'He's gone and hung the crockery shelf with a single nail.' Thankfully, that was one conversation that was ended. The parents, they lived in a semi-detached bungalow on the outskirts of Pune and led a social life so hectic that slots in their engagements diary had to be grabbed months in advance or I was forced to rely on the off-chance that something might get cancelled, something that was more important than I, their firstborn offspring, was.

Aaarrggh! There was a fancy wedding to be attended that evening and I needed to make myself presentable enough to not scare off unwary onlookers. I bathed and got dressed to get to the salon before it opened in order to be the first customer on the premises and be able to pick and choose who would attend to me. I was already sorting through my saree collection and wondering mentally what saree would go with which jewellery and wasn't it a great thing that I had gone in for a workshop on how to make one's face up professionally, never mind that the hand was so unsteady that eyeliner and mascara application was precariously poised between professionally made up and drag levels of expertise.

Attending weddings did not figure in my favourite-things-to-do list. I was the kind of wedding guest who was distracted and vacant and just that bit on the edge, almost like I was looking for an escape to a deserted corner to snort up a couple of lines. I sat uneasily through the speeches, and the dance performances, and the checking-out of what the other women were wearing and which of them might have had her upper chest area enhanced. I looked around shiftily if people approached me with the seeming intention of engaging me in conversation that could keep me from getting to the buffet counter the second the fires beneath the chafing dishes were lit up. I also edged away from hearty aunts bearing tidings about their US-settled sons, and their PhD-qualified daughters and assorted nephews and nieces, who had reached exalted positions in multinational corporations, where they had a minion rolling on the floor before their every step to clean the ground 'exalted position person' would step on, or things to that effect. I usually sidled away stealthily, or grabbed an unsuspecting random acquaintance floating in the vicinity and planted them in front of the gabbing person to make good my escape. I was known to grab the round table closest to the start of the buffet and stare daggers at any random soul who hovered near the stacked plates, willing them to steer clear and allow me first shot at the spread. I was also known, much to the cringing embarrassment of the spouse, to walk up and down the buffet line-up, checking the fare on offer in advance, so I could, ermm, plan the meal, to the point where the starters and the dessert battled for preference.

And when the buffet was finally open, I did the mile in a minute to hit the stacked, warm plates before going down the line with the hushed reverence pilgrims reserve for touching sacred relics within a temple. Then I ladled out the spread onto my plate and searched for a corner that allowed easy refilling by cutting through the line, and which was also sufficiently away from the public gaze, offering protection from well-meaning folk who intend to carry on a conversation through the meal. The spouse pretended he was not with me in a buffet situation and we agreed to meet at a fixed spot at a fixed time outside the venue once I was done with the seconds and thirds and, as embarrassing as it was to admit, even the fourths.

The child was spending his Sunday morning in an overwhelmingly unproductive manner by scooter-racing with his friend from the neighbouring house and decimating the plaster on the walls of the passageway to whoops of blood-curdling laughter. I plucked the child off his scooty and hauled him into the premises to the accompaniment of random squeals of protest. 'I wantu play, I haven't broken the scooty wheel yet!'

'Get in the house, bathe, breakfast and sit with your homework,' I decreed sternly.

'Okay,' he said with the kind of grave-faced earnestness that harked back to the child in *The Sixth Sense* who Saw Dead People. 'I'll do my bathing and breakfasting. Homevurk I'll do wid yu wen yu come back. Where are yu going widoud me on Sunday morning? I wantu come wid yu to the mall.'

'I'm off to the salon,' I announced to the dear husband. 'Shall be back by lunch.' He stared at me sternly with the eye he condescended to shift from the newspaper.

'By lunch?' he snorted with choked laughter. 'Just make sure you're back in time for us to reach the venue in time for dinner.' How well he knew me, the spouse. I had already planned in my head that I was to get all the overdue treatments in a single day.

It was strange that a wedding was happening in July. It was not kind weather to wear one's finery or to get one's hair set and sprayed into place with the kind of spray that morphs hair into a concrete helmet, which would see hatchlings emerge flapping nascent wings once one had managed to break it down with concerted effort. The season had the kind of wind and humidity that made everything flop down into recalcitrant mousiness. This was not the kind of weather that regular folk in India got married in.

It must have been a wedding planned in a hurry. Was the bride pregnant? Surely not in the days of the morning-after pills.

The mobile shrieked as I stepped into the corridor. Runa.

'What?' I answered, in a muted hiss, aware that I wasn't out of earshot of the spouse and two calls from Runa in the span of a single morning would have his antennae set to high alert.

'I'm here, in your lobby, Squealie. Come and get it and make it snappy, you don't need to slather on the face paint, it's just me.'

She had no sense of occasion, this woman. I could meet a random handsome stranger in the elevator, going down. Who was it who said always dress like you will bump into the love of your life, never mind if it was just running down to the store? I followed that maxim, even though the love of my life was unshaven and grouchy, back in his reading armchair, carefully emptying out the contents of his nostril when he thought no one was looking.

As I reached the lobby, I spotted Runa lurking around the premises looking threatening enough to have the security supervisor of the complex stop by and make polite enquiries with her in the 'to what do we owe the pleasure of this visit' sort of way. This was not surprising, given that his previous encounter with her had her flashing a fake CBI card and totally getting him to click his heels at her command.

'Here,' she said, handing me a suspicious-looking brown envelope, folded in half. 'Keep it in your handbag. I've written out all the instructions. Study them. Remember to switch it on when you sit at the table.'

I nodded, because she gave me no opportunity to interrupt with speech. 'Did you get it? Did you get it?' She did have an infernal stuck-record manner. Of course, I got it. I was just to place the mike and wire within my clothing, tape it up properly and switch on the recorder when I sat the table and introductions were being made. How difficult could that be? I'd seen enough detective serials on television to know how this worked, hadn't I?

'Of course, I know how to work these,' I replied, waving to her as she stomped out to where she had parked her motorcycle – disdainfully right next to the entrance of the lobby and not in the visitors' parking, as was mandatory.

'Don't mess up,' she warned me, in dire tones, and kick-started her ancient Enfield into eardrum-cracking levels of roaring, and then roared off into the drizzly morning, leaving the rest of us shuddering from the sonic boom that ensued.

When all my bones had stopped rattling and my eardrums returned from the coffee break they had gone off to, I took myself to the local beauty salon down the road, which welcomed me with open arms without an appointment. I was, what they called, a standing. It had nothing to do with the upright state of my limbs, and everything to do with the fact that whenever I went there I required they drop all else and attend to me in droves. I also tipped lavishly enough to ensure this.

'*Haanji, didi, bahut din ho gaye*,' said the aunty who owned the place, I misheard *bahut* thin *ho gaye*, and beamed happily until she followed it up with: '*Thoda aur* healthy *ho gaye*,' before telling me, in her mandatory sales pitch that I was looking tired and I needed to do shirshaasan to get the glow back to my face, failing which she had a 'pearl glow' facial that she offered which could do the needful in a more convenient manner.

I listed out the services I required, which had me breathless when I finally paused for air, and she deputed a small army of efficient workers to take each limb individually and one to administer to the hair, while the limbs were being defoliated, manicured, pedicured and the face was being attacked with the thread and the face pack, and the hair colour being slapped on, I found myself in the pedicure basin next to Swati from B wing, 804. With cordial relations being maintained between the two of us, and nothing in common to discuss, we turned our discussion swiftly to the various denizens of the building complex, settling on Mrs 504.

'Do you know she has, ermm, mental issues,' Swati hissed in an undertone that the entire parlour in all its fifteen-by-twenty foot plus mezzanine floor heard with complete clarity. 'Tell, tell,' I pleaded, not that she needed much cajoling. 'She's seeing a skykatriss. That *dimaag ka* doctor kind. You know.'

'I know,' I admitted, unwilling to out myself as someone who knew how to pronounce. 'But what for?'

'*Usko daure padte the*,' she hissed again before going through thin partitions where waxing of unknowns and facials were being conducted in strict privacy accorded by board and curtain. By the time I emerged, buffed, polished, hair set and limbs defoliated of enough undergrowth to reforest a small nation, I had learnt that Mrs 504 was a dangerous creature indeed and had to be kept placid with constant force-feeding of pills by her spouse, who was half her size and would be crumpled like a sheet of paper should she decide to take him on in hand-to-hand combat.

I informed Raji about this latest nugget of information as soon as I got home, before the spouse managed to drag me off the intercom, by pawing at the ground and snorting out little puffs of steam, and tapping at his watch in an officious manner, which I'm sure any self-respecting executive assistant would avenge by spitting into his coffee when he got it for him.

'It's almost 3 p.m. You left home at 10 a.m., Seriously, Kay, all day at the salon?'

'Did you miss me?' I cooed in sultry manner, hoping to deflect his anger into more constructive pursuits and whispering about Brazilian experiments with waxing strips into his ears. The offspring emerged from his room where Doraemon dubbed in Hindi had been rattling the plaster.

'Doraemon became a ghoss tuday. Like Goosebumps,' he declared. 'Ghosties everywhere, in the staircase, in the road—'

I stopped him short.

'Why ghosties in the staircase, son?' I asked, holding my breath for what I thought the answer would be.

'One aunty is always crying in the staircase. Especially when we play chor-poliss. Bud we can't see her.' I shuddered and quickly changed the topic to the wedding reception we were to attend and whether he wanted to accompany us or stay home, and finally concluded that there would be a dessert counter with as much ice cream as he wanted. Needless to say, he was tempted. After all, he had inherited his sweet tooth from his X-chromosomal donor.

We draped ourselves in our finery, which entailed me spending one hour rolling myself into and out of my saree, with Jamuna at hand with safety pins and for pleat-holding assistance, and then employing the cover-the-bulge camouflage technique where I pulled in my stomach and found that nothing moved. I added some danglers to the ears, which weighed the lobes immediately to the knees, slapped on make-up that did not paint the face a shade of hideous bilious yellow, and was finally satisfied with my reflection in the mirror. The spouse was showered and dressed in ten ticks of a duck's tail and was looking all unfairly scrumptious and dapper in biscuit-coloured jacket and brown trousers with a V-necked white T-shirt within, which wasn't standard wedding-reception dress code but then men got away with worse when they wore dupattas round their necks with ethnic wear. I poured the squirming child into his best dapper sherwani, ignoring the protests of it being scratchy and irritating and 'I don laikeit, I wantu wear my Ferrari racing jacked wid jeans', and assured him he was looking the 'han-somest' thing since Hrithik Roshan in *Krrish 3* made Mamma's eyeballs pop out and roll to the floor and an involuntary wolf-whistle escape her lips.

'Mamma, where we is goin?' asked the child, to which he received the appropriate response.

'We're going to a wedding, child,' I replied.

'Dat I know,' he replied scornfully, his gaze making me feel like the village idiot. 'Where is the wedding?'

I named the five-star hotel that was our destination.

'Wat we'll do there?'

This was going to be a long conversation, and I could feel my hair greying in anticipation.

'Hmm, we'll wish the bride and groom and then we'll eat dinner.'

His eyes lit up with the sparkle of someone who had just realized that forbidden goods might soon be within reach. 'An den I will ead ichscream? Lods of id?'

I assured him that the quantity would not be rationed in miserly manner, never mind the throat infections and coughs that plagued half the populace during that miserable time of the year.

I dragged him behind me, tripping over my stilettos as they got stuck in the edge of my saree and almost put me in close proximity to the ground in a manner not too dignified. The spouse marched ahead, jabbing buttons and going forth to get the car out of the parking while I minced along painfully. Why did I choose to wear these stilettos that were garrotting my toes to certain death or gangrene? I cursed as I made my way across the vast expanse of marble floor made slippery by wet feet and dripping umbrellas.

As I scurried past, I saw Mrs 504 sitting on the floor in the lobby. In the most peaceful manner. Like it was the exact place she was supposed to be sitting in. In a meditation mudra. While the floating population of watchmen, drivers, handy men and random maids walked around her gingerly, gawping and wondering whether to intrude on her closed-eyed peacefulness. Folks entering and exiting the premises gave her the quizzical eye and let her be.

The child went up to her before he could be pulled back, and tapped her on the shoulder with the complete lack of reticence and complete confidence to speak his mind that every child should have. 'Aundy. Gerrup,' he stated plainly. The child was a plain speaker. He inherited it from his mother. His father could talk a horse around a racecourse before getting to the point. 'Is dirdy on the ground. Yer clodz will ged dirdy.'

The aunty in question opened her eyes and looked at him with a blank gaze, as if emerging from a trance, then got up silently and made her way to the elevator without speaking a single word. We looked after her a little open-mouthed, too stunned to react. A sudden buzz of conversation descended on the, till then silent, lobby with assorted drivers and support staff suddenly chattering about the strangeness of a resident sitting cross-legged on the floor slam dunk in the midst of a bustling building lobby like it was a terminus for long-distance trains, where everyone sat cross-legged and waited till their train arrived.

The child marched on towards the car much in the manner of one who had done his good deed for the day, and was now assured of points marked in his favour when Santa Claus peeked at the list with his name on it. He settled into the back seat with the air of a long-suffering martyr, a soft sigh escaping him. The long suffering occasioned undoubtedly by the sherwani ensemble, which had been resisted valiantly given its pokiness quotient with all the embroidery layered on. He tugged at his collar uncomfortably.

'I is lookin very hansome?' he asked for validation that all his suffering was not in vain.

I hastened to reassure him and even clicked a selfie with him.

'Wai we habtu wear fancy dress fer weddings? Wai I canna wear shird an pant. And jakkid wid jeans?' This was truly a question to which I had no answer. The husband also refused to answer, concentrating grimly on the traffic and cursing two-wheelers that swerved in suicidal manner into his path with the kind of language I said I would not stand for in the presence of the child and could he wash his mouth with soap, etc.

The child had inherited all his mother's sartorial inclinations. To this end he had a wardrobe that consisted of distinct segmentations: clothes he would deign to wear only in the house and clothes that were relegated to be worn down in the park – of which synthetic costumes of various superheroes comprised the prime components.

And then, of course, were clothes meant for the various birthday parties he attended, which were the highlight of his social life, comprising jackets fit for Formula One racing, in puffy fabric so he walked around like a mini astronaut (minus the goldfish bowl for his head) and dapper corduroy jackets in shades ranging from sombre browns – befitting English lords, with leather patches on the elbows – to self-selected shades of orange that would ring alarm bells if ever found in a food product.

On this pyramidal hierarchy of clothing options, ethnic wear that included poky and itchy sherwanis ranked amongst the lowest of the low, probably at the evolutionary scale of primordial slime containing single-cell microorganisms that floated around having sex with themselves and reproducing at obscene rates.

My concept of mothering, you see, was that of laissez-faire. While other moms would be going around their offspring in circles trying to regulate or limit the unhealthy stuff they shovelled into their gullets, I let the child eat what he wanted until he tired of it and never wanted to see said item of food ever again for the rest of his life. I did it when he went through a 'chickabuggawidcheez' phase, which lasted months and involved one chicken burger with extra cheese from McDonalds every single day to the point where we couldn't drive past the golden arches without ducking in quickly and emerging with said item. Today, he would probably barf when confronted with said chicken burger with extra cheese and my task would be done. The more I sang and danced around him, forbidding him to eat any item of edible stuff including rubbery Chewits, I noticed he got all fired up to insist that his system needed it. Then we would end up in a total 'assert parental authority' scrap, which pretty much finished with him sobbing, me fuming and then thawing and letting him have his way, negating the entire purpose of the denying of said item of unhealthy food to start with. In an open forum on mothering practices in the contemporary age, I would be drawn and quartered. And probably hung out to dry in the blazing noon sun for the carrion eaters to get at me.

Coming back to the wedding at hand. I detested attending weddings. Especially with the child in tow. It necessitated that I spend the evening like a meerkat on guard, craning my neck to spot him racing through the crowds in search of other pint-sizes to gang up with and wreck mayhem and destruction. Ever seen them meerkats on Discovery or Animal Planet or whatever channel it was that the child resolutely refused to watch despite me insisting that it would do wonders for his general knowledge and suchlike? One of them is deputed to stand watch, and the poor critter stood on its hind legs surveying the horizon for any sign of a random predator approaching. The expression on its pinched face that of acute tension. Well, that was me at a wedding with the child. I would make sure to dress him in eye-popping colours. I also offered him my phone to keep him in one place and Temple Run proved to be effective. At family weddings, I breathed a sigh of relief because he had other pint-sizes from within the family to run around with and one could imperiously command the teens within the immediate family to keep an eagle eye out for said child, and restrain him physically from getting into fist fights over who could tear down the marigold strings the fastest.

We stepped out gingerly onto the hotel porch, which was thankfully dry enough to keep the saree border of my sequin-encrusted chiffon number untouched by mud and other repulsive must-avoids of the monsoon. The strappy gold stilettos I had on needed to be placed with much care, seeing as they had caused the spouse to choke a bit when faced with the bill.

At the entrance to the hotel, the boy developed an immense fascination with the rather impressive moustache sported by the turbaned chappie at the door, and whispered that he needed to investigate the authenticity of it right now, and began to tiptoe towards him. '*Kabbbiiiiirrrrr!*' I yelled.

I managed to steer him banquet-hall-wards, aided by a sharp glance from his father who gave me the single eyebrow raise, which translated to his usual, 'I told you to leave the child at home.'

'Wai dis aundy is coming so angrily?' he squawked in return, spotting the rather hefty Runa, draped for a change in a saree which looked as awkward and unfeminine on her as it would have on a six-foot All-American Basketball player. He hopped nimbly behind me for protection from what he surely perceived as an immediate threat to life and limb. 'Kaaaayyyyy,' sang Runa in dulcet tones. 'Fancy meeting you here.'

I inched back. Runa singing in dulcet tones meant there was an agenda underfoot. She moved in on me, saree notwithstanding, like a quarterback ready for a bone-crushing tackle. 'I'm here on a case.'

I should have guessed. Runa wouldn't do social gatherings unless they had threatened her with thumbtacks and the iron maiden.

'Should I know anything?' I asked. The spouse had floated off, in the terribly rude manner he had when we were at a social event, and was now in deep conversation with a man in a suit whose belly preceded him.

It's better to be informed beforehand if one would be required to flee the premises in a hurry, which was always a possibility given Runa's professional calling of a private detective, and the fact that she had recently decided to employ me on a non-payable basis as an occasional sidekick. This seemed like a professional assignment, and Runa probably needed backup.

She spoke into my ear while leading me towards the banquet hall, where no doubt good folks were assembling as we spoke to walk onto the dais and hand over little envelopes bearing cash as tokens of goodwill. 'I'm helping an investigation into a gang of thieves who walk into wedding receptions of the well-heeled and make off with the gifts or with the jewellery of the guests. I've been hired by the hotel, they've had it happen four times in the past couple of months.'

I felt my skin convert into gooseflesh immediately. I reached out to grab the child, who was contemplating the distinct possibility of dunking himself head first into the fountain that was gushing forth in the marbled corridor. I contemplated a turnaround back to whence I came from. It had been a long and tiring day, the child would thankfully not be expected to rise and shine at the crack of dawn the next morning for school.

As we entered the banquet hall with its mock fountains trailing flowers down either side of the entrance, two girls smiled and splashed us not so gently with rose water, over which I promptly shrieked out in horror, fearing the chiffon I had on would be stained. Instinctively, I raised my hands to protect the make-up and the saree from further essence of rose water landing on me and the child grabbed his God-sent opportunity to vamoose into the crowd, burrowing through the suits and the sequined sarees draped into overstretched perfection.

I dived right behind him with a yell that startled many a conversation into silence, and had heads turning to my general direction.

'*Kabir!*' I yelled, in a manner which was supposed to be threatening enough to have him return tout de suite, tail tucked between his legs, but which obviously wasn't working. 'Come here right now, and hold my hand.' The spouse, having heard me air my lungs, gave me a stern look from ten feet away, where he was again in deep conversation with a chinless wonder in pink shirt with purple tie, and then beckoned me across to make a polite introduction. I smiled politely, murmured the 'How lovely to meet you' and such, with one eye trained on the fleck of brightness that was the child. I caught a flash of him running towards the stage, and I dashed after him, leaving the spouse staring with creased forehead and an expression that was closest to pain that I had ever seen on his face.

I closed in on the boy with lightning reflexes and strong thigh muscles, which developed only after he gained mobility and became the kind of toddler that made gentler mothers than me sit in corners and sob. Girding my loins, metaphorically speaking of course, I resumed the chase with renewed determination to administer spanks. I raced as fast as the shiny four-inch-heeled footwear and the five yards of fabric draped and pinned around me allowed, until an errant wire snagged on the heel and made me lurch precariously forward, and crash-land into a thinly pinstriped navy suit with fabric so smooth, I almost apologized for creasing it up. In true filmi fashion, a firm hand steadied me and I found myself in a semi swoon when I saw whom I had crashed into. My hands remained frozen into clutch-the-lapels position from which black-T-shirt-wearing muscled types firmly opened each finger and propped me in standing position. *Be still my beating heart*, a slight squeal escaped my lips, and all thoughts of finding the errant child flew out of my head much like them doves hightailed it from the to-be Mughal queen's hands.

'You!' So much was encompassed in that one word.

The object of my inelegantly gasped 'You!' smiled politely and handed me over to the hulking bald creature who was positioned at convenient arm's length and who promptly sat me on a chair while I recovered my breath and picked my jaw off the carpeted floor.

The child stopped in his tracks when he realized he wasn't being chased and made an about-turn to come gawp at the object of his mother's attention. 'You is Amar Khanna. Where is yer gun?' he asked without preamble, while I attempted hard to stop looking like a goldfish struck with a bad case of the hiccups.

Amar Khanna, the superstar, smiled warmly at him and picked him up in the manner of a man who has young children. I melted into a puddle of mush on the floor. There was something to macho men who could be nice to small children. Certain women would happily lay down in their paths, begging them to fertilize their eggs NOW.

'I've hidden it now,' he said. It brought me out of my trance-like state, and I smiled warmly at the child, perfectly unaware that he was in a position that 90 per cent of India's female population would slice out body parts and offer them to gods without hesitating to be in. The child was set down, patted gently and told firmly that running around in a public situation was not a great idea. Said child displayed great presence of mind and introduced me, proprietarily, by expediently grabbing my hand. 'Is my mudder.'

The boyish dimpled grin happened.

Be still my beating heart.

I had to prop myself up by holding onto the proffered hand and hanging onto it like a limpet. Anyone attempting to separate us now would have to do a surgical procedure involving scalpel and other sharp objects.

Runa's baritone cut in. 'Kay.' She inserted her formidable presence between me and *the* Amar Khanna, with not so much as a momentary glance at the heart-throb positioned for CinemaScope close-range drooling purposes. 'When you're done being such a drooling fangirl, come left of stage. I need your help.'

I gave her one of my patented knife-stab gazes that barely grazed her retreating back and fell, unheeded, to the floor.

The superstar got swept away into the crowd and moved swiftly towards the exit. I clung onto the child's hand staring at them broad retreating shoulders with a mixture of awe and regret that I hadn't been able to move out of goldfish mode for a moment to have carped the diem and made scintillating conversation.

I cast a longing look at the extreme end of the ballroom, beyond which the buffet was seeing the chafing dishes being filled with steaming hot delicacies, where plates were already clinking with the pleasant sounds of cutlery against porcelain. The mandatory chaat counter and the sushi counter already had a straggling motley bunch of first movers who were clustered strategically around them.

Runa had positioned herself left of stage, trying hard to look inconspicuous and succeeding just about as well as a steamroller in a line-up of racing cars. The spouse plucked me and the child out of our current position, placing us in the line meant to clamber onto the stage, convey our wishes and stand for the mandatory photo op. The bridal couple seemed young and pleasant looking, rather like a pair of kids playing dress-up in their parents' fancy wear. I wondered if the bridegroom's voice had broken yet. We went up on stage, smiled, shook hands and posed for the photographs and made polite chit-chat. Kabir examined the ceremonial sword at the groom's waist, worn to either reflect a warrior heritage quite at odds with his current stick-insect format, or in deference to some mandate that prescribes swords as an essential accessory, which the Stylish Modern Groom must wear. Hunger pangs were rumbling in deep thundercloud formation within my abdomen, and lightning in the form of the beginnings of a migraine attack began zinging my brain.

The spouse helped me down the steps, aware that unsteady steps, a saree, high heels and me all thrown together was a recipe for ungainly falling-down. I had spent enough time shoving bones back into sockets after having them dislocated in previous such episodes.

'Now, can we eat?' I asked, raising an arched brow in what I hoped was a sufficiently intimidating manner. And as I lifted a plate to serve myself, I spotted, from the corner of my eye, a child whom Kabir had made what he called 'frenship' with. He emerged holding a wrapped gift – which I hadn't seen him enter with because it was the one *we* had entered with – and proceeded swiftly through the crowd towards the exit gate. I blocked his path.

'Where are you taking the gift we brought?' I demanded, rather loudly.

When I blocked a path, it stayed blocked. Runa stared at me over the heads of the crowds. I raised my free hand and beckoned her over. Suddenly, the premises were a maze of people in blue safari suits speaking into walkie-talkies and circling us.

'Dat oney I wuz telling dis boy,' Kabir added kindly. 'Wai are yu taking the geefs outside. You habtu take dem inside. And he tole me it was for anudder pardy.'

6

In Which Kay Is Pursued by Manic Killer Lady on the Stairs

MONDAY

I woke up to a drizzly Monday morning. The previous evening was still fresh in my head, and I perused the details lovingly, over and over again, until the entire sequence of events had morphed into a CinemaScope presentation with appropriate intimidating background music by Hans Zimmer. The boy stopped from fleeing the premises with the gift was one of many children used by a gang of well-heeled thieves, who made it their modus operandi to visit venues with multiple wedding receptions on and wander from hall to hall transferring gifts without folks getting suspicious. Runa had even sourly granted me a 'Well, well, I wouldn't have put you down to be so alert,' as the General Manager, Banquets, had wrung the bones of my right hand to pulp in gratitude. The spouse, most annoyed at spotting Runa on the premises, had frogmarched me out in what could only be embarrassment.

'What was the need to play detective there, Kay? The place was swarming with my business associates, and I'm dreading to think that they think you work as an undercover detective,' he had said on the way back home.

'I wasn't playing detective, for God's sake! I just stopped that child from taking the gift we had brought out of the hall,' I had replied, stung to the bone that he had been embarrassed by what I thought was keen presence of mind.

'You could have done it in a dignified manner instead of yelling at the kid like a fishmonger. It was most embarrassing, Kay – you must learn to not get hyper and overreact.'

'What do you mean "overreact"? I busted a gang of wedding-gift thieves with my overreaction, and people thanked me for that ... but of course, you would find something about what I did not to your liking.'

He harrumphed and turned to the window. I harrumphed and turned to the other window.

The offspring sat between the two of us looking at our faces in turn and then gave up all attempts to play peacemaker and demanded a phone from either of us to play a game. The cold silence between the two of us all through the drive home had the boy playing interpreter in the manner couples have when they want to communicate a message but aren't in conversation with each other. It ended with the child telling his father, politely, 'Mamma sez to tell yu to go to hell.'

'Yes, I heard that.'

The white flag of truce had still not yet been flown by either of the warring factions. We had slept turning cold, unrelenting backs to each other.

The sky outside was in the kind of bad mood that had thunder growling occasionally at us, and the light wondering whether it was worth the effort to break through the cloud cover, and then giving up all pretence completely. I drew the covers over myself and snuggled back deeper, until the devil prodded me in my now-very-corpulent behind.

'Gerrup,' hissed the small, still voice of conscience and calorie-counting in my inner ear.

'You can't let rain keep you from working out.' I pulled the covers over my ears, and luxuriated in the warmth of sheer laziness until a random memory from a couple of days ago made it to the screen of the mind theatre: that of a glimpse of self in silhouette chanced upon during a random, unwary moment, where I wondered why the lady reflected did not use tummy-control foundation garments. This was followed by the horrific realization that the reflection was that of me. A glimpse that rattled my teeth and set them on gnashing edge, so distinct and well-formed was the little rotundity that is known in some circles as a paunch and in yet others as a pot belly. I thought back to the dress-up-in-saree moment last evening, where I had sucked in my belly and nothing had moved at all.

I sprang up, as the sharp cattle prod of guilt had actually made physical contact with behind, dragged myself to the bathroom, jumped in shock at the hideous visage reflecting back at me, with bags under eyes I could pack for a trip round the world and hair in wild disarray. All I needed to complete the look was to perch onto a broomstick and take off, holding on tight to my pointed hat.

I dragged on my velour hoodie and trackpants – in a vile shade of purple that had seemed interesting under the fluorescent lights but which the maid called 'baingani', robbing it of its allure – and slipped my reluctant feet into running shoes designed to add a spring to my step and help my cellulite rejig its way to nothingness.

I stepped out of the door, wondering where I should do my daily constitutional rounds: in the park or on the deserted streets that were probably overflowing with residual garbage and rainwater. That was when the heavens suddenly split the darkness of the morning with a finger of lightning that would have been more effective in an Armageddon-themed movie. Right on cue, as I took a wary step towards the elevator, a sonic thunder boom cut the air and landed on my eardrums, making me wish I had carried the home keys and would therefore not need to ring the doorbell, and in turn wake the spouse since the girl, Jamuna, was normally impervious to doorbells rung before her deemed wake-up time.

I girded my loins and decided that pounding the stairs would be my routine for the day again, unless I wanted to risk the parking lot and the dog turds deposited at regular intervals therein. I set off down the stairwell, prepared to encounter the occasional milkman and newspaper-delivery person who might be traipsing around the premises before the crack of dawn. Ever go down the staircase in a multistorey tower? It was always a voyage of discovery. On each floor you would encounter disused furniture, odds and ends that were too decrepit to be kept in the house but too emotionally relevant to be disposed of heartlessly to the bangarwalla who made his rounds of the area every morning.

Old stools, with one leg gone off to that place in the fifth dimension where single socks disappear to, and assorted cutlery leaving you with a set that is full of odds and ends whereas once there was an entire service for a seating of six, mattresses which have been propped up against the wall and which are now sagging in repose, threatening to collapse onto the stairwell if not re-propped up to stable levels, and the occasional remnants of carpentry and interior work that needed to be trashed: the jute bags comprising nails and odd ends that needed sorting out by the man of the house who, of course, was always really busy doing important things in the office and which are, stereotypically, believed to be beyond the ken of the woman of the house who dare not dispose of said gunny bag without the go-ahead from 'lord and master' because it might just contain some item of earth-shaking relevance to future home-improvement projects, like a nut or bolt that could make all the difference between a good table and a great table.

Naturally, much dodging and avoiding comprised an essential part of the manoeuvring. I quite fancied myself like Akshay Kumar in the cola ad where he parkours his way through a city, all to get to a bottle of said beverage, which is actually quite conveniently available at any corner grocery store. Some of the junk on the stairway, I was convinced, had entire early-life-on-earth ecosystems flourishing beneath it.

Exercise was meditative for me. I could get the feet moving to a rhythm, lose myself in my thoughts and come back to the real world only when the beeper alerted me that my hour was up. Today, I didn't have the beeper, it was just my counting of the stairs that was going to make all the difference to my glutes and my thighs and, hopefully, the rippling deposits on them that could only be eradicated by tubes attached to vacuums to suck them out of the system and churn them into fat cubes to be shipped right back to junk-food manufacturers to use in their food, which then caused us to become fat all over again and need the services of them liposuction experts. I digress.

I had reached the eighth floor after cheating and going down to the ground floor by the lift. It would be nice to start from the bottom without panting halfway through, I had thought. As I neared the eighth-floor landing, I felt the presence of something behind me. It was not even 6 a.m. Cleaning folk did not get into the act until it is well past 8 a.m. I half turned around, expecting the milkman. There was no one. Just a slight shadow. I blinked and turned back to the task at hand, namely to get myself up to the twentieth floor without collapsing by the end of ten minutes. I thought about the wedding last night and the swiftness with which the gang had been busted, and with a soft smile playing on my face, of how I had thrown myself unrestrained, at the buffet table, and needed to take my heels off to get to the car without toppling over with the excess poundage.

I knew the newspapers would have the details today, and I thought I might apprehend the newspaper guy on the stairwell itself and glean details of what had happened yesterday. It would be a snippet buried at the bottom of the city pages. Would there be a mention of me as the brave guest who noticed something amiss and apprehended the child burglar, never mind that she was now having afterthoughts about the apprehended delinquent being packed off to some gruesome remand home and child shelter, stories of which made her queasy?

Crime sniffed me out as an innocent bystander at most times. A year ago, there was a murder in the building complex and a corpse I chanced upon in the neighbourhood that I had gotten vaguely entangled with. I had been the last person to see the recently deceased alive and the police had asked me many questions; it had been my moment of fame in the society complex. Ever since I had developed a totally unhealthy interest in the components of a murder, a nice grisly murder witnessed first-hand would have probably freaked me out into cuckoo land, but being on the fringes and witnessing how a crime was solved was something I was quickly finding fascinating.

As I reached the twentieth floor, I felt the slight presence of something behind me yet again. I stopped in my tracks and turned around. Maybe it was the newspaper vendor doing his rounds. There was nothing. Totally clear. The stairs were lit up brightly by the multiple tube lights dotting every turn. And then the lights flickered. Like they do in them horror movies. I should have screamed but I was made of sturdier stuff. A sudden palpitating uneasiness took up residency in my chest. I carefully made my way back down the stairs in the deliberate manner that cartoon characters adopt when they don't want to make any noise.

Again, I felt someone behind me. I peered up.

Mrs 504 was standing there in her nightdress, staring down at me from the landing between the twentieth and nineteenth floors. A gaze so fixed and vitriolic, she only needed pig's blood all over her to be a dead ringer for Carrie. I squealed in horror and scooted down the stairs to the eighteenth floor, where I rang my doorbell one zillion times and hammered at the door in a frenzy, totally unconcerned about the inevitable grumpiness of his spouseness when awoken before his mandated hour.

'What the ... Kay?' The door was flung open angrily, a mood that no doubt changed rapidly no doubt seeing my pale face and shaken expression. 'What happened?'

I collapsed onto the sofa, panting heavily – and not from the physical exertion. He checked my pulse, checked my brow and, having ascertained I would live, continued with the inquisition.

'What happened to you? Are you all right? Do you feel a pain in your chest?'

Having caught my breath adequately enough to compose a coherent sentence, I gasped out, 'Mrs 504 was on the staircase. In her nightdress.' Why I felt compelled to add that sartorial detail, I did not know.

'And?' he asked, wondering why it had caused me to have a mini cardiac arrest.

'She was staring at me,' I gasped.

The procession of expressions on the man's face needed a video to be preserved for posterity. A handy cam video, not a cell phone one. If I hadn't been in such a state of shock, I would have run to the cupboard and done the needful myself. The first expression was that of bewilderment, followed in rapid succession by confusion, and then a spreading expression of wariness.

'Drink some water,' he urged, pressing a glass on me. The spouse has a standard solution to every situation that has me in a panic: drink some water, he always urges. If I were to be fished out of the sea, gasping and choking, having inhaled half the ocean into my lungs, he would still urge upon me the need to immediately ingest a glass of water upon which all would be well with me and the world at large.

'Now tell me,' he said in the calm, competent manner that made me realize why the good Lord above had thrown the twain of us together, why yin needed yang, why north needed south and other such polarities of nature. If the spouse was confronted by manic-looking lady on a stairwell, he would get into a detailed discussion about the reason for manic-looking lady's presence on said stairwell, along with added inputs about the cleanliness factor of the stairwell and the need to up the ante on the monthly washing of said stairs with requisite industrial cleaner and disinfectant.

'Why are you so freaked out if she was just staring at you? Did she try to harm you in any way? Was there anything about her appearance that was alarming?'

Put like that, it was difficult to pinpoint what it was that had freaked me out. Other than the rather loud orange flowers on her blue nightdress, with that appalling smocked yoke, the only thing that was alarming was the expression in her eyes.

'She was staring at me weirdly,' I replied.

The husband gave me his long-suffering sigh and put on his dealing-with-an-idiot face. We were interrupted by Jamuna emerging from the child's room nervously, realizing that the household was awake and buzzing and that undoubtedly the doorbell had been rung for the spouse to be awake at this hour. '*Bhaaaabbbbbhiii!*' she squealed, undoubtedly realizing that said bhabhi was shaky and needed gentle administering to for edgy nerves, which would undoubtedly be calmed down by screeches of '*Kyaaaa huaa*?' on a loop.

I smiled wanly in her direction much in the manner of the Christian martyr who had emerged from before the starving lion not a pile of white bones scraped bare, but in full health and unscathed, if a little shaky in the limbs. 'I was climbing the staircase,' I began, and the spouse settled himself comfortably knowing that a long narrative was in order, and demanded the girl rustle up some tea to fuel his brain cells so horrifically awakened by multiple doorbell rings. 'I felt someone behind me from the eight floor. I turned around but there was no one to be seen. When I was at the nineteenth floor again, but going down this time, I felt someone behind me again, so I turned around and saw this lady standing up there near the door to the terrace, in her nightgown, such an ugly print by the way – who wears cabbage roses on nightgowns any more? – just staring at me with the most evil stare possible. Like she wanted to kill me.'

Like Mrs Rochester, I wanted to add, but was overwhelmed by the ugliness of said nightgown, so violently hued, it assaulted the retinal rods and cones, and could cause an eye bleed if one came across it in bright light without requisite dark glasses on. What kind of women came out in public in a nightgown, I itched to add. I thought my social commentary on women who wore nightwear in public would not reach receptive ears at the moment, so I reined myself in with great difficulty and just touched upon it sparingly. The spouse wasn't interested in my thoughts on sartorial preferences and asked, relevantly, I thought, 'Why would she follow you on the stairs? Did you have a run-in of any sort with her?'

I thought long and hard if my encounters with her could be considered run-ins? 'No,' I replied firmly. 'I had just once hopped across to enquire kindly if all was well, given that folks were hearing screams from her floor, and she had been reportedly beaten up by her spouse, according to the watchman-maid-car-cleaner grapevine.'

His face turned stern and his jaw began its clench act. 'With Raji,' I added hastily.

The spouse shook his head. In a clearing of his head or a sorting of his thoughts, I couldn't tell. I braced myself for what I knew was coming: 'Why do you always need to poke your nose into stuff that is no concern of yours?'

He shook his head some more. 'Now stop climbing the stairs at odd hours and stick to your routine in the park or in the open.' He looked a minute at the sky pouring furiously outside, grey and grim. 'Or just go the gym! Good knows that membership has been languishing for months and they won't give me a half refund given you never use yours.'

I nodded in terror. This was not the best moment to bring up the point that I hated going to the gym and exercising in a public situation where everyone seemed to be much more competent at operating all the machines than I was.

All thoughts of further exercise banished, I went into the bathroom to splash some water on my face with trembling hands. The face in front of me was ashen, terrified, the roses blown off the cheeks by a fear that still tickled my spine. I was still shivering. Something about Mrs 504 was shiver-inducing at that moment, strange, given that on a regular day she was a regular woman. One who wouldn't cause hyperventilation in an ant even if she approached it with stated intention of stomping it to a pulp.

The child awoke and immediately demanded cavity-enhancing sugary stuff, which the dentist had declared verboten, and was yelled at for his temerity at being so selfish when I had obviously just saved myself from a serial killer. He shuffled back into the bedroom and put the television on at full volume to make his opinion of my sudden escape from death's hands very clear. The intercom rang. Insistently. Jamuna answered it, like she answered all telephone instruments, at volumes ascertained to wake the dead from their graves and send them fleeing.

'*Haaaallllloooo*,' she screeched. The child shut the door to the bedroom, to ensure he could listen to the dialogue of whatever cartoon character he was watching, undisturbed.

'*Kyaaaa bolaaa?*'

I rushed up to take the instrument from her as the spouse winced at the obscene decibel levels. It was the security personnel from the building lobby demanding immediate discourse with the spouse. I handed the phone to him. The spouse was on the managing committee of the society and consequently among the Persons Who Must Be Informed Immediately whenever things of consequence happened on the premises.

'*Kya?*' His face drained itself of all colour, which definitely was a difficult task given that on any day, even without alcohol to add an additional tint of the rose, his face was ruddy enough to shame any sunset into declaring it would only incorporate pastel shades.

'*Kabhi hua?*' he continued. I sidled up next to him, hoping to glean information through osmosis because, of course, he wasn't still communicating what had happened to make his face drain itself of all available blood, making him a sure candidate for the next vampire role to come along, with adequate glitter powder painted on. '*Aap* sure *ho, aadha ghanta ho gaya? Main aa raha hun.*'

With that, he hung up and looked straight at me. 'I didn't do anything,' I said, in immediate reflex action.

'The lady from 504 jumped off from the terrace. Half an hour ago. What time did you see her?

I looked at him in shock. I looked at the wall clock. I looked at my wristwatch, which never left my wrist unless I was in the bath. Fifteen minutes ago, I thought. It could have been half an hour. Time swirled. Half an hour ago, according to my wristwatch, I had been pressing the buzzer on the lift that had glided up to the eighteenth floor and had gone straight to the ground floor where there was absolute peace and calm and errant milkmen entering the premises clanging their cans of milk to much disharmony. There was definitely, at that point, no hullaballoo normally associated with a person flinging themselves off the twentieth floor of the premises and spattering onto the paving below. Unless the watchman and I had watches set to different times.

The words were icicles on my tongue: 'Perhaps twenty minutes ago.' Luckily, the chair right behind me was positioned to catch my frame as it sank rather heavily into it. It groaned in protest, though. No piece of furniture would like me to sink heavily into it, especially not a delicate Louis some-number-in-French reproduction chair. The spouse winced just that little bit as it creaked. He was rather fond of those chairs, he was, and had scoured the second-hand furniture markets in Oshiwara long and hard to find exact replicas. When he finally found them, he almost did the funky chicken dance on the streets.

'The watchman says she jumped half an hour to forty-five minutes ago. Behind the building. She almost flattened a car cleaner, who was narrowly saved by his quick reflexes.

The spouse slipped his feet into his slippers and prepared to descend to the lobby to confront the chaos. 'I'm coming down too,' I said. He didn't try to dissuade me. Not that his dissuading me would have worked. I am, what the elders in the family have long called, without embellishment, dheet. Roughly translated, this word meant stubborn. Resolutely stubborn. Stubborn to the extent that no amount of persuasion would get one to change one's mind. This particular quality served me well whenever I was on a track that was right and leading to concrete action with positive results, but not so useful when it consistently came to issues like insisting on a fringe when the entire square area of the face was about the size of a hand, resulting in me looking like Samara crawling out of the well in *The Ring*. Nonetheless, I did spend most of my adolescence under a fringe and spectacles, which meant very little face surface area was exposed to the elements. That was actually a kindness done to society. On the occasional events when I was compelled to sweep the fringe off my face, folk quickly requested me to mercifully let it fall over half my face again or risk an outbreak of pink eye.

Therefore the husband went off to investigate people flinging themselves off twentieth-floor terraces which were supposed to be kept locked at all times, and only opened for official purposes such as cleaning of the water tanks or the glass facades or very important official reasons as spotting the moon on Karwa Chauth which in turn meant that one watchman was permanently stationed on the terrace in the event that a hungry, irate wife decided that flinging herself over the side was a preferable option to seeing her husband's face through the sieve and getting saddled with him for the next many lifetimes.

I wondered if I should call Runa on this. The timing bothered me. I was probably the last person to see this woman on the stairs barely a few minutes before getting told she had smashed herself to smithereens on the paving in the compound an hour earlier. I wondered whether the smashed person had been suitably removed from the public gaze, and whether I would be strong enough to stomach the remnants of blood and tissue which undoubtedly would be scattered all over the place. Unless of course, some kind soul had done us all a favour and cleaned up the place.

Nonetheless, with a show of courage I did not possess, I meekly followed the spouse down to the elevator bank, where he stood pressing the buttons with the kind of impatience that clearly denoted that someone was going to have to pay for a messed-up Monday morning. And with Mrs 504 being dead, I was the only available scapegoat he could turn his wrathful gaze on. And so he stared at me wrathfully until I felt around two feet tall, and in a particular situation: like when the hand of an irate progenitor was about to descend upon my cheek.

When we reached the ground floor, the lobby was buzzing with folks in various stages of déshabillé. The venerable Colonel Pandit from the ninth floor was in a pair of violently striped green-and-yellow pyjamas that had the eyeballs shivering in their sockets. The assorted car cleaners in their shorts and T-shirts were clustered around what seemed to be a heap of clothes at the extreme end of the paved compound. Only the tiles cracked under the impact and what seemed to be a dull brown river flowing down to the flower beds gave me any indication that this was indeed the body of a person who had thrown herself from the terrace of a twenty-floor building. Add to that a double-heighted lobby, which made it effectively the twenty-second floor. The rain had thinned to a drizzle, and the sun was pushing curious rays through breaks in the cloud cover, feeling around for the earth below.

I scurried across with the fascinated terror that made me watch horror movies from behind the cushion with the volume on mute. I found myself drawn to it, yet my weak heart could not take too much of the gore. I was known to pass out during a viewing of *The Amityville Horror*, and was revived with much hooting and 'water on the face splashing' that cruel friends are fully capable of doing rather than the loving 'head on the lap' and 'gentle wiping of face with damp towel' that a mother should do. I was convinced that in an earlier life I was a Victorian lady, trussed up in corsets so tight that the distress caused me to keel over and faint, crushing whatever unfortunate creature happened to be in my path.

I held onto the spouse's hand for support as we approached, much to his disgusted look at this unseemly display of affection in such a situation. The wailing sirens of the approaching police vans grew stronger, and a sudden rush of activity broke out in the complex. The rains had made the tiling wet and slick with running blood, and Mrs 504 was lying like she had fallen unexpectedly to the ground and was looking up at us in a very surprised manner. Almost as if she expected to be picked up, and was puzzled that none of us were offering to help her. Only if you looked closer you noticed that her limbs were splayed in an awkward manner and the angle of one leg was at such a degree that no surgeon would ever be able to manoeuvre it back into the position the good Lord meant it to be in. I felt bile rising in my throat. Pulpy bits of what seemed like brain tissue were floating in the blood that ran out towards the plant beds, mingling with the run-over from the rainwater, seeping into the soil, no doubt destroying evidence.

A police inspector hopped out of the jeep, his face a mashed, complex crease of sleeplessness and irritation. And the kind of suntan that went beyond any redemption with anti-tan creams. Not that he would be requiring any for application. '*Kone hai yeh ladees*? *Kidhar hai phamily*?' he asked randomly at the crowd. No one volunteered to impart information or take on onus of the family ties enquired politely after.

The security rounder, Mr Rathore – him of the rodent teeth, slicked back hair and sharp safari suits at 6 a.m. – hovered around surreptitiously and muttered that the husband of said unfortunate demised soul was apparently on tour and therefore unavailable and that he had been called and informed of the incident by a neighbour and was starting back from whatever place he was supposed to be in, and would be back on the premises by the afternoon. All this was said in one soft low breath, at which I looked upon him in shock and awe for his calmness and seeming control of the situation, which admittedly was getting a little too runny given that the rain had begun falling with even greater ferocity.

The situation in question had by then been clicked from every possible angle by the forensic photographer, who had an assistant with umbrella held hovering over him and his camera. A stretcher was brought out from the police van, and a discoloured sheet – once white in its youth, and now an indeterminate shade between beige and coffee – was used to give the poor woman some dignity in her death. A team of policemen had swarmed over the premises with disembodied walkie-talkie conversation going on between those positioned on the terrace and those on the ground, checking angle of fall and trajectory and suchlike, I presumed.

I stood, hand over my mouth, in silent horror. My stomach, with nothing ingested, was doing an evil dance with my gastric secretions, which were threatening to rise to the throat. The sub-inspector (SI) was jotting down names and contact details of all those present on the spot, and promised to visit us later for further insight into what they were terming a possible suicide. I nudged the husband, gently, and then with a rather sharp jab, when he didn't respond with the alacrity I would have liked. 'Wha … what …?' He jumped and turned round.

'Should I tell them I saw her on the stairs before or after she had supposedly jumped?' It was a valid question. I wanted to help with the police investigation.

I also had rainwater pouring down me in the most unflattering way, given that neither of us had thought to carry an umbrella. And I would have liked to do all my helping of the police investigation in dry locations, preferably within the lobby.

The spouse gave me one of his looks. The kind of look he reserved for moments of serious doubts about whether I needed to book a consultation with a psychiatrist. He had an extensive collection of many looks to give me, and I had deciphered them all. This look also meant that I would do well to keep it zipped.

I scooted back to the relative dryness of the lobby area, where a majority of the residents were already congregated much like a flock of pigeons in a 'let's figure out which statues to bombard with poop right now' strategy meet.

This was looking to be an eventful week, starting off with a gang of wedding-gift thieves and the suicide off the roof of my own building. Heavens. At that rate, I wouldn't be surprised to find corpses emerging, slimily green and decaying, from my bathtub. Which reminded me: I had a kitty lunch the next day and a suicide to investigate.

7

In Which a Catfight Ruins a Lunch

TUESDAY

The previous day had gone by in the kind of surreal daze that set in when the person who passed away was not one you knew well enough but could still mourn in a manner that clouded the mood. It also made you feel a little guilty while devouring a boxfull of red velvet cupcakes when in troth you had no business donning the sackcloth and ashes.

But I was nothing if not a diligent detective-in-training, and I would rein in my natural black mood and be the life and soul of the lunch I had to attend, I told myself. Then I did a couple of rounds of testing to figure out if the contraption Runa had given me for recording purposes was indeed functional. Of course, I could just set the phone on record and keep it in my handbag, but who was I to argue with Runa when she insisted on going all high-tech-gizmos on me.

Getting dressed for a ladies' lunch was a big deal. For one, there was the pressure to look good and with it wear sufficient caratage of compressed carbon on one's person to have people donning sunglasses to protect their eyes from glare-induced blindness. Then comparisons of caratage of the rocks on one's fingers and ears would be done, albeit without actually calling for a pair of callipers. That would be followed by spot X-ray-vision label-reading of the clothes to determine the exact number of kilograms gained or lost since last inspected. Given that this was my first encounter with this lot, the last one could be skipped over peaceably. For the first one, I loaded my person up with solitaire earrings, pendant and matching rock on finger, and added to my light-refracting properties with a tennis bracelet that could, if properly twirled in the light, cause serious retinal damage.

I donned a blood-red, tie-neck balloon top that fell gracefully to my hips, and paired it with a pair of tan skin-fit trousers and nude stilettos. The trousers, while supposed to make me look slimmer, ended up making me look much like a chicken drumstick post some time spent on a tandoor. What had compelled me to wear this ensemble had been the premise of expandability as promised by the Lycra, and the girth of the balloon top, which I hoped would adequately conceal the spread of the abdominal girth as one ate and ate and ate to one's heart's content as one is supposed to do at an all-you-can-eat buffet – and that, to my parsimonious mind, entailed licking the chafing dishes clean at the counter and needing physical assistance to stagger out of the restaurant, maintaining dignity by not keeling over with the imbalance of food (ingested and undigested) inside my person.

When Devyani met me at the lobby, she had poured herself into a skin-fit top and a pair of trousers so tight, they'd probably have to contemplate surgery by the end of the day to get them off her. Not to mention that I was acutely jealous of the fact that she had a stomach so flat she probably had her child by Amazon delivery.

As we drove towards the suburb where the lunch was to be, she briefed me quickly – or was it debriefed? – on the people we were to meet with. There was Jahnavi who was the head honcho or the de facto leader of the group, who was the most important person. Next was Mili, who was her sidekick and flunkey.

'You'll know them when you see them,' she said mysteriously. She then rattled off a list of names, taking the total to ten, excluding the two of us. 'Today,' she informed me, 'is Mili's turn. She always picks this restaurant because her husband knows the owner and she gets a discount and can even have the leftovers packed to take home.'

I empathized. I was rather miffed with the new policy the rather spiffy places had about not packing doggy bags. I imagined staffers rolling joints and downing the perfectly edible remnants of my paid-for meals after the shutters were downed. I had the kind of relationship with restaurants that most people had with places of worship. I always entered hesitantly and looked around in wonderment. I savoured the aromas of food wafting through the holy portals. I looked for a buffet along with the à la carte, and if there was one, I gravitated to it to check out what was on offer and whether it was worth opting for. As you might well surmise, dear reader, my days of fine dining have long gone the way of the waistline when I came forth with child.

When we stepped into the dimly lit restaurant – the soft music playing in the background, the chatter of high-pitched voices drowning said soft music – the table was full.

'Arey, why so late?' boomed an authoritative voice, and an imposing woman hauled herself out of her seat and air-kissed Devyani, who then introduced me to the owner of the voice. The personality, as they say in the colloquial, matched the voice in its imperiousness.

'Jahnavi, meet Kanan,' said Devyani doing the honours. I smiled and extended a paw delicately, conscious that if Jahnavi applied her strength, the paw would be a crumple of crushed bones. Jahnavi was what they termed Amazonian: tall and solidly built. She had the refined features of a fine genetic inheritance, grey-green eyes and a mane of brown hair (whether natural or bottle-bought I could not tell in the dim lighting) that a lion would have given a canine tooth to own. She smiled pleasantly, running an appraising eye up and down my person, stopping momentarily at the diamonds, with the circuitry in her brain almost making visible estimations of net worth.

A thin, anxious-looking face popped up next to Jahnavi inserting itself between the three of us, insisting on an introduction.

'Mili, Kanan,' Devyani said politely, inserting a short speech about where the spouse worked, and the fact that I had also been a career woman before taking a break for child-rearing, and that the spouse was a hotshot in the corporate echelons and steadily clambering upwards and onwards, validating my credentials as worthy enough to join their closed ranks.

I smiled tautly, stretching cheek muscles to tearing point, and air-kissed all and sundry. That was when I spotted Runa hunkered down in a corner behind a pillar and a potted plant, sticking out like a sore thumb with her mistrustful gaze no doubt souring everything lactic on the premises, including the offerings at the dessert counter. She gave me, what they termed in the books, a loaded gaze. I was sure that the backpack she carried everywhere had something equally explosive and loaded nestled within. A shiver ran down my spine.

'Excuse me,' I said, wriggling my way out from the midst of the banquette I'd been squeezed into, displacing three graciously accommodating women, and hotfooted it to the restrooms. Runa followed quickly, stomping the ground with the footstep of one who owned it.

'Are you set?'

'Yes, yes, I am.'

She took the recording device, shook it, put her ear to it, commanded I say something, decided it was functional, and warned me not to do something stupid or sit on it.

'Take notes, just in case this doesn't work,' she said, handing me a pen and a notepad.

My jaw dropped.

'How can I take notes at a ladies' lunch?' I protested, valiantly. Runa just didn't get these things.

'Of course you can. Say you are writing down names and details so you remember them or something, since you're meeting them all for the first time. And get them all to talk about the dead woman.'

'But how am I supposed to eat and take notes at the same time? I'll call you and you can listen into the conversation. That would be easier.'

She fixed me with the gorgon's eyes. 'Yes, that's a good idea. But take notes too.'

I was powerless to protest. I took the pad and the pen wordlessly and shuffled out of the restroom, a broken woman. How was I to do justice to the meal with the right hand occupied with note-taking? The table had commenced playing a rather raucous housie, giving me a legitimate excuse to keep pen and notepad on the table, although there seemed to be nothing legitimate worth scribbling except a heated discussion over who called the Jaldi Five first, which almost led to a fist fight, and a challenge to guns at dawn, failing which drawing of the butter knives at close of play. When that was settled, a round of quick gossip happened about one member who hadn't attended, and the ladies were all grateful that she hadn't come in, so they had at least one person to tear to pieces collectively.

'Do you remember the time before last, when everyone was present?' said Devyani, with a slight shudder. 'It was so boring, we couldn't discuss anyone. We had to wake folks up to stop them falling face first into their salads.'

After having learnt that the absent party had an issue with food, and she had been known to finish a lunch and trot off to the bathrooms to put a hand down her throat, and that this was the only secret of her rather enviable slimness, not to mention a good surgeon who offered her a bulk discount since she had got liposuction done almost all over her body.

'Remember how she was after she delivered her second?' cackled one lady in the corner, whose name evaded me and who could have rolled downhill with just a slight prod of a finger. 'She looked like a balloon. And then within three months she was size zero.'

'And Jaya?' cut in another one, from the other extreme of the table, so effectively making me ping-pong my head in order to follow the conversation. 'What about her? I saw her come out of the VeriSlim clinic across my house so often I thought she'd moved in there.'

My senses went on alert. 'Isn't she the one who passed away by suicide?'

There was a sudden hush at the word suicide. Then the buzz of voices broke out all at once. With parties for and against the deceased person. 'She was such a wonderful person, I wonder what happened to tip her over the edge?' said Mili, sighing deeply.

'We never know what goes on in someone's head,' said the corpulent one at the far end, who was concentrating fiercely on hacking a stubborn piece of animal protein into bits.

'She was a nasty, mean thing, good riddance,' piped up another pinched-looking person, who was called Jolly by the rest of the clan, nomenclature that was most ironic given that her face was anything but.

'Don't speak ill of the dead, Jolly,' a voice of caution piped in, casually parting the crowd of voices, clearing its own path with its sweetness. The owner of the voice was delicate and soft faced, and sat as though a shield protected her from the rambunctiousness of the others. Another more aggressive voice took up cudgels for the dear departed, and this degenerated into another loud argument and we were but seconds away from the bread knives being put to efficient use as maiming devices when they announced that the buffet was now open.

The herd stampeded to the chafing dishes, snorting, and for some time the only sound at the table was that of cutlery clinking contentedly against the plates. Five refills of my plate later, for which I had cleverly positioned myself at the end of the banquette, I sighed and laid the fork and knife down. The discussion regarding the deceased was picked up once again and I listened in, my ears aflap.

'I heard she lost a lot of money betting on the IPL?' speculated another, her eyes lighting up at the prospect of a vicarious spin at the 20-over series betting tables. 'No, no,' interjected Jahnavi, who had just polished off a mound of ice-cream and cake that had almost hidden her face from view across the table. 'She was in depression. Post-partum.'

'But her baby was born ten years ago,' piped in a surprised voice from indeterminate source.

'Arey, my post-partum lasted till both the kids entered college,' stated another slightly senior personage, with both overflowing personality and cleavage, firmly, in a tone that brooked no debate.

Mili decided that she must add her two bits to the entire thing. 'Perhaps there is something we don't know. There was no suicide note found, right?'

'But since when has that stopped us from knowing everything,' Jahnavi answered to a burst of approving laughter. The topic veered to another hot suicide, that of a television actress who had put rope and ceiling fan to use. All that iced tea I had ingested in the run-up to lunch was pressing excitably on my pea-sized bladder and I excused myself to go to the ladies' room.

As I sat on the pot and puffed at a sly smoke (what? A girl needed some nicotine in her system to stay alert and to kill the appetite), I pondered about the nowhere this investigation was leading to and figured an alternate track needed to be taken and taken immediately. Just then, the click-clacking of heels signalled the arrival of feet into the adjoining powder room. I rose to exeunt right, in case the smoke was reported to the authorities.

'You better stop discussing Jaya,' hissed a familiar voice, 'or I'll tell everyone it was you who forced her to kill herself.'

I held my breath and sat as still as I could manage, trying to figure out who the two women were. The voices were muted, almost as if they were speaking from behind a wall. I then realized that the voices were not coming from within the ladies' cloakroom but from outside and through the exhaust vent, which was located conveniently near the parking lot. I wondered whether, by the expedient method of removing my heels and clambering onto the pot, I might just be able to see who the two voices belonged to.

'Stop behaving like a bereaved widow,' said the other voice, now hissing too.

'You have no proof except your suspicions and your nitpicking. She was just as good a friend to me as she was to you and you need to stop this obsessive imagining about what drove her to suicide, okay, *okay*? It is not healthy …'

I began removing my stilettos as stealthily as I could and clambered precariously on top of the commode, peering through the slats of the exhaust fan vent. I could see nothing except cars parked in the regimented lines of the parking lot that stretched out for yards and yards of what seemed to be unpopulated-by-humans territory, except for the occasional driver sleeping deep in the arms of air-conditioned Lethe. *Perhaps if I stood on my toes and angled my neck a bit* … the voices were beginning to fade, they were walking away, I needed to do something quickly and so I did: I lost my balance and crashed down in the most horrendous way that led to shrieks from the adjoining cubicle and the cleaner rushing in and banging on my locked door.

'I'm okay, am okay,' I yelled back, picking myself and my dignity up, and slipping feet back into my shoes, opening the door, while checking if all my limbs were still in working condition. Thankfully they were, and I opened the door to the curious gathering of assorted faces that had accumulated outside.

'But, how did you fall?' Devyani had landed inside the ladies' room. 'Did you black out or something? Low BP spell?'

She took my wrist with the authority of one who has done the mandatory first-aid course and knows how to check a pulse. 'It seems high, if anything,' she said.

'Widen your eyes.' She looked into them deep. 'You seem okay. You must really rethink wearing such high heels, I think it is a trifle difficult for you to balance your, errm, weight on them.'

I gave her one of those looks that, had she been made of wax, would have instantly melted her.

'Shall we leave? We're done here,' she said. Her face had an odd look to it, which did not brook any argument, although there was a second helping of the tiramisu calling out my name in dulcet tones from the dessert counter.

Runa entered, hulking in a corner, and made to straighten what was there of the hair on her head by running her fingers through it. When Devyani stepped out of the powder room, Runa hissed at me.

'What happened in here?'

I gave her an abbreviated report of all I had heard.

'Do you know who it was?' she hissed.

'Nope, I couldn't see them,' I confessed sadly, displaying the patch of blue and rapid swelling of the ankle from the fall. This detective business was rough on the limbs. I would have to wear comfortable shoes for the next few days, and this did not augur well for any social occasions that might crop up unexpectedly.

I rummaged around the handbag for the recorder but couldn't find it. A sudden brainwave and I looked into the stall I had been occupying, and sure enough, there it was, floating where no hand would dare to retrieve it. That was what came from not closing one's bag when one clambered onto things one was liable to fall from.

'Dammit, Kay, not one simple thing you can get done.'

'I helped you nab the thieves at the wedding reception.'

It had the effect of shining a torch into the eyes of a stampeding bull, making the beast do an instant backflip and charge in the opposite direction, tail tucked between rear legs.

'Okay, okay, that was just beginner's luck. Don't read too much into it.'

'I also ...' I began, just getting started on listing out all the numerous small incidents where I had been of invaluable assistance to her. That included the time when she was given detention in fifth grade for bringing a dangerous weapon to school and I'd helped her by saying a strange man had come into the grounds brandishing it and she had bravely divested him of it, saving the lives of us hapless ones cowering and bleating in terror on the fringes of the playground. It had all ended with her being honoured with a bravery certificate, given that the watchman had been fast asleep on duty and couldn't corroborate my version of events.

'Later, Kay,' she cut in. 'They're all leaving now, go, go, go. God, how they can eat.'

I shrugged. I had barely eaten. I had been too busy trying to remember who said what. And now I had forgotten everything. I scampered out, walking carefully on my ankle that was threatening to swell into a fine medium-sized orange. I took the stilettos off and held them in my hand with all the suaveness I could muster. Luckily, people around were sympathetic. Except Runa of course, who slunk off like she had no truck with me.

Jahnavi was waiting at the table, and tut-tutted about my hobbling arrival. 'Oho, that bad? The strap snapped, did it?'

The remainder of the coven still not dispersed cluck-clucked sympathetically and yelled for some ice, pressing an unused napkin into service. I gave in to their ministrations happily. Then, a voice spoke: 'Let's leave now, okay?'

I looked up. The 'okay' was unmistakable. I'd heard it one second before I'd crash-landed in undignified sprawl onto the tiling of the tiny WC cubicle. The faces around me were dispersing, who was it who had said the sentence? The 'okay' disappeared into a sea of bye-byes peppered with air-kissing. All I knew was that someone from this very group had probably pushed Jaya into taking her own life, and that Jaya's husband's suspicions were right. But I had absolutely no clue who it could be. And soon, helped by Devyani, I made my slow progress to the exit, where the petrol-fuelled chariot arrived, and we made our speedy exit. The phone pinged. Insistently. I fished it out, while making the smallest of small talk with Devyani, which revolved around the price of vegetables having reached such stratospheric levels that eating animal protein actually felt cheaper.

The screen flashed. Runa. I disconnected the call, with the auto message going out saying that I was in a very important meeting and would call back later. A few seconds later the WhatsApp vibrate shook the handbag lying in my lap in a manner only demonic possession could rival.

'Kay, *YOU NUT*,' she had typed in capital letters. 'You're in the car with one of the women who was in the parking lot. That's the one you need to be asking questions to.'

8

In Which There Is Yet Another Gluttonous Lunch

WEDNESDAY

The next morning was dark, dank. I was still recovering from the ear-lashing Runa had given me for being elementarily idiotic in not being able to recognize voices or remembering to make that call to her as promised so she could listen in to the conversation at the table.

Perhaps I was not cut out for this detective business, I thought. Keeping eyes and ears open wasn't enough, one needed to do a short course in How to Operate Tiny Gadgetry without Being Spotted.

The spouse and the child were sleeping in. It was a public holiday in deference to a national leader who had either been born or had died on that date, and consequently, we were at the loose end that we generally ended up at on enforced holidays, which occurred unseemingly in the middle of the week, and ruined one completely for additional hedonism on the weekend.

As I flipped through the newspapers, the mobile buzzed. The mater. It was something urgent for the mater to be calling at the crack of dawn. Ah well, 9 a.m. did constitute the crack of dawn on a public holiday, didn't it?

'You didn't tell me you were going for a page-three wedding,' she began without preamble. Her tone the accusatory version which would, in the course of three sentences into the conversation, get in to 'This is what I suffered pre-eclampsia and had an episiotomy that got reinfected multiple times for.'

After I had calmed her down a bit, it emerged that photographs of the wedding had been splashed in the social section of the newspaper and she had spotted me looking confused behind one of the Bollywood actors who had been in attendance, for whom she would have slit her veins in the days when she was young and gullible and hadn't yet plighted her troth to the pater. I flipped through the newspapers too, and realized that the newspapers in Pune generally had the social pages a few days later than the ones in Mumbai and went hunting for the previous day's newspapers, which Jamuna kindly informed me had been used to dry out the spinach leaves on and had been disposed of with the stems. There was a lesson here. My one moment of fame, albeit by virtue of being in the same frame as a celebrity, was disposable. I could have sobbed.

When the duo awoke, it was just about time for lunch, and the consensus was that it would be buffet lunching because the child was terribly miffed I had partaken of the calorific stuff the previous day without including him in the party, no matter that I tried patiently to explain to him that the lunch was only for aunties and there were no children present, nor life-size animal replicas moving their trunks or growling threateningly, nor a sound-and-light show to keep pint-sizes like him occupied while the accompanying adults threw food down their gullets, without chewing, at the acute risk of choking, in order to leave the premises before boisterousness took over the momentary onset of good behaviour in public situation.

We rarely went to restaurants that did not have novelties placed in situ to grasp the attention of the juvenile diner. And most of the times, our culinary excursions were limited to places where the crockery was disposable, and a man with a painted face and a striped suit sat on a bench without to serve as warning for those headed within to check if they were carrying their migraine medication, because the child-induced chaos within would be louder than the red and yellow of his suit.

The child bounded around, looking his dapper best in clothes that were two sizes too small for him but currently in favour because they were his current favourite outfit, one that he had worn everywhere for the past couple of months. The ensemble included a bumblebee striped fleece hoodie, which was totally inappropriate for the Mumbai climate but had been bought on a shopping whim in foreign climes. Ten minutes into it and I would be mopping the sweat off his brow and begging him to divest himself of it or risk perspiration-induced dehydration. He also had on a pair of jeans that were so tight he had to be pulled into them inch by inch, and then told to suck his little stomach in to get the button and the buttonhole to meet – worn primarily because they were the only pair of his jeans in stock which met the mandatory requirement of being slim-fits, 'sukdu' jeans as he called them, which were currently in vogue. The zip of said pair of jeans had already given way, thanks to the frantic pulling that was occasioned every time the need to empty the bladder hit, and given the climate, coupled with the child's manic intake of cold and sweet non-nutritious drinks on the double.

'Why don't you throw those pants away,' the spouse growled. 'He'll damage some delicate parts if he continues wearing them.'

I sighed and tried again to convince the offspring to shift legs into roomier trousers but he kicked and screamed and threw the kind of tantrum that had me reaching for the Disprin in vodka before ingesting anything solid as a buffer. We reached a happy compromise: he could wear the sukdu fits when we returned home, now he could wear the elastic-waisted trousers so he had space to eat. He agreed and I handed over the offending sukdu fits to Jamuna indicating through mime that she was to dispose of them by either cutting them to bits or burning them without setting the place ablaze.

'Let's eat food,' said the child most eloquently when we entered the portals of the hallowed food place. We did our mandatory tour of the buffet spread, his little hand tucked into mine, for him to investigate what it was that would slide down his gullet with the minimum of fuss and the maximum of speed. Any animal protein normally did the trick. The child was blatantly carnivorous. 'Gimme chikkin. Gimme muttin,' was the normal refrain heard during mealtimes in the house. One of those instances that would go down in the annals of recorded history would be the one where he held up a polite hand at a party and instructed the server to not even bother approaching him with something that had not been alive and running around at some point.

We moved purposefully to claim a vacant table. The spouse sat back and relaxed with the bar menu and I sat down graciously as the man pushed the chair back in gently for me to make a graceful descent and not land smack bang on my butt in ungainly manner. I looked around to suss out the competition on the premises, and content that there was none, let the stomach relax. The restaurant had still to fill up. Of course, once it filled up I would have a plate full of edibles in front of me and wouldn't care a damn if the most beautiful woman in the world was at the next table, except, of course, if the spouse's drool dripped onto my foot from indiscreet staring.

The child pulled my hand. 'Lookit there. Is dat gurl frum dat serial?' The jaw hit the floor. How did my child, who got an hour or so of rationed cartoons, ladled out in miserly manner, know about 'gurls' from TV serials?

I swivelled my head in said direction with the kind of suddenness that was a red-carpet invitation for a crick in the neck – which I did get. Surely and sharply enough for me to gasp out loud. The spouse looked at me quizzically. 'Stop staring, Kay,' he said in the quiet tone that was used as a warning in public spaces.

'Don stare, don stare,' exhorted the child. 'Is very bad manners.'

I sputtered in exasperation. The face was pretty but unfamiliar. Was I the world's worst television serial watcher?

'I wantu ged an autograff,' spake the fruit of my womb. 'Wid my name. I will showtu my frens in skul.'

The handbag, cluttered to the point of having alien life forms growing in it and threatening to take over the world, yielded, after much shaking, poking around and emptying all contents onto table, a scrap of paper that could be used for procuring said autograph. The boy calmly picked up a pen, which had fallen out from the debris, and marched up to the pretty face with the self-assuredness that comes from the knowledge that, unlike a male approximately a couple of decades or so older, he would never be slapped when approaching a random female at a restaurant.

I watched with interest. Some flattered giggling and flibbertigibbeting happened, and the hapless male accompanying TV serial girl sighed deeply and then turned around to look at our table as the child pointed us out to the person who was signing autograph.

It was a television serial man with the copper highlighted curls. Veer. Or Rana. Or whatever his current small-screen character was called. He lived in our tower and had already had a couple of close encounters with me in the elevator. He raised a polite hand in acknowledgement when he saw us. And then – the horror! – pushed his chair back, rose from it, and firmly escorted the child back to our table.

I got into the kind of lather I always did when a good-looking person of the opposite sex was in the immediate vicinity, that is, I sucked the stomach in and wondered if my pores were as dilated as my pupils.

'And your son, Kay, takes after you, he does,' he said, in the smooth non-gravelly voice that belied the number of times one had seen him puffing away on the evil sticks in the building compound. 'Complete charmer.'

'Hello,' I said, as the spouse reluctantly struggled to his feet to handshake in the excruciatingly polite manner one reserves for folks one knows not too well and can't confess to being too glad to meet.

'BTW,' said he, the man whose character was named Veer, and whose real name was Rana something I couldn't recall earlier. I'd had some conversation a few months ago about some other murders in the vicinity with him. I so needed to take those memory-enhancing pills hawked on television by white-haired grannies who solved calculus problems in a jiffy. He addressed the spouse: 'I thought I'd bring to your notice that there seems to be some problem on the sixth or the fifth floor. Sometimes there is screaming on the stairs, a woman's voice really loud, just screams. I know because sometimes I climb the stairs home instead of taking the elevator. You know, try to pack in as much cardio as one can on a working day when one can't hit the gym.'

The spouse looked at me at the same moment I looked at him, no doubt thinking thoughts of Mrs 504 spattered on the paving.

Rana continued sanguinely, 'Also, you really need to do something about the security, they're sleeping on the job. I return home late from shoots most nights, and they're snoring complacently in their chairs. I have to keep buzzing non-stop before they wake up and press the switch to open the doors to the inner lobby.'

The spouse thanked him politely for letting him know about the hapless security personnel snoring on the job and promised to conduct surprise checks. Being on the managing committee of the society had its deterrents, with people waking one up at 3 a.m. to complain about random folk having usurped their parking spots, or worse, about watering plants from flats overhead causing acute trauma of levels so intense that they would immediately need ICU intervention. This was the latest manifestation of 'grab the committee member when you've got his attention and file your complaint verbally'.

For now though, we smiled politely and promised to drop in for chai-shai and the child tucked his precious autograph into his pocket, not trusting me or his father with the custody of the precious scrap of paper. We then turned our attention to the goodies on offer at the buffet. I thanked the good Lord and whoever the genius was who had invented Lycra.

The restaurant we had taken refuge in from the pouring rain, which thankfully had died down to a trickle, called itself Beach Hut. The interiors had no resemblance to a hut of any kind, which was a good decision given the weather and that the soup would probably be *Poisson Avec L'Eau de* Monsoon had it been hutlike. In fact, another very good point about this restaurant, and a point which made it far removed from any resemblance to any kind of a beach hut, was the absolute lack of sunlight. The dim lighting did wonderful things to conceal the repeat helpings I was piling onto my plate and wheeling towards my table on those little trolleys meant for waiters to serve the really heavy stuff on. And with the child accompanying us, it always gave me more leeway to pretend that not all the stuff going onto my plate was exclusively for me.

The phone buzzed violently in my handbag, which was hung onto the back of my chair, making it leap about animatedly, like I had imprisoned a sprite or some such being within. I fished it out with utmost speed. 'Twas the mater. 'Where are you?' she said at volumes I was sure the next suburb could hear. 'Why didn't you answer the phone?'

'I've answered it now. I'm talking to you, aren't I?'

To the mater, the phone had to be answered on the first ring itself, or else it meant trouble was afoot. If a phone call went unanswered she would call back multiple times until you answered. If you still didn't answer, she would call on the landline to investigate whether you had fallen in the bathroom and cracked your spine and therefore couldn't get to the mobile. And if the landline wasn't answered for whatever reason, she would then call the spouse. Who would, of course, be at the office and have no clue about the possible reason behind you not answering the phone – and who would then, in turn, call you up to inform you to call your mother.

It was just easier to answer her call on the first couple of rings.

'Where are you? Jamuna said you had gone out?'

'We're out for lunch, Ma,' I said, my voice declining into the plaintive whine of the sixth grader I felt like whenever the mater called. 'Can I call you back in a while?'

The plate piled up in front of me was calling out my name. Loud enough for the entire restaurant to hear.

'Hmm,' said the mater in disapproving tones, given she firmly did not condone that sort of weekly indulgence of blowing them credit-card limits on meals at fancy restaurants. 'Anyway, are you going to attend any more weddings this week? Weddings with an interesting guest list. And I read also they busted a gang of thieves at that wedding.'

Errr, that was going to be sticky to explain. 'Actually, it was me who helped them catch the thieves. You know Runa, from school?'

There was a dry pause. The mater knew Runa from school. Runa had once given the mater the shock of her life when she had introduced her to Albie, her pet albino grass snake that she kept in a small shoebox in her school bag. It had taken some persuasion to get the mater to agree to climb down from the top of the refrigerator once Runa had left the premises.

'Erm, yes.' The tone of her voice had shifted to permafrost levels. 'Don't tell me you took Runa to the wedding and didn't even think it necessary to ask your own mother, the one who gave birth to you, whether she would be interested in attending.'

'You're in another city, Mother,' I said drily, knowing, of course, that this was no deterrent when it came to the mater and matinee idol.

'It takes three hours to reach Mumbai by the expressway. Of course, not when your dad is driving, then it would take eight,' she said, her volume-control knob turning itself onto high with her escalating excitement.

'Okay, Ma.' I decided it was easier to cave in than to resume the circular arguments. 'I will let you know about the next wedding I plan to attend and smuggle you in even if you are not invited.'

The pan-fried basa was going cold and glutinous on me. The dumplings were winking at me lasciviously.

'I'm losing signal,' I said weakly, as pangs of hunger overcame me. 'I'll call you later.' With that, I disconnected the line hurriedly.

The husband was at the buffet counter, his plate in hand. 'There, Kabir, what a good boy you are, now shall I get you some more?'

The child had cleaned his plate to reflective-surface levels of cleanliness. He nodded violently, his mouth too full for him to give a coherent answer. He so took after me, that darling child. I marched off purposefully towards the buffet counters with the child leading the way, much like them massive cruise liners being led out of the docks by them little tugboats. I heaped up his plate to his eye's content and led him back to the table and out of the way of other innocent diners who might not appreciate a six-year-old sticking his head into their plate and enquiring politely, 'Whashthat? I wantueadit.'

We reached our table and found the spouse in deep conversation with a stranger. A stranger wearing a floral shirt. And with not much hair on his head. The kind of stranger you edged away from on a flight if he happened to take up the seat next to you. The kind of person who you assumed would be dripping with bonhomie, jollity, adipose and stinky perspiration. I edged carefully and warily to the table. I was not comfortable with being interrupted in the midst of a meal, especially by overweight men in floral shirts and what seemed like Bermuda shorts sitting in my chair.

I hovered around quite confused as to what I should do and where I should place myself and my plate, until I finally decided to keep the laden plate on the table, and seat the child at his seat and wait for the floral-shirted giant to realize I needed my chair, and that by God I was not going to stand and finish my meal.

The child slithered into his chair with the ease children have in not caring whether their presence had been registered or not, and began a two-handed effort at tackling the contents of his plate.

The spouse and fat man continued to converse, until the spouse suddenly noted my presence and looked up at me as if in a daze, and then smiled like I was the person he least expected to see around.

'Oh, Kay,' he said heavily, 'meet Mr Bhatia.'

Mr Bhatia rose to his feet graciously, almost lightly for a man for his weight, and turned towards me. His eyes were a brilliant blaze of green, and his skin swarthy. It was a strange combination, which had me disconcerted and almost checking at close range for evidence of coloured contact lenses being jammed into said eyes. He took my hand and bowed low over it in a cavalier fashion that made me wonder if he was going to do something really old-worldly and terribly repellent, aka kiss the hand, but he resisted and rose back up. Standing, I was amazed to see he towered over me. Which wasn't a difficult task to do given that I wasn't wearing heels, thanks to the sore ankle, and stood not so tall at 5 feet and a couple of inches.

'Mr Bhatia has just purchased a flat in our building,' said the spouse wearily, making me want to run a sympathetic hand over his ruffled hair.

'I'm so sorry to be intruding on your lunch, but there is some inordinate delay with the transfer and when I saw Mr Mehra here, I had to grab the opportunity to chat with him about it, given he's always busy when I try to visit him at the society office ...'

I smiled grimly, with the tight smile intended to tell the recipient I didn't appreciate being kept from ingesting my food. My stomach growled in appropriately threatening manner, my hand began clutching my fork in dagger style. This was not lost on the man and he backed away from my seat, apologizing profusely.

'Let me call you sometime this week, Mr Mehra,' he said, as a parting shot. 'Let's come to an amicable conclusion about this.'

The spouse looked weary and hassled, as spouses are meant to look when they come back home from the office, and not when they are out to lunch with the family on a public holiday and have downed a couple of beers to smoothen the mood out.

'What was that all about?' I asked, sensing the prickliness in the air.

'This gentleman bought the flat from the owner, who sold it to him without permission from the society, and we've been doing some background checks and ...' he lowered his voice, and looked around furtively before continuing in the kind of low tone he used when he wanted to convey something not for ears of the child, '...he is not the kind of person we would like living on the premises.'

I agreed absolutely. For one, he was horribly out of shape. He burst out of his clothes in a way no human being who had not been spattered down from a skyscraper should. And for another he had terrible dress sense. Imagine being accosted by floral shirts and Bermuda shorts in the lifts every single day! I would need to carry vials of smelling salts with me in my handbag to keep me from blacking out from the assault on my fashion sensitivities.

The spouse continued before I could add in my points of agreement, which included the very pertinent observation that he was wearing sandals and his toenails needed a pedicure. What? I checked out people's feet – a person could be dressed to the nines, but if their feet weren't well-maintained or well-shod, they were automatically persona non grata for me. I had also been known to reject suitors who wore brown socks with black shoes.

'He has a criminal record …'

I sat down in my chair with a thud, all thoughts of food and corpses dismissed from my mind. 'Now what will you do? Has the flat already been sold? Will he come to live in the building?'

I feared for my innocent child, being surrounded by criminals with evil intent. I had visions of police snipers taking positions in the lobby and the stairs in order to ambush and arrest the man, and a den of vice with molls and drugs in a dark room, luring little kids in with promises of unlimited Cartoon Network and forcing them to run drugs. A cold finger of dread walked at leisurely pace up my spine. Was the air conditioning turned up all of sudden? I looked back at the retreating floral shirt, who had gone to the other end of the restaurant and was squeezing himself, centimetre by centimetre, into a banquette while three waiters hovered around judiciously trying to assist him by moving the furniture, while what was really needed was a hole cut into the side of the table to accommodate his belly.

I looked away in embarrassment when he raised a hand in acknowledgement, with a cheeky grin as he caught me staring at him.

'Anyway,' said the spouse, sipping carefully from his pint. 'We plan to discuss it at the next committee meeting and take it from there. We have to find a diplomatic way to refuse to acknowledge the sale.'

I shovelled the food into my mouth and found it strangely tasteless, like I was eating desiccated cardboard that had been carbonized to eliminate all residual flavour from it.

'And which flat has he bought?' I asked gently.

The spouse laughed hoarsely. 'You won't believe it if I told you. It is 504. That place is jinxed.'

9

In Which a Lift Crashes Down

THURSDAY

School day mornings were tough calls when one had spent most of the previous day ingesting copious amounts of food, rising only in order to refill one's plate. The alarm rang with the sadistic kind of incessantness that demanded whoever invented the damn device of torture be drawn and quartered and hung out to dry in the hot noonday sun on a spaghetti western filmset.

The ringing had woken me from a deep, dark dream that involved much running up and down stairs being chased by a spectral vision of Mrs 504, her arms appropriately outstretched in true *Ringu* fashion. *Note to self: stop watching horror movies, especially when you have enough of real-life horror to see you through your days – like catching a glimpse of yourself in a mirror at an all-you-can-eat buffet.*

I jumped up at the 5.45 a.m. buzz and dragged my finger across the screen to get it to shut up. The spouse opened one reluctant eye. 'Don't even think of the stairs, Kay.' He closed said reluctant eye. And then opened it again to add an afterthought. 'And no need to go out in the rain. If you must exercise, take the car out and go to the gym.'

I sulked. For a moment. And went right back to sleep. *Half an hour*, I told myself, *just half an hour more*. The next thing I knew the child was shaking my shoulder and prising my eyelids open with pincer grip and demanding pupil-to-pupil eye contact. 'Mamma,' he said, 'tuday is a holyday?'

My eyes flew open. The clock on the wall had its hands at 7.30 a.m. The spouse was nowhere to be seen, his squash kit was also nowhere to be seen. I had been abandoned, snoring, and folks had tiptoed around me for fear of waking me and facing my wrath. And now I had ten minutes to get the child bathed and into his school uniform. I decided to skip the bathed part of that list.

'Kabir, come.' I trundled to the bathroom, and picked up a nice soft hand towel from the towel basket. 'Let's do a sponge bath today.'

'Nooooooo,' he squawked in protest. 'I wantudu a properly bath. Udderwise everyone will say "you is smelling badly".'

The hand itched to administer a smack and restrained itself with immense self-control, self-control said hand never showed when confronted with a pastry liberally endowed with calorific constituents. 'Kabir,' I pleaded, in the midst of wringing out the hand towel with warm water and scraping off layers of dirt from his face. 'Please, child, you are late, there is no time for a proper bath today. Why did Jamuna not bathe you?'

'She is headaching.'

Jamuna's headaches were a euphemism for her getting her menses and this news relieved me given the long conversations she seemed to be having with the driver from B-303 these days, especially in secluded corners when she needed to be out in full sight, preventing the offspring from inflicting physical harm on himself or another down in the park. Alas, on the days she was 'headaching', she took herself to the distant corners of the apartment and generally played grouch until her 'headache' had abated sufficiently for her to resume normal programming.

The child squirmed out of my grasp with the kind of slitheriness that had me convinced he could be an ideal candidate for the political world once grown up. 'No.' He sat cross-legged on the bed in yogic pose. 'I wantu hab a bath. Now. I is nod going widaoud a bath.'

I put a bit of toothpaste onto his brush and stuck it into his mouth. He moved it around slothfully, masticating the bristles. 'Jamunaaaaa …' I yelled. She could headache later.

I needed her and her extra pair of hands.

'*Aa rahi hoon!*' she screamed back at equal decibel level, which quite shattered the peace of the neighbourhood. Finally, between the two of us, the child was dressed, spit polished and combed with side parting, and led firmly through the passage to the elevator bank.

'Mamma, yu drop me down tuday?' he whined uncharacteristically. 'I is frightened of the dead peepul.'

Mamma was frightened too, not that she was about to show it to a six-year-old. And Mamma wondered how the child had been informed of potential supernatural entities on the premises when he himself revealed that the under-eight-year-olds had been having a spirited discussion on the possibility of Mrs 504 making it to the other-worldly realm of disquiet spirit entities who haunted the premises from where they'd made an exit from the world.

'What is there to be frightened about dead people? When people die, they go to heaven or hell,' Mamma began her theological explanations as she shoved her parcel into the yawning mouth of the lift.

'Den whu become ghoss?'

Complicated theological questions were best not dealt with when one had barely washed one's face and was still conscious of morning dragon breath fumes lurking in one's mouth. Still, Mamma made an attempt as the lift shuddered its way down from the eighteenth floor. 'Ghosts are people who die suddenly, either by accident, or by committing suicide or those who have been murdered or the folk who have desires yet to achieve in their lives …'

'…when I die and if I don ged my own iPad will I become a ghoss?'

The bent of conversation was not to Mamma's liking, especially not after the previous day when Mamma was convinced she had had a close encounter of the other-worldly kind.

'Let's talk about it when you come back from school,' I said, hoping against hope that the topic would die a natural death in the course of a packed school day, which included the dreaded swimming class the brat hated, having inherited hydrophobia undiluted from his mother; his penchant for 'forgetting' his swimming bag at home was stuff that had even the bus driver on high alert, with the said bag being found mysteriously abandoned in the school bus on swimming days, ergo leading to no swimming class happening in school.

The lift whirred threateningly and lurched downwards with a sudden unpredictable kind of random speed that grabbed my throat. It moved. It shuddered. It moved again. It stopped between floors. I did what any calm, rational and sensible person should do in such a situation. I screamed loudly. The child pressed the alarm button and the intercom crackled into the ethers. Sometimes I wondered who was raising whom.

The watchman's voice floated eerily into the steel coffin lurching down frantically. 'Haaayloo? Haaaylo?'

'*Yeh* lift *mein kuch* problem *hai, shuru-band ho raha hai aur* floor *ke beech mein ruk raha hai* ...'

The child held my hands, which were now clammy with sweat. 'Mamma, don worry. Da watchmanz will switch it off. Den da repair manz will come and open the top and pud a rope laddur. An we will clim outofdlift.'

The lift gave up all attempts at pretending to be well behaved and threw itself swiftly to the ground, aided effectively by gravity. *This is it*, I thought, and prayed for forgiveness for having overshot my credit limit, exhausting my mobile data, and for not visiting the parents often enough. We were thrown around mildly and the child was most amused to see me lose my balance and fall awkwardly, screaming in terror. Then, for a strange moment, it stopped moving, and gently seemed to touch down, soft as a caress, almost as if a skilful pilot, with many flying hours under his or her belt, had taken charge of the controls. Thankfully, apart from a rather sudden jolt when we stopped, we didn't seem to have much damage done. He patted my hand in calming manner, much like one would pat down an overexcited Great Dane. I refused to calm down.

I was a non-calm person to begin with. I hyperventilated when doorbells weren't answered in a single ring, when phones went unanswered in two rings, and when lifts didn't arrive at a single jab. I could hear vague voices outside. I waited for the lift doors to open, clutching the child's hand for moral support. But they didn't. I realized we were stuck between floors. I yelled, I exhorted the child to yell too, in the hope that someone from the floors we were stuck between would hear us. We were lucky we weren't a mangled mash of steel and concrete in the lift well.

'Let's sit quiedly,' the child said with calmness never in evidence on normal days. I did as told, not the sitting part, but the quietly part at least. The darkness was womblike. I could almost fall right back to sleep if I wasn't meant to be panicking. *Damn.* I stomped my foot for not having carried my mobile along with me to call the spouse and demand that he get the lift fixed immediately: 'I don't care how you do it, and do it now.' The child mused about how if Krrish, the action hero, was around he could have solved the problem in a jiffy and not only lifted the lift into place, but also torn the doors open and deposited him directly into his classroom, without him having to scrap for a window seat in the bus. A sudden whir and a click and the lights began flickering within the lift again, and the disconnected voice of the watchman crackled, '*Madamji, liftwalla aa raha hai. Aap baithiye.*'

We didn't have many other options. And so we sat. And heard the spouse calling out to us from the floor above. We replied, and I realized that the child had long missed not only his school bus but also his school bell and therefore, I was now doomed to spend an entire day entertaining him at home, and my knees shook in horror at the thought. And the need to visit the loo was dawning pressingly on my bladder. In acute cross-the-legs-awkwardly fashion. I squirmed. This was just punishment for me not getting up at the scheduled time in the morning. I yelled up at the disembodied voices asking if we were ever to emerge blinking into the daylight or if they would be sending in food and liquid nourishment down on a rope, and also perhaps that book on by my bedside table with a torch while they were at it.

A sudden grating noise.

We heard the top of the elevator being lifted away. A face peered in: the worried-looking face of a man who flung a rope down and informed us we had reached the elevator pit and would need to climb out. We had been very lucky, he told us, to not end up pulp. I asked, validly I thought, if they had enough strong men to pull me out.

He laughed nervously and without the necessary reassuring manner requisite in such circumstance and clambered back up, presumably to get reinforcements. I tugged at the rope and yelled out again into darkness. 'Is anyone there?'

Nothing. Not even the beloved spouse, who I had presumed should rightfully have been clambering down like Prince Charming albeit in shorts and sweat-drenched T-shirt, dri-fit notwithstanding. The child added his treble to my screech. 'Pappa,' he yelled. No response. I began trembling. Perceptibly.

'Is coming,' the spawn of my womb told me calmly. 'Is gone to ged stronger ropes and ladders. Dis one is very thin. Will break.'

What had I done in a previous birth to deserve such a gloriously rational child? I looked up again and the blood froze in my veins.

There it was: a face. One that I had seen attached to a body on the stairs, standing behind me, now looking down at both of us with an indeterminate expression. Not the anger of the previous time we had bumped into each other, which had led to me scooting up the stairs like a live wire had come into immediate contact with my person. This time, it was a more wistful, concerned gaze. Some male voices came down the shaft, and slowly a tiny person, the approximate size of a small chimpanzee, slithered down the rope, which he kept yelling at the male voices above to hold onto and keep tied to the railing.

The face above disappeared. Into the air, literally. I felt my arms prickle up with fear. The child had not seen her – thankfully, he was looking intently at Tiny Tim, who was skidding through the hole and landing appropriately at my feet in appropriately reverent Hanuman pose.

'Madam, let the child go up first …' he instructed us with all the calm of knowing that he could fit through the tiny hole in the roof, and which I feared would have me stuck – unless it was cut wider – as the rest of humanity witnessed my humiliation.

'Kay,' yelled the beloved spouse. 'I'm here, send Kabir up first.'

The rope was tied, double-knotted and tested for firmness, around the child's waist. And he was instructed to hang onto the fibres for dear life, never mind the potential beasties in the darkness he was about to be hauled into.

'Okay Mamma,' he said cheerfully. 'I is going. Take care. Bye. Cee yu later.'

I hastened to reassure him that I was scheduled next on the rope up to level ground. He swung upwards with the kind of blind trust only a child who knew that he would not be allowed to fall down and injure himself had. I heard with pleasure the sounds of the reunion between father and son at the upper level. I could vaguely hear the son talking in high-pitched animation about how he defeated the monsters in the dungeon, but the buzz of the crowd of onlookers drowned him out.

It was my turn now. I gulped. I hoped the men who were doing the hauling were used to lifting heavy weights. I implored the spouse to lend them a hand. He assured me that there were enough and more hands for the task at hand. A ladder had been lowered and positioned carefully on the roof of the elevator and was held with firm hands.

It was probably my National Geographic moment. Rescued from a fallen elevator. Not that I had set out to find adventure. One moment you are traipsing around in my part of the suburb minding your own business when: voila! you fall into the elevator pit, your life flashes in front of your eyes, and you decide you should have been nicer to your mother in your teenage years, and should have spent more time playing with the child rather than dumping him in front of the computer with the Jumpstart educational DVD. But then, when my life flashed before my eyes it made for quite dreary watching.

The squeaks of what seemed to be itinerant rodents in the vicinity had me leaping up and grabbing the rope for dear life and yelling at the unseen hands hauling me out to work faster. 'There are rats here,' I squeaked much like a rodent. 'Get me out of here.'

The spouse yelled back in True Rescue fashion, 'Keep shut, Kay, let the people do their work.'

It was a tight fit through the hole in the roof, but I got through. I smirked down in triumph at the rodent face looking up at me questioningly and then looked up again. The ladder was makeshift but functional and I began my slow ascent. The darkness was like a tunnel, a pretty wide tunnel nonetheless, and I thanked my lucky stars I had no fear of either darkness or tunnels and the squeaking rodents were far below me and I needed only to fear if I fell right back through the hole.

I could see a sliver of light and slowly, feet came into view, as did the rest of the assemblage.

The spouse cheerfully helped me off the ladder, untied the rope around my waist and gave me one of the rare public displays of affection by squeezing my hand. He must have been really moved by the prospect of me dying for such an emotional display.

'Did you know you could have been killed?' he said in the same matter-of-fact tone he used to inform me that I had over-salted the omelette.

'Come on,' I said, trembling with a mixture of rage and fear. 'It wasn't something I did deliberately.'

'Freak accident,' said a man in a kind of uniformed overall ensemble, who I took to be the mandatory representative from the lift company, but in effect turned out to be the local power-supply representative. He happened to be lurking around in the neighbourhood and was duly summoned by the security men because he looked like he could be of some help in case of lift crisis.

The spouse was barking into a phone about servicing and suchlike. I looked at the big clock in the lobby and saw it was a good part of an hour that we had been stuck in dungeons to be tortured by squeaking rats, so to speak. The child had been dispatched up home to the care of the very vocal and concerned Jamuna, who was, undoubtedly by this point, busy shoving high-sugar candy pops into his mouth in her idea of a treat while the harridan mother was away, and swearing the child conspiratorially into secrecy.

'Err …' I tugged at the spouse's sweat-drenched T-shirt, acutely aware and thankful that he had just landed back from his morning squash session, and therefore was at his most aromatic, and also his most grouchy until bathed and fed. 'I saw her again.'

'What? Who?' said the spouse, stopping mid-conversation to look at me with an expression of complete confusion on his face.

'I saw Mrs 504.' God save me, I still couldn't recall her name. The spouse looked at me with an expression that bordered on the murderous. The handsome face furrowed into the kind of frown that totally ruined his forehead. 'Kay,' he began thunderously, 'she is dead. We saw the body. This is no time to be joking. I have to get to office. We'll discuss this later.'

I trudged off cheerlessly behind him, acutely aware that I was at my sweatiest, or at least, as 'sweatiest' as one could get. I discreetly raised an arm to sniff the armpit and was almost thrown off by the stench. Being stuck in a dark, dank lift was definitely not conducive to hygiene. And caused serious odorific issues. I wondered how folks managed to have romantic encounters while stuck in lifts. I would have shrunk into a corner acutely aware of the fumes wafting from my person. I so needed a bath. With scented oils. I could definitely do with some aura cleansing. Too much negative energy was clouding my aura.

And then maybe, to lift my spirits, I could go out to lunch or go shopping. Depending, of course, on which friend was available at short notice to do the rounds with me. The trouble with being a corporate woman out of the workforce was that most of one's friends were chain-balled to their desks during the work week and couldn't escape even for a miserly hour of a lunch break without agonizing about dragon bosses and time cards and suchlike, and the other bunch were the school-gate moms, who normally had intricate domestic arrangements to be balanced before they could schedule a shopping getaway.

The spouse was summarily dispatched to the office, from whence he was supposed not to show his countenance back home until the night had fallen. The child was fed and placed before the Jumpstart DVD, from which much excitement and squealing in joy assured me that he had got the hang of all the games on the CD and needed some new ones to graduate to.

As I twiddled my manicured fingers, Keys to My Karma red, if you must know, I contemplated what could be done with my day spread ahead. The newspaper was lying in disarray on the coffee table and was just begging to be read. I would need to read the newspaper regularly, something I promised myself. I couldn't really snark past every deep conversation at a get-together with a wide smile and nod intelligently at random intervals when folks discussed topics like interest-rate hikes and the Naxalite insurgency movement and things like that made me tune out completely and wonder when to schedule my next appointment at the spa.

I demanded a cup of tea to accompany the newspaper and settled myself down in the cane settee in my balcony, overlooking a spread of landscape being ferociously drilled and foundation-laid into.

I suddenly realized the phone had been ringing and I had not answered it. It was not a good feeling. I jabbed at the instrument to find out it had been Runa calling.

'Yes, Runa, you called?' I said hastily, being aware of Runa's penchant for getting irritated if the phone wasn't answered in the first ring. 'Where do you keep your phone, Kay?' she muttered most predictably. 'Anyway, any progress with Devyani? Did you meet her after the lunch?

I had completely forgotten about the case and my need to gather details. 'I haven't had the chance,' I said, blandly. 'I can't keep inflicting myself on her at all hours, can I? I had just spent the previous day's afternoon with her.'

It was terrible work, this private-detective business. People kept dying at any odd hours and one couldn't even schedule a respectable manicure without being certain one wouldn't be dragged off to look at someone with a knife in their gut. And speaking of knife in gut, I really didn't have the stomach to stomach the resultant not-very-pleasant sights one invariably encountered in such situations. I had lost count of the number of times I had, much to Runa's cold eye of disgust, spattered the pavement with uncontrollable barfing.

'Err, Runa,' I said hesitantly, thanking the good Lord that I had the good sense to do this telephonically rather than in person. 'I'm dropping out of this detective thing … I don't think it quite suits me.' I had, what they called, cold feet. She snorted in disgust at the other end of the line like a hippo in labour underwater.

Lady detectives were supposed to run around in smart suits and full stilettos like in *Remington Steele*. They were supposed to have Pierce Brosnan around to perk up their day, not a hulking grim-faced 5 ft 10–ish hirsute lady in khadi kurtas and boyfriend jeans to accompany them on their investigations. I gulped and continued bravely, 'I mean, I really don't have the stomach for it, and I can't do the legwork you need me to, and I keep dreaming of all the dead people …'

'What???' she exploded. My eardrum had probably been shattered by that one word.

I held the phone away while I joggled myself back to hearing clearly. 'Okay, call me when you get more information, you're free to stop working with me once I've got the information I need from Devyani,' she replied.

I had said my piece. I was free. I disconnected the call.

I then promptly called Tanaz, the friend who would drop everything, including new boyfriends, if offered a shot at a 50-per-cent-off-everything sale and an all-you-can-eat buffet.

'Want to do lunch?

'Does a fish want to eat worms?' she screeched. 'Of course I do, babe, name the joint and the hour and I will be there. Keep it reasonable, like ten minutes away from the office, okay?'

Luckily her office was in one of those newfangled high-tech parks, which was ten minutes away from where I lived, so distance was no hindrance to us breaking bread together during the lunch hour.

Tanaz had the kind of job I liked. She was a retail consultant. That basically meant she wandered around malls for *The Entire Day*. And could buy stuff and charge it to the companies she consulted for under the pretext of doing shopping-experience research. I could do her job. I could be a retail consultant. Being a detective was so … so … drab. I could see myself in smart suits researching the cosmetic-buying experience at the Clarins counter. Or the Lancôme counter. I could do that.

'And I have something to ask you,' I added. 'But that's for later.' I had a smile on my face that refused to fade as I showered and decided what could be the outfit du jour for an innocuous lunch with a friend where I planned to ply her with sumptuous food, and break down her defences, and – *No, eww, what were you thinking* – get her to promise to help me get a break into the retail-consulting business.

Maybe I could intern with her. I could then start my own consultancy, jet-set around the country advising corporations on how they could better connect with the consumer. From the consumer perspective. Maybe I could convince them to pay me in kind. Shopping vouchers would do. The child ambled in, fed and sated on cheese paratha deftly rolled out by the cook, and sat on the bed watching with wide eyes, waiting for the wriggling-into-the-pant dance to happen. I was determined to circumvent it; also, he was older now and I changed behind closed doors.

'Kabir, go out of the room, Mamma wants to change,' I commanded in clear tones.

He looked puzzled. 'No. I wantu see yu fighting wid yer pant button.'

'No, Kabir, leave the room now. You are a big boy now. You cannot be in the same room as Mamma when she is changing.' I widened my eyes threateningly to indicate I meant what I said and that I would be firm in implementing the statement.

'Now wen I change my klodz, I won't led yu come in the room,' he grumbled as he went out. And as a parting shot he threw, 'Den wai Pappa be's in the same room wen yu change klodz? He's nod a big boy or wot?'

I ignored his whining, picked up my sadly non-Birkin bag – nonetheless, a lovely burnt orange Hidesign – informed the girl Friday vocally that I would be back in an hour or two and closed the door gently behind me to insistent squeals from the fruit of my womb that I return bearing a Rey Mysterio action figure. I would get into a toy shop, I promised him, through the closing door.

'Don forged!' he yelled at my fleeing back while he continued to rip them little infernal circles of fire all on my polished Cappuccino Italian marble with his cars. The whirring sound stayed in my ear like some earworm until the warm glow of the last remnants of the rabidly-spooned-in tiramisu effectively drowned it out.

By the time we were done with lunch, I had convinced Tanaz to take me on board in her retail consultancy as a gofer to start with and then at the higher positions that I would no doubt climb to, given my extensive experience in retail (being primarily that of one who could go through any sale like a Cyclops and sift out the true bargains from the rubbish). 'Only for a couple of months to start with, Kay, okay?' she said warily, even with the carbohydrate overload in her system, which should have softened her up, knowing as she did my penchant for Quitting jobs that bored the bejesus out of me, especially when it came to legwork.

We air-kissed and went our respective ways, with me promising to come into work at her office, which was luckily a ten-minute drive from my home, beginning the first of the next month. That was still a couple of weeks away.

'Think about it again,' she said, as she teetered away. 'It isn't all the fun and games you think it will be.'

I was resolute, I was going to do something interesting with my days and playing detective was not proving to be my cup of cappuccino, two pellets of Sugar Free notwithstanding. As I strolled through the mall, darting swiftly into stores to check out the merchandise on display and the offers contained within, I spotted a familiar face sitting at a coffee shop, with another familiar face. I peered hard, squinting because I refused to acknowledge that I needed to use spectacles on a permanent basis, and functioned much like a bat relying on sonic radar.

I carefully fished out my distance-view spectacles, languishing neglected in my handbag, and put them on, hiding myself behind a huge 'Up to 50 per cent off' sign in the show window of the store I was in. The couple was engrossed in intense conversation, which was veering into teary territory.

One was Jahnavi, from the kitty group. And the man in deep conversation with her was a face I had seen before, though not in person. I thought long and I thought hard and then decided to click them surreptitiously and WhatsApp the picture to Runa, and so I did. Never mind that barely a couple of hours ago I had given her a resignation speech.

The phone rang infernally two seconds after the second tick mark, against the message informing her of where I was and where I had clicked the duo, confirmed it had been delivered. 'Kay, stay on their tail, don't let them get away.'

'Sure,' I replied, in hushed voice, given that an irritated salesperson was hovering over my left shoulder, undecided whether I was a genuine customer with a kleptomaniac itch for the On Sale sign or whether I really planned to lighten my wallet in a legitimate fashion at her store. 'But who is this man? He looks familiar.'

'Kay,' Runa yelled at levels that pierced my tympanic membrane and made a direct assault on the cranial nerves. 'That is my client. The husband who has asked me to investigate the suicide of his wife. I showed you the picture. He told me he barely knew any of her kitty group. I'm reaching there in ten minutes, stay put.'

If he barely knew anyone from his dead wife's kitty group, what was he doing having an intense conversation with Jahnavi, one that involved much handholding and intense conversation, with some tear-wiping thrown in? I was staying put. Did I have a choice? I froze myself in the best statue-for-pigeon act behind one of the pillars, casting a regretful glance at a pair of shoes in tan suede with the most comfortable-looking midsized heel that was on half price.

But then, it would barely take a minute to try it out, pay and come back to my vantage point, I told myself. Jahnavi was busy sniffling inelegantly by now and the bereaved man was comforting her in a manner that did not indicate a lack of familiarity. They would be there for a while, I rationalized. I nipped back into the store and tried on the shoes. It turned out they were made for me, so I handed over the credit card. It was duly swiped, the message sure to ping on the spouse's phone. But I would deal with the inevitable 'What do you need so many shoes for?' question when it came.

I took my new acquisition and turned back to hot-step into my spying position, only to find the table they were sitting at vacant. I looked up and down the length of the stores to find no one resembling them anywhere. Just then, there was a tap on my shoulder.

'Gone, aren't they?' said Runa, in the voice of one who had just chewed glass bottles in place of an after-meal mint. 'I should have known you would have gotten distracted with all the sale signs. Anyway …'

I quailed.

We went into the cafe they had been sitting in and investigated the now clean and empty table they had once occupied. 'Why would he be chatting her up?' Runa wondered, sotto voce.

'Look here, Runa,' I began weakly, 'I've already told you I don't want to do more detective work, I'm not cut out for this.'

The gorgon's stare did not waver and I could feel my extremities petrify in place. Then she laughed, a laugh that could break rocks better than a crashing wave. 'Squealie,' she said, using the fond moniker that had haunted me from the primary section when—*never mind!* Those were tales meant to be buried in the past and never brought to the fore again after one had a child and they could be used to undermine your authority. 'You don't have a choice as far as this case goes. You're already in it up to your neck. Whether you like it or not.'

10

In Which Yet Another Person Goes Missing

FRIDAY

The morning was nothing like its predecessor. For one, the clouds had melted away magically through the night, and the sun had made a valiant brilliant stab at yellowing up the sky.

It was a needlessly bright and sunny morning. The occasional bird was chirping away incessantly in the kind of manic frenzy that made one conclude it had ingested prohibited substances along with the early worm. The child, I could hear – from the strained, high-pitched voice begging to be let in and the knocking on the bedroom door – was awake and alert and fully charged for a day of education and learning in the hallowed halls of his school. Or rather. Not.

'Mamma, Mamma,' his voice was hollering, as much as six-year-old voices could holler without losing out on their childishness. 'Am nod going to skul tuday.'

The spouse uncurled himself from his covers and threw the door open. I opened a reluctant eye and looked at the wall clock, which told me it was barely 6.30 a.m. It was no time for a child to wake on his own. I felt a little deprived at not being able to yell him into wakefulness.

The father all but grabbed the child by the scruff of his neck and lifted him up to eye level. 'No school today? Why?'

'Because I want the lift to fall down again, and make it a haw-lee-day for me.'

My eyes opened wide at the memory. 'Hush, child,' I said, my voice hoarse from sleep. 'It isn't a nice thing for the lift to fall down, we could have …' I trailed off, not willing to put the concept of dying in a lift crash in the mind of a child morbidly obsessed with the various ways people give up their mortal bodies, and an expert teller of tall stories that had various people shuffling off their mortal coil in gruesome manner which normally involved much blood flowing: the result of spending too much time bonding with the father over action movies.

I rose from the bed like one of those beached whales, from the National Geographic channels, carefully being pushed off the shore and back into the sea. The head was groggy from the hectic events of the previous day. I needed coffee, strong and dark and instant, to clear the clouds in my head and let the light stream in.

'Jamunaaa …!' I hollered, pulling the folds of the dressing grown I had shrugged on, as I rose, closer towards me. 'Coffee, please.'

'Bhabhiii…!' came the responding war cry from the inner recesses of the house.

I materialized by her side immediately to prevent further waking of the dead. 'What is it?'

'*Who waali bhabhi ka* phone *aaya tha,* intercom *par, aap so rahe the …*' Which *waali bhabhi*, I asked. The trouble with Jamuna was that all the women who were of my immediate acquaintance in the complex became bhabhis and she would only deign to specify by distinguishing physical characteristics, always of the unflattering kind. Often we had gone round in circles while she tried to convey a message when her concept of unflattering did not align with mine, until we found a common point of agreement.

'*Woh waali bhabhi, jiska muh ghode ke jaisa hai, woh jiske saath aap takrakar gir gaye*?'

Devyani. I looked at the clock on the wall, it was seven in the morning. Why would she call so early in the day? I decided to call back and so I did. I noted, as I went towards the intercom, that Jamuna was wearing on her nails a polish that looked suspiciously like a Dior nail polish specially brought down for me by darling friend from London over the previous weekend. Bond Street. It was a dirty smoggy grey, which appropriately encapsulated the London look but made my hands look viciously cadaverous and thereby had been consigned to the corner of the nail polish drawer. I refrained from comment on the grey nail, and rather focused my attention on the phone ringing its head off at the other end of the line.

The voice that answered belonged to someone on the verge of tears.

'Whatever happened, Devyani?' I asked, unsure whether we were close enough for me to offer to rush across with my shoulders available for crying on.

'Kanan, can I ask you a favour, please?'

'Of course,' I replied grandiosely. It was rare that folks used my given name. This had to be a serious favour.

'Divyam will be back home at around 1.30 p.m. If you are home, could you collect him from the gate and take him home with you for a while? I need to go out for something urgent and have no clue when I will be back. Hopefully it shouldn't be for more than a couple of hours.'

'Of course,' I replied. 'Don't you worry, just message me the necessary bus details, etc., and do inform the bus that he will be collected by someone other than you.' I then asked, gently, 'Anything serious?'

There was a long, pregnant pause, and then she decided to answer. 'Something has come up with one of the ladies from the kitty group. It is an emergency of sorts; I just need to go sort things out.'

The long, pregnant pause returned, firmly putting up the barrier between me and her and the amount of information she was ready to dispense.

'Thanks so much for offering to watch Divyam. He has dal-chawal when he returns from school and at four, he has a bowl of Chocos with some fruit ...' She rattled off instructions that went into the night, which left me wondering whether she needed to send along an overnight valise with the boy's clothes and blankie.

I informed Jamuna that she had one additional pint-size to haul upstairs from the school bus, and realized that there was a scrimmage happening between the cook and Jamuna that needed a whistle and red-card level of intervention. After the kitchen was sorted out, the child dispersed to school and the spouse packed into the bathroom for his shower, I pulled out the phone and hastily dialled Runa with the latest development.

Runa sounded annoyed at being called. 'I'm doing my yoga. I'll call you back.'

I stared at the phone screen and got back to organizing my day. Fifteen minutes later, while we were sitting down to breakfast, the phone rang again. Runa. I disconnected it, seeing the spouse raise one sardonic brow when he saw her name flashing on the screen.

'Why don't you answer it?' he ventured, helpfully, when the phone continued to scream her name, despite the call being rejected twice. So I did.

'I have news,' I hissed in an undertone that might have given a less trusting spouse cause to believe I was conducting clandestine liaisons with folks whose names I had saved under pseudonyms on the phone. The spouse stared on, his fork playing with the fragrant eggs and sausages on his plate, his expression curiously disinterested. He then switched his attention to his phone where he began going through his messages with a frown on his face and grim-set lips, which could only indicate that workday mails had begun to pour in.

'Devyani told me there is some emergency with one of the ladies of the group. Which one, what emergency, she specified nothing. And what's more, she's asked me to watch her son all day because she's going to be out for she doesn't know how long because of this emergency.'

'Sounds interesting, try and extract more information from her when she returns. Ask her about Jahnavi and Jaya. Try to figure out why Jahnavi would be having coffee with Jaya's husband, whom she supposedly barely knows. Okay? Write it down, Kay, don't forget. Don't tell her directly that you saw the two of them having coffee – you're not supposed to know who Jaya's husband is, or anything about Jaya.'

'I'll do that. I'll let you know if I find anything,' I replied and said my polite goodbyes, to which she harrumphed and disconnected the line. Mandatory courtesies were always dispensable by Runa's book of social niceties.

The spouse lifted his eyes from the screen of the phone he was scrolling through and fixed them firmly on mine. I quailed a little. It was the kind of stern that no amount of gentle smiles and judiciously employed flattering terms could subjugate.

'Kay,' he began, 'have I not told you before that I would rather you found a proper job than get into this hare-brained detective business with that Runa?' He spat out the word Runa in the manner of one getting out a hock of phlegm from the windpipe. 'You know how much I dislike you getting wrapped up in all those murders and cases of hers. You need to find something more constructive. Get back to work. Apply for jobs. Companies are taking back women who have less than eight years of career gap now, and offering flexitime, and no commute days and whatnot.'

I scuffed my heel like a truant schoolgirl before the headmistress. Preferably a nun with her starched habit. I pictured the husband in a nun's habit and was overcome with a fit of giggles which promptly had him burst into the kind of ranting that had even the sparrows in the balcony fly away in fear. I looked at him cautiously, making a random, topic-deflecting remark about the sparrows chirping in the balcony. The man was immune to the birdsong, his eyes still of the gaze that could crack a walnut at twenty paces.

'I am, I am,' I interjected before the argument escalated to levels that had the cook and Jamuna discard their tasks at hand and settle down in ringside seats to watch the words fly in the best manner of the never-ending rallies between the top-seeded ones in tennis matches.

'Kay,' the spouse began, in the soft slow tones that were generally an indication for me to discard the slippers and flee for my life if I knew what was good for me. 'Do you realize I have no idea what you do with your entire day, except when I get a message on my phone that tells me you've bought something? I hope they're a nice pair of shoes, and you will use them a couple of times at the very least.'

I turned a bright red, it was evil of him to bring my shoes into the discussion. It would be only fair of me to bring in the set of Jack Nicklaus signature series golf clubs he had bought and which were languishing in a distant corner of the loft, gathering dust and other unmentionables. I hoped to God that the spouse didn't open the overhead shelves where he stored his disused cricket kit, which would now result in a shower of newly acquired footwear and bags, carefully ferreted away for removal into public usage one at a time. I needed to find new hiding places for new purchases, I needed to put the ladder out and clamber into the loft to figure out if I could earmark a space for new purchases to be put out of sight before it would be safe to air them a bit, nonchalantly, and pray like hell that the man didn't notice it was something new on the person.

I was lucky like that. Mine – much like the spouses of most women, who were married ten years or longer – didn't notice anything new on me. Nor anything old. I had once stood in front of the spouse with a brand-new head full of platinum-blonde highlights (looking what I felt was leonine, but was informed later by unkind friend – who found it essential to prick multiple holes in my newly emergent bubble of high self-esteem – was more skunk stripe) but had failed to elicit even a vague grunt of approval. Ergo most purchases passed unnoticed.

Coming back to the current crisis regarding my purpose of existence on this planet: 'I met Tanaz yesterday,' I interjected quickly before things degenerated further, 'and I'm going to start working with her on the first.'

The spouse knew Tanaz and had high regard for her entrepreneurial skills, which had basically included setting up shop in a sphere that was just getting off the ground ten years ago and now reaping the benefits of being an early mover in the business.

His expression softened. 'As what and what will she be paying you?'

'We didn't discuss that,' I replied, in a small voice.

'That's okay, as long as it is something constructive, not this chasing dead bodies and ferreting around trying to get out personal information from folks you don't know.'

I smiled quickly and handed him his briefcase, pecking him dutifully on the cheek in chaste manner that the dog watcher from the opposite flat, now cleaning out the contents of his ears, would not consider worthy of whispering about. In general, wives kissing husbands in public made for zero gossip value – unless said husband was not theirs.

In the course of the day, after one had bathed, breakfasted and gently painted one's nails a subtler colour to go with the mood, the infernal phone screeched again. It was the lady from the store, insistent on sending me to Bali with a husband who had no time to go to Bali with me.

I apologized for the delay and promised to get back to her in a couple of days, buying time with the barefaced white lie that the spouse was out of town and I would need him to be back – even in the age of WhatsApp, Skype and Viber – to have a conversation with him.

She swallowed it with the calm acceptance that must come about through dealing with difficult customers at the store and signed off, informing me that in the event I was not able to give them a date by the end of the week, they would be forced to offer the prize to the second runner-up. This, I was told, when I squawked very vocally in protest, came under the 'terms and conditions apply' in the fine print. I cooled my seething rage with some iced tea, peach flavour. I dashed off a message to the spouse, in the same 'seething with rage' frame of mind – the kind that drew a red curtain over one's eyeballs and could have brave matadors quail before – demanding a fixed date he could free himself of office duties by in order for us to make the trip to Bali, or I would take off with a friend, gender unspecified.

His reply came within two seconds. 'Do that.'

I fell to the floor and gnashed my teeth a bit, until I remembered I had a recently installed cap and it would do my dentition no good to damage it, given that I lived in morbid fear of being held captive in a dentist's chair.

I risked calling the mater and pater again, to check whether they would be up to the task of getting themselves into the city to babysit their only begotten grandson in the event that the spouse and I went off for a foreign trip. 'But why can't you take the boy with you?' the mater said, her voice plaintive and pleading, wondering how to squirm out of being the one solely responsible for the tyke in my absence, given that he held quite a record for getting her to tear her hair out in one single day of sole custody. Also, the mater had pretty much channelled the 'warden of a borstal' act while the brother and I were at knee height, and her haplessness in dealing with the grandchild had me quite amused.

'Ask your father,' she said, throwing the receiver at the pater, 'he is the one with the umpteen meetings and dinners and circles that he has to juggle.'

I sighed. It would be better to just deposit the child as a fait accompli on them and hotfoot it out of the country. I had till the end of the week. I would figure out dates by then.

The kids, Divyam and Kabir, came in off the school bus, sweaty and bursting with unresolved disputes that only fisticuffs could settle. Jamuna ladled their nutrients into plates after divesting them of their school bags and water bottles, and resolved efficiently what was threatening to trigger World War Three – the issue of 'Wai yu gave him Spiderman plate and wai yu gave me Badman plate' – by the simple expedient of switching the plates between the two who promptly, in competitive spirit, finished all that was placed on the plates in quick unchewed bites.

I put them into Kabir's room, put on a CD of *Happy Feet*, and resolutely closed the door, leaving them to themselves, and giving myself some breathing space. I had dropped off into a deep afternoon nap when the intercom rang and Jamuna bellowed through the walls of the house, demanding my presence beside the infernal instrument. I rubbed my eyes awake and hurried over to answer. Devyani was at the phone.

'Thanks, Kay,' she said, 'for keeping Divyam. I hope he didn't give you any trouble.' She sounded on the verge of tears.

'No, not at all,' I replied brightly, looking daggers at Jamuna to go check what the blood-curdling yells emerging from the boy's room were all about. 'They've had a great time playing together and now they're watching a movie.'

'Could I trouble you to send Divyam down to the lobby? I'm waiting here for him.' Her voice, at this point, quavered and then cracked. A small sob escaped unwittingly.

I pounced upon it like a leopard, on a week-long diet, sniffing prey in the immediate radius. 'What is it? Are you all right? Is everything okay?'

There was the briefest hesitation. 'Actually, it isn't.' She paused, unwilling to go into further detail. I could visualize her, standing in the lobby, noting the flotsam jetsam of crowd around the watchman, wondering whether she could bare her heart in such a public situation.

'Why don't you pop up for a moment, have some coffee and settle yourself. Divyam still has a bit of time to go before he finishes watching the movie.'

She seemed to debate the pros and cons of the invitation for the briefest of moments, before throwing caution to the winds and agreeing to come up. When the doorbell rang, and she stepped into the house, she looked a defeated woman. The roses, if they had existed on her cheeks – either naturally or through judiciously applied blush – had faded to a waxy pallor and her shoulders drooped.

Divyam popped his head out of Kabir's room, in response to her call to him to present himself, and muttered a not-very-welcoming 'Oh, yer back alledy.' He took himself back into the room, where the volume was raised to plaster-falling levels and the door pointedly shut behind him.

I bade her settle herself comfortably in the armchair, which was designed to trap any person who sank into it, and was not conducive to an easy exit, it being so low and encompassing and cosy. She accepted the cup of coffee I put into her hands gratefully and took a deep, contemplative sip.

'Do you need something stronger?' I asked, in case the inner turmoil could only be assuaged by fermented spirits of the grape that cheers.

'No, no.' She waved a distraught hand in distracted manner. 'I'll be fine. I'm just a little overwhelmed by the news I got today.'

'What news? I hope everything is all right?'

Her face crumpled like the proverbial sheet of paper and she put the cup down on the coffee table, without placing it on the coaster, which was a cardinal sin in my books, but I wouldn't get into that right now, seeing as this seemed to be a moment of emotional upheaval. I supplied her with the box of tissues, kept handy, left of sofa on nesting table set.

'I've lost all my money, Kay. I don't know what to do, what to tell my husband.'

I arranged my face into the appropriate concerned expression and patted her on the back at periodic intervals in empathy, until the honking sobs got Jamuna out of the kitchen and staring at her with the trademark open-jawed stare she adopted when she had too many questions to ask but dared not. I shooed her back out of the immediate line of vision and asked for some more coffee.

After around five minutes of uninterrupted sobbing, punctuated by some inelegant honking of the nose and hunting around for a convenient spot to discard the used tissues in, she was composed enough to speak.

'You know Jahnavi, right, we met on Tuesday? The lady who is the de facto head of the kitty group? She also runs a BC scheme, where we put in any amount and she pays us fixed interest every month. All based on trust, you understand. Nothing with receipts, only kachcha receipts.'

My ears, if they could be seen beneath my hair that covered them, were flapping wildly at this point. I wished I had that recorder Runa had handed across to me.

'I know about these schemes, but I've only heard the sad stories when they go kaput,' I replied, and honestly I'd never had the courage to divert funds into something so risky without the consent of the spouse, and given that the spouse had a penchant for needing everything signed on revenue stamp and in triplicate when it came to money being handed over for safekeeping.

'She hasn't paid you for this month, is it?' I asked gently, wondering how far it was acceptable to probe into sensitive issues like personal finances, given that I barely knew her.

This triggered a fresh round of 'bawling at top of her voice', which brought Jamuna and the kids out of their respective rooms. They stared at her in puzzlement.

'Mamma,' asked Kabir, reticence not being part of his genetic inheritance, 'wai her nose is Rudolph d reindeer red colour?'

I shushed him frenetically and instructed Jamuna to take both the pint-sizes back to their movie and promised them popcorn and marshmallows in huge tubs if they stayed within until I announced they could emerge. They charged into the kid's room, back to the half-watched movie, with the grace of stampeding elephants.

Devyani sniffed into a pristine tissue, it did not stay pristine for too long. I indicated to her that her eyeliner had gone panda on her and she plied the offending under-eye region with a determined hand, fishing out a compact mirror from her rather huge tote.

After she had resettled and arranged herself into a modicum of composedness, she took a deep breath and closed her eyes.

'I don't know what I am going to do. I had deposited a huge amount with her, money I'd got from the sale of a little shop I'd owned. You know how it is, she offered more interest than the banks and she had been giving us our monthly interest for years and we trusted her. And now, she's just disappeared. She was to hand out the interest yesterday afternoon, at her residence as she always does, once a month. But she's been unavailable on the phone since last evening. No one can get in touch with her. And her landline's just ringing and ringing. So we landed up at her home yesterday in the evening, and she's gone. Disappeared. Her neighbours have no idea where she is. Her husband is abroad, and we have no contact for him, her son is studying abroad. He has no idea where she is, he claims he hasn't heard from her since Sunday, when they last spoke.'

'Perhaps,' I ventured, 'she's gone off for a small holiday and will return soon.'

She honked her nose again, before speaking. 'It isn't like her to have her phone switched off, or to go away without handing over her keys to her neighbour to water her plants, or even inform her maid and driver. And she has a stocked aquarium. She didn't ask her neighbours to feed the fish either, nor tell the milkman and paperboy to stop delivery. The packets of milk were lying outside her door uncollected this morning when we went there again.'

It definitely sounded suspicious, I concurred.

'Anyone knows how she went and at what time?'

'That is the surprising part. No one saw her go away. And she is not a person you don't notice. You know.'

I knew. I had spotted her sobbing in a cafe yesterday at around 3 p.m., on the very broad shoulders of a man she was supposed to barely know. And she had disappeared after that.

'Could she be lying dead in there?' I asked, wondering if more corpses were littering this trail.

'No, the neighbour had a spare key and we had the door opened this morning when the milk packets were uncollected till 10 a.m. The house was empty.'

She shuddered deeply and began wailing again. 'My money is gone. All of it.' If there was ever a shortage of rudaalis in the country, I had just the right candidate rocking back and forth in loud mourning in my armchair.

'How many people have deposited money with her that you know of?' I asked, my natural curiosity about how many people got cornered by greed and such, and threw caution to the wind, taking precedence over the proper thing to do – which was to cluck in sympathy.

'Almost all of us in the kitty group. And many more.'

'Jaya too?' I asked, my voice hesitant to be bandying around the name of a dead person in such circumstances.

'Jaya too,' she admitted in a small voice.

'How much do you think she has as total investments from everyone?' I asked, mentally toting up figures in my head.

She shook her head. 'I had part of my sale amount, the cash component, with her. Around forty lakhs. Everyone had similar amounts, little less or more.'

'How many people do you think had given her money?'

She sat patiently and explained the structure to me. The person who brought in a depositor earned a commission on the deposit, and those who were already depositors brought in more. It was Hydra-headed. 'God knows how many.' She shuddered. 'Over a hundred for sure. She never called all the groups on the same day.'

Then she blinked, as if something had just struck her. 'You know, Jaya and she were having an argument of sorts, at the last meeting. Jaya told her she wanted her money back because they wanted to invest in some property. She flat out refused, saying the term of the deposit was not up. I've heard that she told Jaya to give her proof that she'd given her the cash. Jaya killed herself some days later.'

She turned the blinking, dazed eyes to me. 'Do you think that's why Jaya killed herself?'

I wondered if it was too. And duly relayed the conversation back to Runa when Devyani had left the premises fortified by coffee and Sula Dindori.

'That's it,' Runa said, drily. 'That is just what I was trying to figure out. Why would Jaya kill herself over money when they are wealthy enough, and have three flats in the city plus a farmhouse in Alibag? Why?'

There was a brief pause, during which Kabir emerged from his room and pulled insistently at my trousers to indicate he needed a refill of the smileys, and would like to top it up with some ice cream, which led to a short, terse conversation about monsoons and throat infections and coughs and which finally resolved with a compromise decision about microwaving the ice cream a few two seconds till it was room temperature.

'Have you finished discussing food, Kay?' Runa asked with the wry amusement of one who didn't have to deal with these issues on an urgent basis. I envied her.

'Yes,' I replied, refusing to be apologetic about my asparagus spine where the offspring was concerned.

'And now Jahnavi goes missing.'

'Yes.'

'Kay,' she said, her voice sounding concerned, very concerned. 'I think we have something completely different here – something right in front of our noses and something we aren't able to see. And don't ask me what that is, because I don't know just yet.'

11

In Which More Bodies Float Up

SATURDAY

Saturday morning is my chosen time of the week for grocery shopping at the local hypermarket, never mind that they tout Wednesdays as the day to get everything and its aged relatives on special offer. Wednesdays, ergo, are mayhem, and you half expect people to pull out machetes or slug bullets into each other in the checkout lines. After having the backs of my knees taken out more times than I could count by the irate elderly shopping-trolley-bombing the aisles, I preferred Saturday mornings, when the world was still dazed and sleepy, and reluctant to step out for constructive work of any sort. It was also when I could go through all the special offers at leisure.

I finished sorting through the vegetables, picking out pre-cut packages which made life simpler on the days the cook decided she was not going to come to work, weighed out the fruits and vegetables, took more than I needed just because something was on special offer, never mind if the family had their eyes bubble over when they spotted broccoli making a special appearance at every single meal in different formats or camouflaged slyly in the soup. Then came the grains and pulses. I turned the aisle with a quickening of the heartbeat; interesting displays told me that there was something exciting on offer with wheat flour and oil and sugar and rice, and it would save me money that I could legitimately then spend on myself without guilt.

It was in the aisle of the breakfast products – while I was contemplating seriously over questions of pressing nature involving organic jam and the preservative-laden kinds I had grown up ingesting – that I bumped into Mrs 501, or Mansi as her passport had her. 'Bumped', in retrospect, was the wrong word. 'Came across' would be more appropriate, for Mansi was of the quiet variety, the kind you never realized was in the same room, even if she crawled up and yelled 'boo' at you. In this case too, she wheeled her trolley up behind me and tapped me gingerly on my shoulder, thankfully not the one attached to the arm holding the jam bottle or there would have been a momentary crisis involving shattered glass bottles and jam expelled all over pristine floor.

'Kay, fancy seeing you here.'

As an opening line, that didn't make for inspiring conversation given that all denizens of our residential complex could give the address and phone number of the hypermarket as alternate address and contact number on official paperwork.

'Yup, fancy seeing you here, Mansi. What are you doing?'

'I'm buying some atta, chawal, shakar ...'

My brain cells began vibrating in protest, and I smiled politely intending to bring the shutter down on the conversation and moving swiftly to the detergent section where I needed to compare prices on fabric whiteners before coming to an informed decision regarding purchase.

'Lovely meeting you, Mansi, see you later—'

'Kanan, do you know, our neighbour went away. With many suitcases,' she interjected, rather sharply I thought, given her nature.

She had only one neighbour on her floor. The female part of the equation had jumped off the roof of the building at the start of the week. The male part of the equation, ergo, was the only part of 'the neighbour' that could pack suitcases and go away.

I drew a breath so sharp it pierced my larynx. 'Her husband?'

She nodded, her eyes bulging with the shock and impropriety of it all. 'With the thirteenth-day function still not done.'

I gasped and put a shocked hand to my mouth. 'Poor thing.'

'No respect for the dead these days,' she said, scathingly. I half expected her to spit on the polished floor to express her opinion of men who didn't perform proper thirteenth-day rituals for their deceased wives. We shook our heads, me a little guiltily because we hadn't bothered to drop in to express our condolences, given none of us really knew the family. They had shifted in a few months ago and pretty much kept to themselves. All we knew, information gleaned through the maid network, was that they had a son who lived abroad.

'Perhaps he has no family here. Perhaps he is taking her ashes for immersion.' I was always one to give folks the benefit of the doubt.

'So many suitcases?' she countered. 'I think he took two cabs to the airport in order to accommodate the entire luggage.'

'Perhaps he is going abroad, to be with his son?' I ventured.

Of course, there were visas that once obtained allowed one to enter and exit for a specified number of years, and some countries offered visa on arrival, but I had no clue which country his son was in nor if that country supplied such visas, and whether, as the spouse of the suicide case, he was allowed to leave the city without proper permission from the khaki-clad arms of the law.

'When did he leave?' I asked, wondering, in my new-found detective mode, whether that was a point to be noted in my little notebook, one that I had taken to carrying around given that often things happened in my immediate vicinity that I needed to put down in writing for fear of forgetting them a minute later and not being able to report to Runa.

'Last evening,' she replied. And, to clear herself of any suspicion of being the kind of neighbour who had one eye permanently affixed to the keyhole to check for suspicious movement in the passageway between flats, she added, 'We happened to go down in the lift together. He put one suitcase on my foot and didn't even apologize.' She divested the offended foot of its slip-on footwear and held it up to display an ugly patch of blue-black where undoubtedly something of crushing weight had been unkindly placed.

'Did you ask him where he was off to?'

She laughed, a bitter, mirthless laugh. 'Arey, for the past six months they have been here, they haven't exchanged even a smile, forget a hello. When I went across with tea on the day they moved in, they didn't even say thank you or invite us inside. We don't speak.'

That was a dead end. I couldn't wait to get home and enquire with the security in charge if they had any information about where Mr 504 had headed to with all his life's belongings in large suitcases.

We said our bye-byes and hotfooted it through opposite aisles, from whence I wheeled my trolley into the emptiest checkout lane I could find, making an almost collision with Velvet Smoking Jacket, aka Veer, aka Rana.

'Whoa. We must stop meeting like this.' He chortled as I did my familiar 'turn crimson all over and need a fire hydrant to douse the burning embarrassment I always felt whenever he was in my immediate vicinity'.

I gave him what, I hoped, was a polite smile and steered my trolley next in line at the checkout counter, while he gallantly let me pass.

'Quite some adventure in the society these days,' he said, conversationally. I nodded. 'There always is, isn't there?'

'Interestingly, though, I haven't heard any screaming on the stairways since I complained to your husband about it. Was he able to figure out what it was all about and get it stopped?'

I furrowed my brow in thought – also worrying about the groove between eyebrows it would cause later, and cursed myself for encouraging facial lining – but I couldn't remember the spouse having taken his complaints about screaming voices too seriously, never mind that I had heard those screams myself and mentioned them to him.

'I don't think he did,' I replied. 'But if they've stopped on their own, well and good. Makes for some peace in the vicinity.'

'And we could do with some. The next to be tackled are the loudspeakers,' he began earnestly. 'Ruin a man's sleep, they do. Five a.m., every morning.' He shook his head, making his curls, highlighted subtly in copper tones – or was that the natural tint of his hair? – bounce in a manner that shampoo-conditioner ads for curly hair would pay a good stylist a pretty packet to achieve for the screen. 'I'm getting dark circles from the lack of proper sleep.' He smiled, in what could be construed as a suggestive manner. It also wasn't becoming of a person to discuss his beauty issues with someone he barely knew.

I gulped and turned back to the business at hand, and checked out my shopping, painfully aware that he was examining all the contents of my trolley, probably judging me on the tub of ice cream and the jumbo packs of chips. His basket consisted of packs of juice and some assorted fruits and a pack of muesli. I stared at the biceps, bulging beneath the thin, white T-shirt he had on, and resolved to cut out the parathas for breakfast and switch to muesli. At the moment, my arms flapped like bat wings in a storm when I waved innocently to the child while wearing anything without sleeves, and I had taken to holding arm up at elbow level and doing a gentle wave in the manner espoused by royalty rather than the entire 'alert the marines version' in a public situation.

By the time I reached home, the sun was blazing angrily through uncertain clouds drifting aimlessly across the sky, apologizing for their lack of monsoon-cloud seriousness. A police van was parked outside the gate.

I hopped out of the car, and investigated with the security personnel as to why the law enforcers had paid us a visit. The man who guarded the gates whispered, 'Her husband has left town without informing the police as to where he is going. He went yesterday, with two taxis because he had so much luggage.' I already knew that.

The police inspectors and constables standing at the watchman's desk in the lobby let me pass by unquestioned. But, of course, I couldn't bear to pass by wihout questions and asked said men in uniform what their purpose was on the premises. I played the card of needing to inform the spouse, who was an office bearer of the society committee, about the presence of said uniformed long arms of the law.

'Madam, *yahaan* murder investigation *chaloo aahe*,' a constable enlightened me. I loved the ease with which he switched languages between the local Marathi and the national Hindi.

'Murder?' I squawked. 'But wasn't that a suicide?'

He smiled grimly at me, his smile splitting his face open much like a watermelon, revealing cheerful pink gums and tobacco-stained teeth. 'Madam, the lady who jumped from your building. She was choked to death and then thrown.'

For a moment, my heart stopped beating. Then it flew into my mouth and hammered at the soft cartilage of my palate. And finally, it decided to be well behaved and fell to my toes where it decided to root me to the spot and refuse to let me follow my flight-or-fight instincts and get the hell out of there. Déjà vu happened and how. Sheetal Jaiswal, the one found with her throat slit some months in the recent past on the back roads of this complex, and now Mrs 504.

The head, which was given to whirring at the best of times, began to spin at giddying levels. I was vaguely aware of putting a hand out to steady myself and found it touching the cold nose of the random adopted stray that always hung around the watchman's desk and skittered away in fear at the touch of my sweaty palms. In a reflex action, I pulled out a wet wipe from my handbag and wiped the palm furiously, resolving not to touch anything edible until the hand in question had been sanitized and washed with Dettol Liquid

Handwash for well over a minute. Those dogs, they put their noses in unmentionable places, especially where other dogs were concerned, not to mention the acts of personal intimate hygiene they seemed to be constantly conducting in public. All thoughts of murder investigations were immediately dismissed from my mind.

'What did you know about the lady who was found on the ground?' asked an inspector with *Dabangg*-style Ray-Bans without the Salman Khan abs to match.

Me, what, little me? I knew nothing about her. I said as much. I repeated it vehemently. All I knew was that she had had a troubled marriage. I'd heard she was consulting a psychiatrist, I mentioned. Someone who lived in the other wing. Maybe she would be able to help them with some information.

The inspector, his smile firmly in place, nodded slowly. 'We know.'

He smiled wider. 'We also know you and another lady went to meet her last Saturday.'

What? Had they installed spycams in the corridors of the building that I knew nothing about?

Would that mean I needed to stop picking my nose in the lifts?

'Yes, I did, with a friend from the same building, because we heard that there had been some screaming from her floor. And we had heard she had been in a fight with her husband.'

'Domestic-violence case?' he asked, his voice dropping down to a whisper.

I was compelled to tell the truth. 'That's what we heard, but when we went to see her, she seemed fine, if a little annoyed that we had come to check on her.'

It had been most annoying, this concern of ours, which hadn't been welcomed. I could have elaborated for the next twenty minutes on why people needed to be more friendly with their neighbours and watch out for them in apartment complexes because then we had cases where thieves dropped in unannounced and slit throats before eating cooked meals and making comfortable getaways because everyone had stopped being concerned about the other. But the good inspector was already not paying attention. A man in a white shirt, which needed introduction to a good fabric whitener, and blue trousers had come up to him and was saying something about the angle of the fall.

'Are you sure?' the inspector asked, furrowing his brow and stepping out to look up at where the terrace was.

'Absolutely sure, and I said it the last time too. The distance of the fall is wrong. If she had fallen from the terrace she should have landed outside the compound wall on the road. The injuries too are not consistent with the angle of the fall.'

My ears pricked up. They were saying Mrs 504 hadn't jumped from the terrace. That her injuries were not consistent with the fall.

'Where else could she have fallen from?' I asked. 'Her flat faced the other side, and she had grilles covering all the balconies, which would need to be cut open for her to get through.'

A small audience had begun to gather. Drivers who, on regular days, hung around in the perimeters of the parking lots, rolling out their tobacco and spattering the fringes of the walls in the area with their streams of brilliant red spittle, moved closer with their ears out on leashes to catch what was being discussed. By the end of the day, the driver-and-domestic-help grapevine would inform residents that Mrs Mehra had been tied to a chair and interrogated by the police in the lobby, with only a 100-watt bulb shining on her face and throwing her T-zone into bright relief.

I turned decisively towards the lift, regretting the moment I had decided to let my curiosity get the better of me. Then a small niggling question made me turn around again, against my better judgement, which anyway was always meant to be gone against. 'How do you know it was murder and not suicide?'

He sidled up to me, smile firmly in place, and said very softly: 'Strangulation marks on dead body's neck.'

I needed something stronger than tea then. I required the spirit that cheered and inebriated. A person with an unstable mind flinging herself off the roof of the premises and someone being flung off the roof of the premises after a pair of hands had squeezed the breath out of her were two completely different things.

I smiled weakly and moved out swiftly before Sub-inspector Wagle, as the badge announced, decided he needed further information from me. The head spun in the giddy way it did when one heard of disturbing portents.

When I finally returned to the security of the home, I jabbed at the phone furiously.

I could not just let go of something like this, which did not concern me at all. A suicide that left strangulation marks around the neck. A husband who ran out of the city without investigating officers giving him the all-clear. I called Runa and quickly filled her in on the recently acquired details, ignoring for the moment her anger at being interrupted on a Saturday morning with information on a case she wasn't being paid to apply her grey cells to.

'How can someone who has been strangled also be a case of suicide, Runa?'

She hmmed and hawed a bit and then adroitly shifted the topic to the kitty-group case. I'd already informed her about the missing Jahnavi, as per my discussion with Devyani the day before.

'Have you spoken with Devyani today? Has she received any further information about Jahnavi's possible whereabouts?'

I was a little abashed. I hadn't. I confessed.

'Tchah,' she said, drilling an acidic hole through the ethers. 'Call her now and report back to me.' Saying so, she disconnected the line, leaving me bristling about her tendency to say jump and expect me to follow instructions.

Nonetheless, I did as instructed.

'No news yet,' Devyani reported. 'I'm terrified. I don't know how I'm going to tell my husband I've lost so much money just because I didn't listen to him about where I should invest and got a bit greedy.'

'Don't tell him now, perhaps,' I suggested, applying my own principle of deferring bad news to be delivered to the spouse until it reached him via other sources.

We ended the conversation with me assuring her blandly that perhaps Jahnavi would surface out of the blue, everyone's money in hand, and to give it a couple of days. After all, who amongst us had not had a moment when one wanted to run away from it all, into the great wilderness, and never be confronted with a bowl of Chocos or a WWE action figure ever again.

'I hope you are right, Kay,' she said, her voice pensive. 'I can't afford to lose so much of money. It was part of my fuck-off money, you know. If I had this, I could say that to the husband any time and walk out of the marriage. I haven't told you about it, but I'm planning to leave him. He's a serial cheat and I've had quite enough.'

I blinked, dazed. I had no such money. Everything we owned was in joint names, including the deposits. But then, I told myself, perhaps we weren't anticipating that things could come to a point where either of us would want to walk out of this marriage. How terrible, I thought to myself, to have money kept aside solely on the premise of the marriage breaking up. Or was that the sensible thing to do these days, given that marriages were breaking up quicker than political affiliations in election year.

'I'm so sorry to hear that,' I replied, racking my brain for appropriate protocol about what was to be said in reply to such revelations. We ended the conversation awkwardly. It was a conversation that could now only proceed face to face.

I turned to the intercom and called Raji, my font of all information.

'Raji?'

'Arey,' she said, sounding surprised, 'you're back? You finished all your grocery shopping before lunch? What's wrong?'

How well my friends knew me. I wish I could have been noble and decried that I had had enough of consumerism and was eschewing mindless purchases in favour of a more noble and spartan lifestyle, but first I really needed to stock the refrigerator with enough provisions to see us through an ice age.

'No, something cropped up and I needed to get back home immediately. Anyway, I'll tell you about that later. Now, listen, Mrs 504 was murdered. It wasn't suicide. What was her name anyway? I keep forgetting. Her husband vamoosed with his luggage. There are policemen down in the lobby asking questions.'

There was a horrified gasp in the static of the blurry intercom line. 'How can that be? Murdered?' She gasped again. 'Her name was in the newspapers, I'll check. Murdered? Not suicide?'

'Yes,' I replied, the horror still lacing my words.

'Killed?' she repeated. Followed by yet another horrified audible gasp.

'Yes,' I replied patiently.

'Homicide? Manslaughter?'

'Arey, are you going to take me through the entire thesaurus now? She had strangulation marks on her neck, a cop told me,' I said.

One more of them horrified gasps on the other end of the line. While she resisted the temptation to add more synonyms to the conversation. I continued.

'What is worse, he even knows we went to her home last Saturday.'

I waited patiently for the next horrified gasp. It came on cue. Gasp dispensed with, the conversation resumed. 'But we didn't kill her, Kay, don't be silly. She could have sat on us and crushed us with no effort absolutely. Whom do they suspect?'

'How would I know?' I replied, mildly miffed that I had no clue and, of course, I wasn't on the inside about this with the cops.

I got off the intercom and dialled Runa, to report on my conversation with Devyani.

The phone rang and rang and rang, and by the third minute I actually got worried. I disconnected the line and dialled her home number, which also rang interminably. Runa lived alone, with only a cat for company. A cat who was, whenever one dropped in, in a perpetual foul mood and inclined to sharpen her claws on whatever ensemble du jour one happened to be wearing. I had, ergo, given up dropping in for a while now. Perhaps she should have trained the cat to answer the phone in her absence. Maybe she needed an answering machine.

I sent her a carefully worded text, knowing she would call back as soon as she could to get the bones of the conversation. That was the trouble with Runa: she wasn't really bothered about the monetary part of it all, she wanted the thrill of solving the jigsaw puzzle of the crime, the whodunnit.

If Jamuna was displeased at seeing me back before she had managed her mandatory post-lunch snooze, she did not show it. 'Bhaaabhhiii!' she screeched in her dulcet tones, which could get ships out of fogs. '*Itna jaldi aa gaya wapas.* I haven't even had my breakfast yet.' An exaggeration of sorts, given that Jamuna's breakfast was an extended meal that began at 7 a.m. and extended to post noon. It comprised all the leftovers of the previous day in addition to whatever had been cooked for the current day's breakfast.

I would have to tell her that there was no additional wardrobe allowance to get her more clothes now that she seemed to be bursting out of her seams. I assured her I would refrain from disturbing her meal and that I had no pressing need of her services at the moment. She settled back to the spread in front of her, which took up approximately a foot in circumference. I glanced in at the spread and almost gagged, and rushed back to my room to breathe deeply and drink down some water.

The groceries were brought into the premises by the trusted driver of my steel grey chariot and put into place. 'Jamunaaa,' I called with a view to demand coffee, black, strong and sweet, just the way I liked it, when the phone rang again.

'Kay,' trilled a 'walking in the park' friend from the other wing, Kavita, she of the body that was slimmer than was mandatorily legal for a woman who had carried to term and delivered two babies, and claimed not to have had a tummy tuck done on the operating table at birth as seemed mandatory these days.

Two, as seemed mandatory these days. 'I have a Mata ki Chauki at my house tomorrow. Please come. Four o'clock.'

Part of me wanted to protest violently given that I had not one religious bone in me, but the other, more dominant part of me was thrilled at the idea of getting together and sharing notes with the other women about who was wearing what, and getting all togged up for the do in my ethnic wear which had, to be honest, been languishing in the farthest recesses of my cupboard, and had most probably been attacked by the invisible creatures that resided in such spaces where they morph perfectly wearable and *en vogue* outfits into outmoded versions of something the chorus dancers in a seventies' qawwali song would turn their noses up at.

I ended the conversation with polite affirmations that I would indeed grace the occasion at 4 p.m. sharp and that she would do well to roll out the rose-petal-strewn red carpet. I then fled to the wardrobe to dig out aforementioned ethnic gear that comprised just one sorry stack of bling so dazzling that I almost reached out for my sunglasses. Of course, there was always 'Sorry It Was That Time of the Month' as a standby excuse in case one wanted to wriggle out of it.

Religious functions in suburbia were 'serious to dress' events that could make or break your standing in the social pecking order within the complex. What to wear was debated furiously, often for days in advance. If it was a big shindig like the annual Navaratri celebrations – which involved lights strung up all around the premises, a hired DJ and catered-for dinner – one might even step out to the marketplace, brave the sweating masses and pick up a chaniya choli for oneself along with appropriate silver jewellery to get the authentic look, so as to ensure that every single one of us looked like we had been airlifted straight from the Rann of Kutch, minus the tattoos, of course.

On a previous occasion, when I had hair and enthusiasm enough, I had even got the hair braided in a bohemian style, which looked great in the night while I hung around trying to look as cool as a thirty-five-year-old urban woman could look when dressed in something that had her six-year-old rolling on the floor laughing when she finally emerged from the bedroom. She, in turn, had then straitjacketed the child into a short orange top with mirrors and a flared skirt much to his disgust, worn with a dhoti which he kept tripping over, and finally divested self of, eventually running around the event looking like a miniature cross-dresser in an orange mirror-worked dress.

When in doubt about attending an event, phone-a-friend was the easiest way out. Ergo I phoned Raji. Her maid, who could have been a twin of Jamuna's, separated at birth, informed me that 'Bhabhi' had gone down to the lobby, adding in a hushed whisper, 'to meet the police people'.

I quickly took myself down to the lobby in unbridled curiosity and the burning desire not to be left out of whatever it was that had taken Raji down to the lobby to meet the men in uniform, who were not even of the dishy variety that I could imagine her wandering down to gaze upon in a hormonal trance.

The lobby, which had been populated by the straggly bunch of drivers, odd-job boys and maids when I had taken myself home, had become, in the span of half an hour, a hive of buzzing activity with what seemed like a representative from every flat present. The gathered crowd looked on as the men in uniform sat asking questions of the security men and the car cleaner, who had found the unfortunate Mrs 504 post her plunge from the assumed height of the terrace, which we had found was unlocked and the key to which had been found missing from the watchman's panel of keys, when searched for.

Raji was sitting on the stone ledge that fringed the vast entrance, making it a comfortable spot for visitors, drivers and other assorted support staff who worked in the complex to gather together for discussions.

Seated next to her was one khaki-clad one, his swarthy face hidden beneath a pair of Ray-Bans with mirror finish. Standing in front of her was the other khaki-clad one who seemed to be of junior rank, and ergo, condemned to stand.

'Kay,' she said, spotting me approach, 'I was just telling this kind inspector that this lady had been taken to a clinic a few days before she died. That there had probably been some domestic violence, but that we don't have the details. Also, that she seemed unnaturally sleepy when she opened the door, like she was on some sleep medication.'

Ah. I needed something to top this now. I couldn't be the lesser person in this 'Tell a Secret' competition that Raji had started.

I fished about in my cranium for something I could share but found nothing. Then a vision flashed across what the good poet referred to as the mind's eye, rather myopic at the moment. A vision of Mrs 504 staring balefully at me from the top of the stairway a few minutes before I learnt she had jumped to her death. And then the vision of her lying, skull cracked and contents flowing with the rain, on the paving in the society compound.

'I saw her on the stairs that morning, some minutes before we got the call on the intercom telling us she had jumped half an hour before.' The throng of stragglers standing around to catch snippets of the conversation had their ears all cocked in anticipation, and drew in closer so as not to miss a whisper.

I needed to explain myself. 'I was walking up and down the stairs because it was raining and I couldn't go for my morning walk, when I felt someone standing behind me. I turned around and saw her standing there. Looking at me. Hard.'

The one wearing the Ray-Bans took them off and looked at me, beady eyes narrowed. 'What do you mean, looking at you hard? Was she short-sighted?'

I felt compelled to do a demo of the narrowed gaze Mrs 504 had inflicted on me that had caused me to run home. It was interesting to see him flinch, although I packed not half the punch into the glare that she had – add to that her dishevelled appearance and bloodshot eyes and the fact that she could have slid straight into the role of Bertha Mason, letting loose some blood-curdling laughs in the process.

'Madam,' he said, with a sudden grave manner that had my heart plummet to my toes, which went icy-cold with tension. 'I will have to record your statement as one of those who last saw the lady alive.'

When I died, if they dug me a grave, I would need one twice the regular size, for me and my big mouth, with my foot in it.

12

In Which Blackmail and Threats Pepper a Perfectly Relaxed Day

SUNDAY

Sunday morning in suburbia was the kind of relaxed that mandated 8 a.m. rising and lolling in bed in slovenly sloth until the prod of conscience dictated one rise and carpe the diem or risk having one's name bandied about in the annals of the house-help diaries as one who could put Rip Van Winkle to shame, with the seven-year fungal growth on the chin to boot.

Barely had I woken and put the flabby grey organ within the cranium to work – trying to figure out how the woman who jumped and the woman on the stairs I saw after she had supposedly jumped could be wearing two different outfits – when the intercom rang.

'Kanan?' It was Devyani. Her voice sounded subdued.

'Did you hear?' she continued, not waiting for me to confirm whether it was indeed me on the line and not the very efficient Jamuna. 'Folks have filed a criminal complaint against Jahnavi for disappearing with their hard-earned money and there's a missing person notice in the papers today.'

I hadn't yet planted the eyeball on the day's news, I confessed, but were there any leads as to what had happened with Jahnavi, and why this entire deposit and loan-sharking business of hers had gone belly-up, given that she seemed to have enough clients content to entrust their savings, in black, to her rather stolid hands?

'You know, I heard she was lending out the money to the builder lobby and the interest was what she was recycling and now that the real-estate scene has gone bust, she had no way to pay the interest and was also delaying repayments of full amount back to depositors. And there was this MLM scheme she had signed many folk up for. You know, the magnetic mattress thing which was supposed to be the next best thing since sliced bread and cure folk of everything from dwarfism to fourth-stage cancer?'

I had heard vague whispers about it, I confessed, and had studiously avoided Mrs Randheria from B-903 who had been trying assiduously to frogmarch me to one of the seminars where a fat, sweating man in a suit gave them a PowerPoint presentation on the benefits of the mattress, and the MLM scheme, post which they literally bulldozed the hapless attendees to hand over signed cheques while they were still glazed from the stupor of a two-hour-long presentation in a room with the lights dimmed.

Jahnavi, Devyani told me, had been pretty successful at converting the hapless ones she took to the seminars into card-carrying mattress sellers. And now that scheme had collapsed on itself and her down-the-liners were baying for her blood and literally picketing her doorstep.

I ended the conversation by promising Devyani I would read the snippet about Jahnavi's disappearance in the newspaper. Page Five, 'City Briefs', she informed me helpfully, to ease the need for me to scour the entire newspaper to arrive at the relevant page.

I picked up the paper, turned to the page and read that the city police were searching for this lady, who had been unfortunate enough to have her passport photograph put on the notice. It said she had defrauded many people of unspecified sums of money. I wondered if the police bothered about checking for more flattering photographs to use when they put out such notices and resolved to have enough flattering photographs of mine easily accessible in the event that any such notice needed to be put out about me. Not that I was planning to defraud people of unspecified amounts of money and go missing. In the kitchen, the cook and Jamuna kept up a steady repartee of insults in the best tradition of comedic double acts. Someday I would find both of them lying comatose with knives stuck in each other's backs, and would need to step gingerly around their bodies to get to the food.

I flitted back into the kitchen, noting that the voluble arguing ceased and desisted immediately in my presence, and checked whether the fruits had been cut to precise chunks, and the sambar tempered with precisely the right amount of snapped red chillies and mustard seeds, the idlis cooked to that precise melt-in-the mouth consistency rather than the 'break the tooth cap' variety that I had managed every time I attempted to make them myself. I was a perfectionist that way.

I moved swiftly towards the breakfast table just as it was being laid. I wasn't looking forward to breakfast-table conversation with the spouse, given that he had made some cutting remarks about me and detective business the previous night, which I had nullified by turning a dignified shoulder and drifting into a deep slumber. I had the feeling that the conversation would be continued over breakfast. He had been giving me the beady eye over the top of his pink paper. It was not the kind of conversation one needed to have at breakfast time, and rather impeded digestion, not to mention the kind of vile things it did to the appetite. I did not take kindly to my appetite being imposed upon the first thing in the morning.

'No walk today?' he asked conversationally, beginning in an accusing manner and setting rather the right adversarial tone for what might follow.

Gah. I stuffed an idli down my throat and refused to think of exercise and bodies given that I was long divorced from the former and the waistline had long divorced me.

'No. It's Sunday.' That explained it. Who in their right senses worked out on Sunday, after all? Even the God who created the world in seven days rested on Sunday, I had learnt at school from the good nuns who did their bit to teach us about everything – except original sin – in happy tandem with Darwin and evolution, never for a moment concerned about the confusion that it would cause innocent minds.

He raised one sardonic eyebrow in my direction and continued buttering his toast with disapproving hand movements. 'Why is Kabir not up yet?'

'Let him sleep in,' I replied. 'It's a holiday.'

The spouse and I were on opposite sides of the sleep divide. He was the lark and I the owl.

He was the 'carpe the diem before the rooster wipes the sleep from his heavy-lidded eyes' and I the 'hit snooze on repeat'.

I had been known, in more languid times, to have slept through an entire night and much of the next day, the kind of story that was aired out at family gatherings and replayed by the pater for communal entertainment.

He went out into the balcony with his newspaper, and then called me to come see. I scampered over.

'Look down, there, beyond the compound wall.'

There was a motley crowd gathered and the scene was dotted with the khaki-clad ones, some of whom seemed to be speaking importantly into walkie-talkies and barking orders to minions. Perhaps a demolishing of the hutments dotting the periphery of the boundary wall of the complex was in progress. That happened periodically, and with some sadistic timing, especially during the monsoon.

My gaze stopped at the bank of the blackened swell of the canal that flowed through this patch of land, turgid with industrial effluent and waste and the kind of toxic stuff that had probably led to radioactive aquatic creatures forming armies, readying themselves to take over the world. A grown adult-sized shape lay on the ground, covered with a sheet. People walked gingerly around it, their hands to their noses. Some had even tied kerchiefs over their noses to prevent further olfactory assault. I gasped. 'A dead body?'

'Yes.' He nodded grimly.

'So probably this was what was making the air so foul, apart from the mounds of uncleared garbage.'

'Probably.' He nodded and began with his 'The City Is Going to the Dogs' speech, which I had heard so often, I timed him to ten minutes uninterrupted on it, when in full spate. Luckily now, the child emerged into the balcony and squealed happily at seeing his first dead peepul and demanded to know if the thing under the draped sheet would rise in horror-show manner and stalk the earth demanding little children to eat. We dissuaded him from that notion, and I was asked sotto voce if I was monitoring the shows the fruit of our respective womb and loin was watching.

He then went on to address, having gained form on a Sunday morning for his weekly session of 'improve Kay', the subject of my determination to put in my two bits of information to the policemen, explaining gently to me that it was best that I stayed out of such things given that I would then be called consistently to police stations which, he explained with even more gentleness, were not places 'people of gentle upbringing' should be wandering around.

I did what I always do when he proffered advice: ignored him while pretending to nod in agreement. Barely had the table been cleared when the doorbell rang and Jamuna announced, in her 'wake the dead from their sound sleep' tones, that a saabji was there to meet 'Bhaiya', as she called the spouse. She added that she didn't know who he was and what was she to do and I needed to talk to the cook soon about her attitude or she, Jamuna, was going to quit and go back to the village and get married. All that in one breath.

I sighed and went towards the door. Mr Bhatia, he of the un-pedicured toes revealed in sandals, and the Hawaiian shirt, was now clad in jeans and an inoffensive T-shirt, which could probably double as a circus tent in an emergency. He stood without and cracked an evil, plaque-encrusted smile at me. I shuddered and invited him in politely, knowing that the houseboy from the flat opposite would have one eye at the peephole trying to ascertain who was visiting us so early.

The spouse emerged from the bedroom, unwarned about the unwanted Sunday-morning guest, and his face visibly blanched, but to his credit he took the knock well and smiled politely at the unwelcome unannounced visitor, calling for water and tea or any beverage of preference, which was declined with equivalent politeness before the discussion got down to the matter at hand, which I surmised would be the transfer of flat no. 504 to his name, which was being consistently stalled by the society committee, of which the spouse was flagbearer.

I took the opportunity to take myself out of the immediate vicinity and get to a secluded corner where I could call Runa to apprise her of the latest conversation I had had with Devyani barely an hour ago. And so I did. Runa, having evidently chewed her mandatory glass bottles for breakfast and digested them without as much as a glass shard of a burp, was unimpressed with the information I dispensed with such glee.

'I already know all that, Kay, surely you could have eased out some more facts from her. Names of people who were her down-liners in the mattress scheme. Names and addresses of those who had lost their money. Find these out and get back to me, we need to do some more talking with more people.'

I harrumphed and disconnected the call. From the living room without, raised voices could be heard. The child, unused to such decibel levels in the a.m., had emerged from his room, enquiring loudly about whether Pappa was about to challenge the fat 'unkul' to a fist fight and if so, could he call his friends to watch.

The Pappa in question gave me a glance that indicated I was to take the offspring into the inner recesses of the house, away from the heated discussion that was getting to the boiling point.

As I steered the child away into calmer zones, I heard Mr Bhatia say as he was being asked to take himself out of our home. 'You will live to regret this, Mr Mehra, I have bought this flat lawfully and you are harassing me for no reason.'

The spouse, I am proud to say, stood his ground firmly. 'Our society rules are very clear on no sale without interview with committee, and you have not had an interview with the committee. I suggest you meet with the rest of the committee to plead your case. I am only the secretary. I wish you all the best and have a good day.'

The sound of the door being closed firmly followed and I emerged from the child's room hesitantly. 'What was that all about?'

The spouse sighed, a deep rolling sigh that had the curtains rustling softly. '504, 504. That flat is determined to be a thorn in my side. Either the residents or the buyers. I wish I could just resign from this thankless position. It is no fun being secretary of a housing society, let me tell you, Kay. You get pounced on for everything …'

I patted his back in comforting manner, glad that his mind had been distracted from my detective apprenticeship with Runa, which he had voiced his disapproval of in very colourful terms along with my conversation with the policemen.

'It's a dirty job but someone's got to do it, right? Think of it as a social responsibility.'

And also there was a certain je ne sais quoi that came with being the wife of the secretary of a housing complex this large, which had the security men kowtowing to me with a deference that was sadly lacking when we were merely one of the many residents of the complex, and I was not willing to give up the trappings of reflected power, albeit limited to being able to get the security chappie in the lobby to abandon his post and go hunt for the offspring in the park on days when he decided he was going down unsupervised because he was now a Big Boy and dare I say otherwise.

The spouse got on to the intercom and bellowed at the hapless recipient of his ire at the other end of the receiver, which would undoubtedly be the security guard on duty in the lobby. The plaster on the ceiling began shaking and a few flakes cascaded down as he yelled queries about why Mr Bhatia had been allowed up without the mandatory phone call requesting permission to send guests, and that too, of such unwanted variety, up on a morning when all good thinking and hard-working folk should be allowed to have their morning cup of tea and browse through the newspaper at leisure.

'And next time he rings my doorbell again without me getting a call from you, you will be fired. Your entire agency will be fired.' The spouse's face had turned a strange shade of purple with rage, and I was sure if it hadn't been for the child peeping out from his bedroom at this latest show of 'Pappa Throws a Tantrum' – wondering whether he could still sell tickets to his friends for it – he would have gone on to sack all further generations of the hapless security chappie, even those who were yet to be hired, regardless of whether they were just a twinkle in the man's eye at the present moment.

Charged with more vim and vigour than should be legally permissible at 11 a.m. on a Sunday morning, the boy declared he wanted to go down to the park. The day, contrary to how monsoon days should be, was bone dry and blazing furiously on the hapless denizens. 'See, is nod raining now. Den if it is raining in d evening I will na be able to play in the park.'

'Kabir, it really is too early to go down to the park. And it's too hot.'

'I'll ged VidaminD,' he insisted, damn the television commercials that had informed him of the necessity of said vitamin to make his bones strong, failing which he needed to ingest gallons of malted beverage.

Since Jamuna had been dispatched down to the vegetable vendors by the corner to procure some of the greens and fruits that would make for the healthy diet we tried hard to pretend we stuck to, I was saddled with the onerous task of escorting him down to the park. There was a silver lining to it though – it got me out of the immediate line of fire from the spouse, who was already pawing-hoof-on-ground post the encounter with Mr Bhatia and would be looking at a 360-degree angle to offload residual anger, and who better than little, ah well, not-so-little but you get my drift, me to be the chosen one.

Kabir, with an alacrity that had me slack-jawed in wonder, showered within record time, changed into park clothes, checked the park for residual pint-sizes for playing purposes, earmarked two who were his current best frenemies and trotted out of the door with a happy wave and 'bye Pappa', to his Y chromosome donor. We travelled down in companionable silence to the ground floor with his little hand cosy in mine paw.

I was suddenly conscious of the fact that I had not even splashed water on my face before stepping out of the house. I retreated into the steel walls of the lift, hoping by some miracle I would be rendered invisible in the event that any of the minor celebrities who populated our building decided that this would be the exact same time they needed to go somewhere.

On cue, the lift stopped on a floor and a waft of men's perfume so strong preceded the wearer that it almost knocked me out cold to the floor. Veer-Rana got in. I skirted the confusion about his name by not addressing him by either. In my head he would always be 'Velvet Smoking Jacket' for the ludicrous choice of attire he had chosen at the glitzy Bollywood party we had bumped into each other at over a year ago. Consequently, he assumed a kinship with me, which discomfited me in the way the scullery maid would feel when the master of the manor insisted on polite conversation, metaphorically speaking of course, given that he was the master of nothing except maybe the 8.30 p.m. time slot on prime time.

'Helloo,' he exclaimed with what seemed to be genuine delight at spotting me with dog breath and tangled hair and definitely the gunk still in the corner of my eyes. I shrank further into the wall in horror. 'And how are we today?'

The child poked him in the gut without invitation. 'It is six packs or eight packs? My fren says it is six packs, I say it is eight packs.'

Rana lifted the thin T-shirt he was wearing and displayed abs so solid, I was tempted to prod them to check if they were real or carved from stone.

'If I give yu a punch in yer stomach yu will all fall down?' Kabir asked, unimpressed with the musculature on display.

'Yes, of course, I will,' he said cheerily, making me wonder what exactly he had snorted up with his morning tea. He had a tennis bag on his shoulder.

In true studmuffin manner he bent down on his haunches to go to eye level with the child.

'Want to have a boxing match someday?' he asked, all attention.

The child punched the air in joy. 'Yus, yus, yus ...' And then he added, 'Can I call my frens to watch? But yu must nod defeat me okay, I is smaller dan yu. Den peepul will say he beat up a smallboy so sad. They will call you a bad peepul.'

'Ah yes.' Rana's eyes widened in mock realization. 'Okay, I will let you defeat me. We have a match on, champ.' They fist-bumped in celebration.

We had reached the ground floor, the date and timing of the match fixed, and the child was already mentally printing out the tickets and selling them at a premium.

The tall one unfurled his length to its fullest and stood up ready for disembarking. 'See you around then.' He smiled.

I smiled and nodded in what I hoped was gracious, amicable neighbourly manner, afraid to speak and reveal morning breath. Surely I had looked like I had sprained my neck or something. And – *gah!* – why had I stepped out in my faded and most tattered pair of PJs? They had originally been a shade of sky blue but were now some colour between grey and dog piss. I wished the steel would melt and swallow me up, I wished I could morph into a more glamorous avatar instantly like Mystique from them *X-Men*, but not in her scaly-blue-with-yellow-eyes form. I was doomed to look like something the family pet regurgitated onto the Persian silk carpet.

'Looking good, Kay,' he said as a parting shot. 'Have you lost weight? And you do look nice without all that' – he waved his hands indeterminately in the air – 'on your face.' And he strode off without waiting for confirmation that I had indeed lost weight. I bristled in irate-porcupine manner, with all quills on high alert. Did this imply that I did not look good earlier, that the excess avoirdupois had robbed me of any pretence towards being attractive? I harrumphed in my head and swore on all that was holy, including the new, yet unopened jar of Nutella in the refrigerator, that I would lose weight and become svelte and attractive so that jaws dropped when I passed and suchlike.

The child raced across the compound to the park, and discovered his true friends for playing purposes. Positioned tactically around the fringe of the park, in the little shade provided by the straggling trees, were the maids in supervisory positions, chatting on their mobiles, while keeping one alert eye on their charges, ready to rescue them from inadvertent scraps or clear and present danger from uncooperative swings and roundabouts that began whizzing too fast thanks to overly enthusiastic playmates hell-bent on getting them to regurgitate their breakfast from the spinning in 'little girl from *The Exorcist* pea soup' manner.

I made my way homewards after ascertaining that Jamuna had returned from vegetable shopping and could be called down on Offspring Watch duty.

I returned home to find a minor battle playing out between the cook and Jamuna, with Jamuna accusing the cook of taking multiple utensils to concoct the edible stuff she made, purely for the pleasure of seeing her spend her entire morning at the kitchen sink scrubbing. I separated the two before hair could be torn off scalps and ordered them to different zones. Jamuna, I decreed, was to step into the kitchen only after the cook had closed the main door gently behind her retreating person, and right now she was to go down to the park. I poured myself a glass of water, and demanded a Disprin be dunked into it instantly.

It promised to be anything but a relaxed Sunday. And then the phone rang on cue, to un-relax it further. Runa.

'Kay, I think we need to have a chat with Devyani. There's something about her that I need to figure out. Set it up,' she commanded imperiously and disconnected the line.

Like all things comprising good intentions, I promptly put that on hold and went back into the kitchen before an all-out conflagration broke out once again between the warring factions, with Jamuna now casting loud aspersions on the cook's method of getting a perfectly round paratha using a sharp-edged round plate. And when I did remember what I had been asked to do, Devyani replied to an urgent WhatsApp message that she was out of town and would probably be back in a couple of days. Which, in retrospect, was a rather strange thing, for someone who had many lakhs disappear in a scam, to do.

13

Of Closed Doors Being Opened

MONDAY

The morning, when it arrived, without ceremony or anxiety-inducing alarm – given I'd changed the infernal intrusive ring to a gentler babbling-brook sound – was dry and calling me to go for a short run. I rushed to the bathroom, splashed water on my face, poured self out of the nightdress that revealed more bat wing on the arm, and pulled on my trackpants and hoodie set.

I stepped into my neon orange running shoes, which had toned my wallet the best so far, before peeping into the child's room to find him muttering in his sleep between bouts of unchildlike snoring. Jamuna, who opened one eye at my entrance, promptly squeezed it shut, in the unlikely event that I had some immediate task at hand which needed to be fulfilled at 5.45 in the a.m.

When I entered the lift I said the Hanuman Chalisa, just in case it decided it was time to plunge into the well again.

For a regular morning walker and runner, staying away from the road was about as torturous as staying away from television would be for a television addict. I could barely wait to get the asphalt under my feet and the wind in my face. I had love handles growing from the month of the 'monsoon of no exercise', which could have me stuck within revolving doors, and which shaved themselves off at the sides when I looked at myself in a mirror, full frontal.

The watchmen were mouth-open snoring at the reception as I walked out into the lobby. I wondered if I should suddenly scream and startle them into blathering wakefulness and then decided against it. I walked gently up to them and prodded one on the shoulder with his baton, which had been helpfully laid on the desk for a burglar to clout him on the head with before proceeding to burgle the premises and all us unwary residents.

'Bhaiya, *utho*.'

He blinked twice and looked up at me. Blinked again and put his head down dismissing me – probably as a night terror – and then jumped up to his feet with a start. 'Madam, madam, *bas abhi neend ki jhapki lagi thi*. I have been awake all night. God promise. I've been doing double duty, *mera* replace *ka*, he didn't turn up.' At times, being related by marriage to the person in charge of hauling up the hirelings was quite a pain at the wrong end of the carcass.

I reassured him as gently as I could that I had no intention of reporting his trespasses to the highest authorities, and for all I cared he could roll out his bedding in the middle of the lobby and snore in decibels so earth-shaking that we could all plug our ears with little wads of cotton right up on the eighteenth floor. All I wanted to know, I asked him, was whether he had noticed anything strange on the morning that Mrs 504 was found fallen in the compound, he having been the one who had reported the suicide to the spouse.

He thought with his forehead creased in the kind of blank, vacuous open-mouthed way that some folk had of denoting that they were attempting to think deeply. I repeated slowly, making sure I faced him in case he needed to lip-read if his auditory senses were still dulled by sleep. 'That day, when Mrs 504 jumped, did you notice anything unusual?'

He thought back, the cogs and wheels and all the circuitry within his cranium whirring and sparking in a bid to recall. 'Anything at all you remember, or were you sleeping on duty that day too?'

'*Arey nahi*, madam, *hamesha thodi* duty *par sotey hai ... aaj thodi si jhapki aa gayi ...*'

'So,' I persisted, with the determination that befitted one on a private investigation of a very public case, 'did you notice anything strange that day?'

There was the briefest of pauses before he replied. 'Actually, I did. Normally husband and wife went for a morning walk together. In fact, for the past few days, the man had been going for morning walks alone. I thought, perhaps, the memsaab was not well or something, and then the next thing I knew was that she had jumped from the building. And all that blood, uff! I still see her corpse in my nightmares.'

I clucked in empathy. Mrs 504 had made her visits to my deep REM dream sequences too, and often was wandering around stairways with a cracked skull leaking brain matter, staring in a vile, accusing manner at me. The newspaper boy came in and dumped his load of consignments onto the floor next to the watchman's table and began sorting them out floor wise.

'Arey,' he added, happily joining the conversation, 'all sorts of strange things happening in this building. All those screams from behind that door between the sixth and seventh floors on the stairs.'

I had heard screams. Veer a.k.a Rana had heard screams. And now this little boy with a face that was older than the rest of him said he had been hearing screams at that same spot too. 'Are you sure about the screaming?' I asked. It was always good to double-check.

'I've heard screams,' he repeated. I almost fell to my knees in gratitude and bowed in front of his straggly frame, but contained my excitement with much effort, allowing only a smidgeon of curiosity to escape and reflect itself on what I hoped was as dough-like a countenance as could ever be found amongst the post-teenage generation, and requested him to elaborate the circumstances.

'Sometimes, on the stairs. I can show you the door from where the screams come. Sometimes, I can hear crying, but the door is always locked. *Bahut dar lagta hai.*' His expression vouched for the degree of terror.

My ears pricked up in 'bloodhound picking up scent' manner. 'Which door, which door?' I was almost holding him by the shoulders and shaking him like a rag doll. 'Show me, show me!'

He led me through the premises to an innocuous-looking door, padlocked, in a little passage off the main stairway between the sixth and seventh floors.

'What door is this?' I asked my captive audience comprising two, the watchman and the newspaper boy. 'And why is it locked?'

'Refuge area, madam,' Ramvilas informed me helpfully. 'Key down with security in charge. It is always locked.'

'Do you still hear the screams?' I asked the newspaper boy, who was a little worried about the time this little detour would take from his newspaper delivery schedule. He scrunched his face up into a thoughtful manner, giving immediate credence to the theory that man was descended from the ape. 'Not in the recent week I haven't, come to think of it. But for quite a few weeks there were screams on some mornings coming from behind this door.'

Curiouser and curiouser. I had a nose that tingled when I was close to discovering something momentous. And it had begun to tingle.

I almost wished I could call Runa in on this, but hadn't the courage to make that call and admit I needed her razor-sharp deductive capabilities and her wide-legged, arms-on-hips interrogative stance, which got her many more nuggets of information than pleasant-faced me could ever extract from hardened nightwatchman types, who were definitely not feeling charitable towards me for commencing the third-degree when they could have been snoring in Technicolor dreams about life back in the village and a romp in the fields with obliging village maidens.

I thought back to the Mrs 504 standing on the landing looking at me like she could have me hacked to small bits to feed to stray dogs and the Mrs 504 floating in the dark space of the lift well, looking on with what could only be an expression of concern and worry, poles removed from the vitriolic stare that made me scamper down many floors like I had snapping Alsatians nipping with feral teeth at my ankles.

And I thought back to the screams that seemed to be selective about who heard them, with me being prime pair of ears bestowed that honour. Ergo, I asked the man,

'And has anyone else heard any screams on the stairs – the housekeeping staff, the security guys, anyone?'

The look he gave me indicated clearly that I was drifting into Loonytown. '*Nahi.*' He shook his head vigorously to underline his point. 'Never heard a squeak on the stairs. Even when I go in the middle of the night to the staff bathroom.'

The door looked innocuous enough. It needed a fresh coat of paint. Also, it was a metal door. Heavy. There was that padlock too. A well-oiled padlock that indicated it was opened often enough and in recent times. A grim-looking padlock of the kind that normally hung outside doors in the era when automated laser-keyed locking systems hadn't entered the country and when telephones were a rarity, ergo one visited distant relatives on the off-chance and was often greeted by locks of this size and persuasion, because said distant relatives had also taken the off-chance to decide to go visit us.

He pointed at the door with one lean, bony-knuckled, trembling finger. 'The screams come from here. Sometimes someone bangs the door. Whatever it is behind the door, it is a ladeez.'

The cogs and wheels rusting in my brain circuitry began creaking and whirring around at the kind of speed they had not seen for the past many months.

I dispatched a general car washer, who had followed the entourage to the room with the big padlock, down to the reception to wake the office bearers of the society and request information about who had the key to this room, since none of the security personnel standing around limply seemed to have it. No unearthly creatures would emerge, I told myself, taking heart from the sun shining in brightly through the slats in the facade glass bricks running up the stairway, which was definitely detrimental to supernatural forces, which my research – by way of watching one zillion horror movies from behind the cushion nearest at hand – had shown. Supernatural ghosties did not wander around when the sun was blazing out in full force, nor when you were in a throng of people. They would lead you off into corners, especially if you were white and blonde, and then do unspeakable things to you which were illustrated by means of wide eyes and screams, and sudden fade screen.

I put my ear to the door. I could hear nothing. The earwax needed cleaning out for sure. Finally, I gulped and knocked at it. Rather ridiculous of course, given that the door was locked from the outside. A bleary-eyed Colonel Singh trickled down the stairs from the higher floors having most probably been called by the random dispatched person, being the person whose car he washed and ergo felt most comfortable disturbing in the wee hours of the morning.

'Good morning, Mrs Mehra,' he boomed in a voice so crisp that anything malevolent in the immediate surroundings would have wet its pants and curled away into a corner until this model of armed-forces efficiency passed the way and was no longer present to fish it out and dispatch it into the furthest recesses of the afterworld. 'What is this I hear about screams from behind a door?'

I quickly filled him in on the details as provided to me by newspaper delivery boy, who stood barely a foot away trembling like the palsy had struck him unaware, and looking at the door with an expression that could be – at best – described as horror-struck.

'Who has the key?' Colonel Singh, having verified with said shaking-leaf person that this was the door from behind which howls of pain and suffering had been heard, asked in raised tone. Sundry watchers were dispatched to the flats above and below said refuge area to enquire kindly with the residents about the: a. screams and b. possession of said missing key.

More people in nightwear, or with hastily pulled on wraps to make them modestly presentable in public situation, appeared. Mrs 303 was in a bright floral nightgown of such a virulent hue and pattern that surely it would keep Mr 303 at bay unless he had no fear of being attacked by stray bees drawn by the florals. '*Kya hua*?' she asked, waddling up to me, her face, un-powdered and un-lipsticked, looked strangely unfamiliar.

I blinked. Took a moment to place her and resolved to get an eye test done that very day – wouldn't do to go flitting around the place unable to recognize folks just because they didn't have their full warpaint on.

I filled her in on the details, asking pleasantly if she had any clue who belonged to the humungous padlock grinning cheekily at us. She shook her head. 'Always thought it to be with the society office.' Which made the good Colonel boom that a refuge area should not be locked or it defeated the purpose in case of a fire emergency. We nodded wisely.

While no screams emanated from behind the door, I noticed a distinctly unpleasant odour. I wrinkled my not-so-delicate nose delicately.

'There's some foul smell here,' I voiced gently. It was like saying there was some water coming into the hold of the *Titanic*. The housekeeping staff, who having just arrived and still in civilian dress and therefore unrecognizable to me, protested violently, insisting that every corner had been cleaned and fumigated just the previous day. Folk around sniffed a little more. The odour was undeniable. And strong.

It was not the stench of damp refuse meeting the rays of the sun. It seemed to be emanating from beyond the metal door.

A hammer was called for, it having been ascertained from all the committee members that the ownership of the key to the door was indeterminate. A strong-armed person from among the ones watching the proceedings was put to use and the lock shattered with a few hard blows.

The door swung open and the stench hit us like a firm, disciplining slap on the face administered by a strict parent. I gagged. Thankfully, I had downed nothing in the morning before leaving the house, or surely I would have heaved it all over Colonel Singh's back as he stood in front of me. I noticed the spouse making his way down as I cupped my palms over my nose.

The spouse, clad in his almost-gone-to-shreds favourite pair of night shorts and a T-shirt – which had, in its infancy, been a shade of pristine white, and was now an indeterminate shade of sepia – looked at the scene and took charge. I wished he had changed the T-shirt, the women would comment about how I hadn't been using the proper whitening soaks with my laundry. He moved up front, as gruff and take-charge-of-the-situation as the elderly gentleman in front of me, and they both ventured into the dark, dank room, with the doors to the open space grilled firmly shut and shuttered down beyond. The air was fetid, miasmal.

The crowd fell about groaning at the reek emanating from the room. Their voices began buzzing like so many bees within my cranium and I could feel the beginnings of a migraine.

I stepped in behind the spouse and saw what seemed like a heap of rags curled up in a corner of what was a room, with a mattress and a trunk and heaps of newspapers. The stench was coming from the room, which had obviously been used as a residence for someone or something, but had not been cleaned too rigorously. I rushed out of the refuge room and heaved out pure, acidic bile onto the stairway.

Colonel Singh turned the kind of purple that indicated either an oncoming stroke or a Very Serious Temper Tantrum. 'This is abominable. Who has been using this place? Why has this been locked up?' he bellowed, rattling the plaster from the ceiling. *'Safai karvao!'* he commanded imperiously in the manner that would, in his days in the army, have had a platoon of jawans marching to his orders.

'Come, Kay,' said the spouse, gently steering me away from the olfactory assault, after I had wiped the mouth weakly with the back of my hand. 'Let's get you back home. And why on earth are you getting doors opened the first thing in the morning? I thought you were off for a run.'

'I was,' I replied, still shaky. 'But I got with the watchman about Mrs 504. And then this boy…' I gestured vaguely at the newspaper boy, who had now given up all pretence of needing to be on his rounds or risk getting his ears chewed off by those experiencing cold-turkey withdrawal symptoms at having been deprived of their daily broadsheets.

I got back home, rinsed out my mouth and took enough medication to quell an armed uprising in the stomach before dispatching the offspring to the school bus despite his protestations that school was 'boreding' these days because the only thing they did was rehearse for the annual day function. They had him playing the role of a tree, which was a trifle brave of the class teacher, I thought, if she expected him to stay in one spot for the entire duration of the play. But then, he could be an Ent, I told myself, and air his legs a bit when it got too cramped.

Having ingested the morning fare, sent the spouse to his workplace with a smile and a token peck on his check – because long, lingering kisses had gone the way of the waistline post the offspring's arrival on this planet – I was just about to take myself into the bathroom and soak in some bubbles when the phone buzzed angrily in my hand. I jumped in fright, looking down at the screen from where 'RUNA' flashed at me in bold capitals. I could almost hear her yelling, 'Answer the phone, Kay!' while sharpening her khukri on a kitchen stone.

'Yes, Runa,' I replied, wondering to what I owed this honour at the crack of dawn, etc.

'I've cracked it, the entire thing, the reason why the suicide happened, why the MLM went bust, everything. Meet me at eleven?'

When Runa asked you, in a questioning tone, to meet her, it was a matter of courtesy and you made yourself free even if you were scheduled for a spine-insertion surgery. I muttered meekly that I would.

'Okay, I'll meet you at the Café Coffee Day down your road at eleven sharp. Be there on time. You know how I hate waiting. And yes, bring Devyani along.'

She disconnected the call without waiting for my reply, calm in the assumption that I would be wearing out the welcome mat of said coffee shop five minutes before the scheduled time, with Devyani in tow, never mind that Devyani wasn't in the city.

I called back explaining Devyani wasn't in the city and that I had already told her about it.

'Well, get her to come back and meet me then.' Runa was a woman who brooked no argument.

Having got my morning organized, I decided to trot down to the local vegetable vendor to check if he had procured the broccoli and the coloured peppers I'd asked him to. I would rather pore over the supply myself than have him send the sludge from the bottom of his basket if I called for it.

In the lobby, the aviator-clad police inspector was present in person, engaged in deep conversation with Colonel Singh, who had since our last encounter changed both clothing and the colour of his face, both now easier on the eye.

I drifted up unobtrusively, my ears out on stalks to catch what was being discussed.

Undoubtedly, it would have something to do with Mrs 504's death.

'Arey, good morning, Mrs Mehra.' Colonel Singh, like any alert army person worth his combat training, had discerned my not-so-subtle approach. 'Nasty business this morning, but I've found the culprit and need to discuss it with the good inspector here.'

'Ho ho,' the inspector said, not in the manner of rotund Santa Clauses circling over the city and not finding the requisite chimneys to drop down, but in the native Marathi, in which it meant affirmative. 'It is all very interesting.'

My ears swivelled around trying to catch every detail in case I had missed something. 'We're getting tests of both the bodies found ...' Their voices trailed off. They looked at me with questioning eyes, and I sidled off without being able to conceal myself behind a pillar or a dog walker or anything conveniently placed, and kicking myself for not being able to eavesdrop on what was being discussed.

I swept out of the premises as regally as I could manage, while wondering whether my trousers had visible panty line – *damn and blast!* – I should have remembered to wear the seamless ones with the white trousers or just different trousers. How much was a woman supposed to remember about her appearance? There should be automated mirror-wardrobe combos that put together the entire ensemble from foundation garments upwards.

The vegetable vendor was still setting up his stall and the sun was playing hide-and-seek in the sky befitting a sixties' Bollywood film song, with the heroine doing the coy dashing-behind-the-trees act, before two flowers were jammed together in order to depict carnal intercourse and, we assume, cross-pollination, and if the drama was to be carried further, fertilization.

As I turned the corner back towards home, the phone rang in the very insistent manner that indicated it could only be the spouse.

'Yes,' I replied, irritated at being compelled to put down bags of vegetables on the pavement in order to fish the phone out, given that phones were now those infernal creatures that needed two hands to operate, one to hold and the other to swipe and, by God, had they taken away from us the pleasure of snapping a clam model shut to disconnect a conversation that had made one frothing-at-the-mouth irate. Swiping a red button on a glass screen didn't quite have the same pizzazz. I was sure people would pay substantially more for the ability to slam the phone off or even to recreate the 'slamming down of phone' sound effect for such occasions.

'What is it?' I barked, aware that the sun was breathing hot and heavy on the nape of my neck, in ways not mentionable in public.

'Kay, that Bali trip you had won? I have a possibility of a quick break of five days beginning Wednesday, after which things might get rather hectic at work. Do you think you could get your parents to babysit Kabir? Or we could take him with us.'

The breath, it caught in my throat. Five days beginning Wednesday? And I hadn't even shopped for resort wear yet. And no, it was to be my 'connect with the spouse again and rekindle the romance' trip, and Kabir climbing all over us, demanding to be entertained even on vacation, would definitely prove to be a dampener to any ardour that might arise. Should we take the offspring with us if the parents declined to play babysitters? Should we postpone the trip to until the parents were able to reschedule their social calendar and give a full week to their only begotten grandson?

Don't be silly, the firm voice of reason said. *Say yes now, or he'll wriggle out of it conveniently and you'll have to either give up the trip or take Raji on the trip with you*, it said in my other ear, not attached to the phone. It actually wasn't a bad idea, going off on a hedonistic girls-only beach vacay with Raji. If only I could deal with the ensuing grief and guilt the parents would lay on with a trowel if I had to beg and plead with them to babysit. Then again, it wasn't the greatest of ideas to go off on a beach vacation with Raji where she would be all svelte and nymphlike in two-piece bikinis and floral sarongs, while I channelled my inner goddess in kaftans a camel could feel at home tethered next to, and a swimsuit with a frill to hide thigh cellulite while doubling up as a flotation device.

'Of course, but what about visa and all that? So soon? Will it happen?' Of course, I was trying to buy time to shop for the trip. After all, what good was a trip you hadn't shopped for – before and during?

'Kay …' said the long-suffering spouse with a longer-suffering sigh. 'Bali has visa on arrival if you plan to stay for long, else no visa needed.'

Ah, of course, that was why the contest was so fluid about dates any time convenient to me, and I only needed to ensure that I had no consignment of the narcotic type snuck into my luggage or I would be condemned to rust for the rest of my life in Bali's notorious Hotel K, where roaches the size of rodents roamed and gang wars would have me dead before natural causes did, given that the only thing I could give a tough fight to was temptation suckering me into eating something calorific.

'Check with your parents if they can come down to watch over Kabir and let me know,' he commanded and disconnected the line. People were commanding me from the early morning and disconnecting calls on me, without even the cursory 'goodbye nice speaking to you have a good day'. I so needed to call a service hotline to the bank to get basic courtesy at the end of a call and feel good again.

I scampered home and placed a call to the progenitors. The mater replied. 'What happened? It is Monday.'

I must explain, the mater was a creature of habit who expected the mandatory phone call on the weekend and, if the routine was disturbed, immediately imagined the worst-case scenario with dismemberment, death and mayhem playing starring roles.

'Don't worry,' I reassured her, and explained the situation, tugging firmly on her grandmotherly chords, implying furiously that if the spouse and I didn't get this alone vacation, our marriage would be as good as kaput and she would need to put up with me and the brat for the rest of our lives, and that this was a great opportunity to bond with her grandchild given that they had last seen him many months ago and he would be asking them searching questions about who they were if he came across them if they let this pass for a few months more.

Given such terrifying options, she immediately consented to arrive in Mumbai on the evening of Tuesday and remain on premises until we returned from our hedonism, never mind that the round table dinner was scheduled for Saturday and she was expected to chair the meeting. As she told me thrice. In a tone so pointed that I was sure my inner ear fluid had drained out.

A few calls later, we were all sorted to leave on Wednesday in style. I rushed home to pack, because, for the love of all that was holy and designer-label, I had limited beachwear and my beach bag packed with all the beach essentials had been tucked away in the high shelves: above the wardrobe where the ladder and stronger arms than mine were required to haul them down. The only way that could be done was to persuade someone of the masculine species to apply muscle and haul it down without cracking his cranium in the process.

I had Bali to look forward to. I wondered if two days on a juice diet would perform a little miracle on the three tyres that comprised my stomach, and put me as a front runner for the model upon whom they would base the female consort of the Michelin Man. Oh well, I could always use them tyres to rest my plate on while sprawled on a sunbed.

14

Of Doppelgängers and Missing Links

TUESDAY

As a day that occurred in the middle of the week, Tuesday did not seem promising when it dawned. For one, the sky was the kind of overcast that begged one to pull the covers over one's head and snore back with the open-mouthed content that only deep sleep brought. But I could hear the pint-sized one hammering at the door, begging to be let in for purposes of snuggling up and being cuddled while he tried his luck at convincing us that today was not a day that was meant to be spent getting his daily dose of the three Rs, and would be spent much more constructively should he be allowed to stay at home and watch unlimited Cartoon Network. He was allowed ten minutes of whining before he was taken into the bathroom, dunked in water and scrubbed clean.

'Wai I habtu gotu skul?' he protested. 'An wai yu can stay at home and nod go tu offiss like Pappa?'

Stung to the quick by this assault on my joblessness by my six-year-old, I felt compelled to defend myself and my lack of occupation. 'Actually, darling,' I said as I towelled him down with more ferocious intent than he deserved, 'Mamma is thinking of starting work soon. Then you can be with Jamuna the entire day after school.'

The spouse, who had hitherto been a pair of knuckles holding the newspaper, lowered it and looked at me, and then raised the paper right back to position and gravely plunged through the narrations of death, violence and mayhem on the stock exchange, reserving comment.

'Really,' trilled the child.

'Really,' I answered, in what I hoped was a reassuring tone.

'Den I can watch Cardoon Nedwurk da whole day when yu are at offis.'

Ermm. That wasn't the positive outcome of getting to work that I was thinking about, but it would have to do for now. And the child had received the news that we would be out of sight for almost a week with the kind of equanimity that had made me sob into the bath towel about being rendered redundant. His only query was if we planned to take the iPad with us, and I had no doubt that he would probably mourn the absence of the television more than he would mine. I could be carried on a bier to the crematorium and the child would wave a cursory goodbye without moving his eyes from the television screen or the iPad. Anyway. Right now, he was poured into his school uniform and dispatched to the gates, escorted by the girl Friday, while I decided to bite the bullet and speak to the husband about my need to do something constructive with my life, either through retail consultancy or the detective business.

He listened, as I thought he never would, with a fair amount of interest and appropriate nodding in the right places and then delivered his opinion, actually laying the newspaper aside to do so, which was a first.

And then he repeated what he had been saying all along. 'I just want you to be constructively occupied, Kay. And if that means doing something as dangerous as detective work, I would naturally be a little wary. You do have a sound background in marketing, why don't you look for some flexitime opportunities in that field? Until then, do whatever keeps you busy. But be careful. Don't get too involved in this police-volice business. This retail consultancy sounds good. Take it up. Tanaz is good at her work.'

I nodded eagerly, struggling to restrain myself from jumping up and slobbering him up with kisses in the manner of a huge rambunctious dog.

I needed to hunker down and pack for Bali, I told him, now that important career decisions had been discussed.

'What do you need to pack for Bali?' He laughed. 'All you need will fit into one duffel bag.' Then he sobered down from his sudden laughing fit from his rare wisecrack, which had me worried as to whether he would crack a rib while rolling around on the floor, and looked at me carefully. 'Perhaps not.'

I harrumphed.

'Kay, be sensible, okay? I'm not putting my back out carrying along stuff that won't even come out of the suitcase, because you thought that climate change would announce itself with snow while we're there in Bali. No stilettos. No boots. No wooden wedge heels. No overcoats. No "just in case". It does not get chilly there. No formal clothes. We are not going to be invited to a black-tie event on holiday. Even if we are, we will find a rental place to rent the clothes from. And, anyway, you can always buy beachwear right on the streets there.'

That put a sparkle into my eye. It was a plan. But I still needed to run out and buy the sunblock. Industrial amounts of it. I did not fancy returning tanned to nutmeg and looking like I'd been ploughing the fields. I could send the driver out for all the essentials, I told myself. I needed to get down to making lists of things to pack. If I had my list in place, all the rest was manageable. In fact, I was a firm believer that if I had a list in place, things would pack themselves.

I began hyperventilating again and barely saw the spouse pick up his squash bag and move out.

'Jamunaaa ...' I called out, to be greeted by silence. The girl had trotted off downstairs to drop the child off, I remembered. I was alone in the house, a situation which in normal course wouldn't faze me but, with the skies growling and spitting rain, was turning out to be quite eerie.

Strong gusts of wind began rattling the glass panes of the French windows. I wondered whether the girl Friday had had the wisdom to cape the offspring in his raincoat, and decided to not leave such matters to chance and called the bus lady to instruct her to extract said raincoat from the child's bag and encase him in it, ignoring all his protests to the contrary.

The stomach growled reminding me that the cook hadn't arrived yet. I advanced warily towards the kitchen, dreading the possibility that it might be one of the off-chance days when said cook decided to take an impromptu leave, resulting in the horrific prospect of me entering the kitchen and rustling up food, given that anything the girl

Friday rustled up was, in normal circumstances, consigned straight to the dustbin.

The intercom rang. Devyani announced herself. She was back. And so she had connected, albeit a day late.

'Hi, I'm back. Actually, I arrived last evening, but was so exhausted after the weekend that I actually slept all day. What was that all about – a friend of yours needing to meet me?'

'She's just someone I was chatting with about Jahnavi's disappearance and Jaya's suicide, and she thought perhaps she could help.'

'How?' The conversation was taking on hostile tones, and had none of the pleasant give-and-take of previous such conversations.

'Well, she is a detective and is generally good at putting the missing links together and figuring out the jigsaw puzzles of unexplained suicides and such ...'

'I don't think Jaya's husband would appreciate the details of why she opted for suicide. You see, no man wants to be outed as a cuckold of the first order. And he has some secrets himself that I'm sure he'd be happier didn't see the light of day. And the police are handling Jahnavi's disappearance. I'm sure they'll find out the truth. Really, Kay, it's quite crazy that you put yourself in charge of something you aren't connected with even remotely.'

Her voice was dripping acid of the variety that could cut through safe doors and eat away marble. I winced.

'Jahnavi should have known better before trying to play a double game with Jaya ...' Her voice trailed off.

'What?' I said, forgetting all the drilling of my distant youth to say 'I beg your pardon', and continued with the 'What,' on a loop, until she put me out of my misery and responded.

'Forget I said anything, Kanan, its best you don't get involved. The one who had to die, died, and the one who was responsible has gone away. It is the best thing that could happen. Except of course, for my money. Which I don't see coming back to me.'

'You never know,' I replied. 'You yourself said the police are handling the case and they'll find out. And probably be able to get your money back.'

She laughed, a mirthless sound that was short on content but long on meaning.

'Has that ever happened, Kay? Has money lost in such schemes ever been recovered by the depositors? I'm not holding my breath.'

There was the sound of something crashing in the background. 'Divyam ...' she screamed. 'How many times have I told you not to swing from the curtains ...' There was a moment's eerie silence.

'Call you later, Kay, he's just managed to crash the curtain rod into the fish tank.'

She hung up, leaving me with visions of fish flapping away frantically.

I had barely placed the intercom receiver back when it rang again, startling me out of my skin. I tucked self back into skin, gently, as I answered it again. 'Yes?'

'Madamji?' said an enquiring voice belonging to the somnambulant one of the previous morning.

'*Haan,* Ramvilas, *bolo.*'

'*Saab hain*?' He had obviously not been perched at his station because the saab in question had taken himself and his squash bag off to the club house barely half an hour ago, and had not brought sweaty self back home yet.

'Nahi, tell me, what is it about?'

'Flat no. 504 *waale saab waapas aa gaye. Aur unke saath poliss aaye hain. Unko lekar aaye hain. Saab ko bata dijiye.*'

The ears, they pricked up. I asked where the prodigal husband was headed with the accompanying police personnel and promptly placed a call to Raji to inform her of the same. We resolved to meet on the floor, where we were told the 'poliss' had taken Mr 504 apparently for questioning, or, as my overactive imagination went, to recreate the scene of the crime. I splashed some water on my face, climbed out of the nightwear into presentable-in-public trackpants and T-shirt, and hurtled down to the fifth floor, beating Raji by a second to the door to 504.

The door was ajar as we approached. We peeked inside warily. Mr 504 was sitting with his head in his hands on a sofa that urgently needed dry cleaning. I was tempted to give him the number of my sofa-laundry-wallah, who would come home and do the needful on a single call. But I desisted. I was not sure that offers of sofa cleaning would be appreciated while it seemed the police personnel in various stages of prowling around the premises were trying to put together a kind of case to help them with their investigation.

One of the party, in as civilian raiment as possible – minus the official shoes that gave him away as being a personnel of the law enforcement – was sketching what seemed to be a floor plan of the flat with many 'X'es and circles and timings scribbled across a sheet of A3-sized white paper. Questions were being rapid-fired at the hapless Mr 504, who looked like he would break into tears at any moment, and I would need to pat him on the back and say 'There, there,' sympathetically.

The police man with the mirror-finish Ray-Bans, who insisted on wearing them even though a) we were indoors and b) it was an overcast day, noticed us peeking in at the door and emerged from the premises, shutting the door carefully behind him. 'Yes, madam, *kaisey ho*?' He beamed, displaying all the thirty-two of his dentition in full paan-stained regalia.

'What is the latest development?' I asked in hushed tones, aware that some sort of an investigation was taking place behind the now-closed door.

He moved to the other end of the corridor and filled us in as briefly as he could with the details, taking off the Ray-Bans and tucking them into his pocket by one handle as delicately as one might handle a grenade with its pin out. The gist of the findings was that Mrs 504 had a twin sister, one who looked exactly like her, and about whom he said, delicately: '*Thoda dimaag ka* problem *tha*.'

That was a shock. A twin. With mental health issues. It got crazier. I needed to sit down and take a deep breath of fresh air and get the oxygen circulating through the bloodstream again. Dizziness, I had read somewhere, was caused by the lack of oxygen in the brain. I deposited myself on a convenient step and breathed deeply. Raji and the inspector looked at me with concern.

'Are you all right, Kay?' Raji asked. 'You must really get a full-body check-up done. You get tired too soon.'

It was not the appropriate moment to tell her I was un-breakfasted and had done the minute-mile down the stairs to get there before her.

'Yes, yes, I'm fine – just a spot of low blood pressure, I think,' I replied, putting my chin up bravely and letting my jaw quiver for a moment to show them how brave I was being by putting all thought of my own health aside in order to poke my rather stodgy nose into matters that didn't concern me at all.

'You must be hypertensive, not low,' said Raji, in the infernal manner she had when anything related to health came up – she was the sort who'd be well acquainted with the encyclopaedia of medical conditions and probably visited medical websites for recreation.

'I'm fine,' I dismissed bravely, not wanting Raji to divert the topic to the lifestyle changes I needed to make while attempting to convince me to give up salt and all things fattening in order to cut down the body fat percentage to zero, which would make me look, in the mater's words from the last time I had dieted down to a respectable BMI: 'TellMeWhatTheDoctorSaidHowLongDoYouHave'.

'Never mind me, Raji, let's hear what the good inspector is kindly sharing with us.'

She cleaned out the earwax, metaphorically speaking of course, cocked her ears and looked at the man with rapt attention. I am sure I bore the same expression as she did.

The man cleared his throat in preparation for what would be, we presumed, a complicated story.

'You remember we found two dead bodies? One from the nala behind …'

'Yes, yes,' I replied eagerly.

'Now, we don't know who is who – who was the one who jumped and who was the one who was fished out of the nala – but we do know that this flat was under the name of the missus and her mister. He wanted to sell and move away, and put the sister into a home. She didn't want to leave her sister. There were constant fights about this. Now who died first, whether the husband killed his wife or she jumped, we are trying to find out. He swears he didn't do anything. And yes, your housekeeping staff was paid off to ensure the undisturbed use of the refuge area. Strange that your committee members weren't paying attention.' He paused for breath. 'You did meet her the day after they had a fight. Did you notice anything strange?'

I looked at Raji, puzzled. I cast my mind back to that day, to the two of us doing our neighbourly duty of going up to the lady and enquiring politely about her and the screams, and all I could remember was that she seemed very sleepy and rather irate at being woken up. I had mentioned it to them earlier.

I mentioned so again to the man.

'Sleepy?' he said. 'What time was it?'

I informed him.

'Yes,' said Raji, backing me, 'it was rather a strange time to be sleepy, unless she was on medications. She did take a rather long time to open the door.'

He nodded his head wisely and scratched his chin, and then proceeded to pick flakes of dandruff off his scalp in the gentle delicate manner which fooled no one that he was aiding thought by the process. I shuddered unwittingly and moved out of speck-falling range.

'Thank you, inspector,' I said, dragging Raji out of his immediate radius. 'I hope you can solve the case soon.'

'What do you think happened, did he kill his wife and her sister?' Raji hissed as soon as we were out of earshot.

'I don't know,' I replied. I seriously didn't. I needed to speak with Runa about this, she would be able to take the tangled skeins and unravel them into something that made sense. Right now, my head was just a minefield on tap dance with women running on staircases and jumping off buildings and into canals slick with dark industrial effluent sludge, which probably had Gollum-like life forms growing within, getting ready to take over the earth and emerge one innocuous day asking to be taken to our ruler, instead of doing the sensible thing and visiting a plastic surgeon.

And then it hit me: the husband of Mrs 504 could probably have pushed her into the canal one morning when they went for their morning walk, returned without her and unlocked the door of the refuge area, letting the other sister run wild knowing she was manic and suicidal. And she had probably run high and low in her disorientation before jumping off, from perhaps the roof or the refuge area itself, given that it was open without windows to keep in those who wanted to jump out, and the fact that the lock was still firmly in place.

And most importantly, the screams had stopped the day she had jumped. And also, swirling, in another case of suicide within my cranium, were thoughts of Jaya Bhatia, who had killed herself because someone knew more than she should have and was blackmailing her about it. And I had a very clear idea as to who that someone could be.

I called up Runa and asked her clearly, 'Who gave you the lead to put me on to Devyani? Maybe you should ask that person some questions to get to the bottom of this case.' For once, Runa heard me out without a word interrupting my sentence before it could end. 'What makes you say that, Kay?' she asked.

'Just a hunch, Rune. Just a hunch,' I replied, feeling all the bits and pieces slide into place, much like the complicated circuitry manning the vault door at Gringotts. And behind the door that was getting locked was a lone figure, one with a history of moving homes too regularly, and a husband whom no one had seen, and no one had heard. Someone who knew more than she would tell, and someone who lived three buildings away from me.

'I had a theory,' Runa said slowly, very slowly. 'But what you just said changes everything around completely. I need to check this out. I will call you back once I do.'

15

Pieces Coming Together Like in the Kaleidoscope of Her Childhood

WEDNESDAY

The news of the police being in conversation with me and Raji had created a buzz in the society that reminded one of bees on street crack. I could hear them in asides when I was on my way to the park the previous evening, taking the kid downstairs for his daily round of unstructured play – aka kicking and fighting with everything under four feet, including a surly little person who was employed as caretaker in one of the apartments leased as a company guest house – and the infinite round of back-and-forth Yo Mamma jokes, which lead to an even more animated round of fisticuffs.

Thankfully, there seemed to be a lull in the monsoon for the past couple of days. This had led to some heavy-duty drying of musty carpets and bedcovers hung out on balconies in the morning to catch the noonday sun, and a Jamuna kept on lookout to ensure that the pigeons didn't decide to consecrate the stuff being aired out with droppings that would then entail another round of washing and airing.

The older, more venerable inhabitants of the building complex conferred hastily about having a havan done on the premises to rid the building of any lingering stray souls that might haunt the place, given that there had been two-odd deaths in the immediate past and one death in the periphery a few months ago.

'Bad Vastu,' Mrs Kapur said, nodding her head in her 'I told you so' manner, her lips pursed so disapprovingly, she could give Mick Jagger a complex.

The spouse moaned and groaned about the complex being in the newspapers twice within the week for all the wrong reasons. 'It's going to depreciate the value of the apartment, mind you,' he moped as he read the report tucked away right at the bottom of the city pages of the daily newspaper, his chin clanging to the floor in disgust. 'Why do they always have to mention the name of the complex? Can't they be happy just naming the locality?'

His cup of tea, strong and sugared, lay untouched and rapidly congealing to the kind of consistency that would ensure it got chucked into the kitchen sink and that a new one was brewed to right freshness.

'Drink your tea,' I urged with misplaced thrift that never kicked into action when it came to 70-per-cent-off sales, which normally left me with more stuff clogging up my wardrobe, given that I was an optimistic soul and estimated it would be a only matter of time before I managed to squeeze myself into the new purchases, give or take a couple of weeks of dedicated running and a drastic cutting-down of all dietary intake. That, more often than not, would result in my crashing down with a nasty bout of some illness, which in turn would result in a weight loss so negligible that it would concentrate its effects on my face – making me look like a famine victim from the neck up, but an escapee from a fat farm neck down.

I was informed in hushed whispers by my driver, who had in turn found out from a car washer who in turn had got it in good faith from the security guard – who had been standing right there unnoticed while the police were confabulating amongst themselves – that the second body, the one who flung herself, or was flung from the stairs, was that of the twin, who had apparently been locked up there occasionally by Mr and Mrs 504 because of a tendency to get violent. She was the one undergoing psychiatric treatment.

Murkier details were emerging. And the cause of the occasional mournful screams was demystified. It fitted in a bit with my theory of Mr 504 pushing his wife into the canal and then killing her sister as well. But the man had been crying so haplessly, it seemed hard to believe he would commit a double crime only to ruin his tear ducts in repentance.

There was also the matter of the strangulation marks on the neck of the twin who had fallen, and the fact that I had seen her on the stairs a short while before she jumped off, albeit in different clothes than her body had been found in.

I could not contain myself any longer and dialled Runa, and despite her initial reluctance to hear the details of the story I had pieced together, she listened with as much grace as she could summon.

'Let me go ask my sources in the police, only for you, Kay, you know I'm not doing gratis work any more,' she said, unable to resist the charm of a convoluted double-death on a single premise. 'Any idea which body was whose, the wife or the sister? Who died first? Did she jump from the terrace or was she pushed off?' I tried mentally to connect the dots, something I wasn't very good at, and just kept wondering whether polka dots were the latest, and whether I really needed a bow-fronted top with salmon polka dots on an off-white base with puffed sleeves, which looked adorable but which I suspected would definitely push me into vaudeville territory.

'The sister, they tell me. The wife I feel was pushed into the canal by her husband or fell into it all on her own and sank quickly and drowned before she could be saved. It is pretty deserted back there in the mornings. And she was rather heavy. I also overheard the investigators say that the landing spot was not concurrent with a fall from the terrace.'

'Which is why I keep telling you, Kay, either stop eating so much or don't wander around water bodies deeper than six feet without a lifeguard at hand.'

I bristled through her chuckling at the other end and informed her coldly that I was off on a five-day break starting that night, and that I wished her luck in figuring out the reason behind Jaya Bhatia's suicide and disconnected the line. It was a first. I had never ever hung up, metaphorically speaking of course, on Runa. Ever. A horrific vision of her chasing me with her khukri, brandished aloft for my impertinence, flashed across the mind's eye. I shrugged it off with new-found insouciance. I was off to Bali. Nothing could faze me.

The child, in the interim, having demolished his mug of warm-milk-turned-ice-cold, strode around demanding from me a firm commitment as to whether he would be taken to the mall in the evening, and if so what was the departure time he should plan for.

'Okay,' conceded the father, after much whining at nose level had reduced him to squinting around head of child to get a view of the newspaper, child having infiltrated the space in between. 'We will see about the mall later, have your breakfast now and get ready for school. Naani will be here in the afternoon and we will be leaving at night, after you go to sleep.'

Having been reminded of the fact that we would be off on holiday while he would be left behind to do 'boreding' things like attend school and complete homework, he frowned and threw one of his rolling-on-the-floor tantrums, which could only be quelled by a slight upward tilt of the father's eyebrow, and then meekly pulled on his school bag and took self towards elevator bank.

'Okay, bud ged fer me two-two toys from yer holyday.'

Two-two toys having been promised generously and two more for good behaviour as conveyed by the good naani in question, he moved off with a sticky kiss planted onto my cheek.

'Mamma,' he enquired kindly, in the commanding tone that only children acquire early before life whoops them one on the butt, 'you will go swimming in the sea?'

I nodded, seeing his eyes widen in wonder. The child was afflicted with an inexplicable fear of the sea. He got it from me. I was afraid of both the sea and the pool and the max I could do without going breathless and having the lifeguards dive in to save me from drowning was to make sure I didn't get into water deeper than my knees.

I was not of the species who inhabited pools as a naiad in a one-piece, colour-blocked swimsuit. For one, I did not swim. In a previous incarnation, I had surely met my end in the kind of watery grave that resulted from being flung off high cliffs. My donning of swimsuits was reserved for vacations, when no one in the immediate vicinity of the pool would hyuck-hyuck uncontrollably and carry tales back to the parents about the 'aunty who was scared of going in the deep', bolstered amiably by the spawn of the womb, who would add his two bits to the discussion by recounting instances on holiday when the spouse had attempted to teach me to swim and ended up being almost choked and drowned as I shinned up his person in a bid to keep my head above the water. Needless to say, swimming classes never happened ever again. I now spent such afternoons by the club poolside downing endless rounds of peach iced tea or cold coffee depending on how guilty I'd been feeling about my lack of calcium.

Speaking of which, I had that appointment with my nutritionist on Monday I needed to cancel. I had not sent in my diet-recall chart. I had not made my diet-recall chart. And for the life of me, I had not stuck to my prescribed diet. I looked around to find a hole in the ground to sink into and pull in after me. I scurried into the kitchen to distract myself with food. The cook was busy chopping some chillies for aloo parathas with the kind of heavy-handedness that was a dead giveaway that some major fracas had ensued between her and the resident domestic help.

'Bhabhi, *isko bolo* to stay out of the kitchen when I'm in it, or else I cannot cook,' she exclaimed the moment she spotted me in the vicinity.

'Arey, are we ever going to get any breakfast or are they planning to spend the entire morning arguing?' grumbled the spouse from the dining table, where he had transplanted himself with his newspapers. 'Why don't you sack both of them and hire two new ones. I am fed up to the gills of this daily drama.'

What was a house without a little raised decibel level, I thought to myself, and where in heavens did he think I would find not one but two replacements: one for a full-timer and another for a two-times-a-day cook who could actually cook? Good cooks and household help were more precious than gold and diamonds and entire war strategies had been plotted to lure the efficient ones from their employers by unscrupulous neighbours and co-residents. Which was why I went around dropping details of Jamuna's inefficiency and the cook's tendency to over-salt and lay on the oils with a heavy hand at regular intervals.

Jamuna, sniffing a fight, marched in from the bedroom – where she was folding laundered clothes and inserting them into appropriate wardrobes – and began spewing out a volley of hissing invective under her breath to the effect that the cook ate up the best of the previous day's leftovers and had left her with no lunch yesterday.

I held the 'baying for each other's blood' parties at arm's length and insisted that breakfast had to be put on the table or else there would be no lunch ever for either of them. Resolving squabbles between domestic help was not the ideal way to spend a workday morning and I hissed at both of them to do the guns-at-dawn outside in the long corridor beyond the front door. I also told them I would personally ration out the leftovers between both of them henceforth to avoid such squabbles and that, seriously, Jamuna needed to control her intake seeing as she had morphed from a skinny wraith into one who needed to go sideways through security gates at malls whenever we visited one. An uneasy truce reigned.

Bathed and dressed in white linen trousers and a white strappy hakoba lace top, I was ready for the last-minute shopping before packing. The spouse was jabbing animatedly into his touchscreen with a ferocity that caused me to look over his shoulder into the screen.

'Flat no. 504,' he said apologetically. 'The new owner is on my case to take possession of that house. God knows why he's so hell-bent on getting immediate possession. We still haven't got all the transfer papers and he wants to move in. And now the police are involved with that case of the suicide of the lady who owned it.'

'The chap who came round the other morning?' I thought back to the raised voices and the veiled threat he'd delivered while exiting our apartment. The stomach churned a trifle in anxiety.

I accompanied the spouse off to his half-day at work, asking to be dropped off round the corner at the hypermarket with the long list he had given me of things I was to pack and definitely not forget. I took myself down to the medical stores to pick up essentials. Sunblock, sun cream, mosquito-repellent spray. Breath mints.

The lift stopped with an infernal chiming and the television chappie, who had housewives swooning and elderly ladies beaming affectionately whenever he came in immediate vicinity, clambered in, bearing with him a cloud of perfume that immediately went hammer and tongs for my limbic centre and roused the migraine demons snoring contentedly behind my eyeballs. I winced, my nose wrinkled, and I retreated into a distant corner hoping to escape the fumes but to no avail.

There were primary lift offenders, like those who emitted noiseless stink bombs and looked you in the eye with the innocent expression of one straight out of the delivery room. The other category of offenders included the ones who refused to make an acquaintance with deo. This man fell into the third category: folks who doused themselves with strong perfumes and then entered a cloistered space with you. While they themselves had no idea about the intensity of the fumes they emitted, the hapless co-traveller in said closed confined space would be dropping down like a fly in a bottle, or feeling the contents of their stomach churn violently and threaten to disgorge on the spanking-new shoes of the bearer of noxious odours. The TV star, his face glowing with the kind of rosiness it should be illegal for men to possess without rouge being slathered on, grinned at us with the kind of winced politeness that could mean either forced cordiality or acute bowel discomfort.

'Terrible things happening here,' he said, opening the conversation.

The spouse nodded with similar winced politeness. 'There's no telling what can happen and where.'

'And where is the husband now?' the TV chap continued.

'The police have taken him in for questioning,' the spouse replied, based on the little information he had.

They both nodded uncomfortably and went back to examining fixed points in the roof and the control panel of said lift. I felt my stomach heave from the olfactory assault. I covered my nose and tried not to breathe in too deep. The spouse looked at me with some concern.

Finally, the lift settled comfortably on the ground floor and the doors slid open. A right ruckus was on, which could have raised the dead. The voice leading the fray was that of Mrs Kapur, punctuated by the annoying yaps of the infernal nipper of ankles, Silky.

As we spilt out of the lift into the sunlight-dappled lobby, me gasping for precious fresh air, we saw a crowd ringed around the security desk with the cowering little man bending backwards as the rather strapping Mrs Kapur held forth loud and clear about how she had almost been killed by the mounds of furniture lying in the lobby, which rightfully speaking had no business being in the lobby but in fact belonged within a residence or within a truck. The spouse went forth to question the logic of random furniture pieces clogging up the premises and who was the human who belonged to said armoires and small sofa with dreadful leopard-print cover.

'*Koi saab hai, kehte hai woh* 504 *mein* shift *ho rahe hain. Par humne* allow *nahi kiya*,' he said with the brave air of the lion heart who had stood steadfast in the face of mortal danger and emerged unscathed. I looked out of the glass pane with horror to see the rude Bermuda man standing outside, puffing away on a vile cancer stick. The spouse blanched visibly. 'Look at the cheek of the man,' he muttered under his breath and stomped off to have a word with him.

By the looks of it, many words would be more like it. My immediate instinct was to exit the lobby and head towards the car, but my eye was drawn to a beautiful armoire with intricate carved work on the doors and gently curved legs. I moved towards it, touching its surface to feel the delicacy of the work. The wood was old teak, solid and glowing, and I wanted to chuck the armoire into my handbag and sneak it home. It was so beautiful.

Out of the blue, the Bermuda man, clad today in a pair of cargos and an assault-to-the-eye fluorescent orange shirt, stomped into the lobby, leaving a flummoxed spouse in mid-sentence, jaw wide open.

'Who is not allowing my furniture to be moved up?' he bellowed, and all that was needed to complete the imagery was a ring through his nostrils and some steam emanating from them. All heads swivelled in unison towards me like I had issued restraining orders and I gulped.

'Well, I was just admiring your lovely furniture, which incidentally is not supposed to be cluttering up the lobby area,' I replied.

Smelling an argument, the crowds swelled. Drivers and dog walkers collected at various porches and jambs. The Bermuda man recognized me. 'Oh, Mrs Mehra, how are you, madam?' The volte-face caused the entire air supply in the lobby to get sucked in by a collective gasp.

The spouse, who had taken a quick detour into the society office, emerged and, with the smoothness that had me fall for him like a sack of bricks all those years ago, interjected himself into the conversation. 'There remains the small matter of you not being allowed to shift into the apartment without the police verification papers in place and society permission letter for sale.'

The porcine man fixed a glare of fire on the spouse, who, I'm proud to stay, did not wither into ash under that glare, which could have burnt a lesser man to a crisp.

The spouse looked back at me and jerked his head towards the exit to indicate I was to move towards the parking lot, and I did exactly the opposite and stayed put in my most fishwifely pose, with one hand on the hip and the other hand tapping the armoire in question.

The spouse, with a jerk of his head, instructed the security to bring in additional forces, and the stand-off looked like it would continue for a while. And I needed to go buy sunblock. I unhooked hand from hip and hailed a passing autorickshaw to take me to the hypermarket. I needed to pick up industrial-sized tubes of sunblock.

Why the obsession with sunblock, you ask? What? Don't you know that ultraviolet radiation is the biggest cause of skin ageing? Each second you expose yourself to sunlight, you're signing up for some wrinkles getting. And not to mention the effects on your hair, it dried it to straw. I reminded myself to pack my sun visor in leopard print and a selection of sunglasses to match my mood for the four days we were there.

Just as I trotted down the aisles, searching for Banana Boat, SPF 50+, the phone trilled in my handbag.

I fished out the infernal instrument of bondage to the world and saw Runa's name. 'Where are you, Kay?' she began without any preamble.

'In the hypermarket,' I trilled back. 'I'm off to Bali tonight, for four days, did I tell you I'd won this trip for two all-expenses paid at the lucky draw, and the husband just wouldn't give me a proper date when he could take off and finally he told me just yesterday that he could take the rest of the week off if I could manage it and so I did?' I paused to catch my breath. I also realized that it had been perhaps the longest sentence I had spoken to Runa without her shutting me up and changing the topic of discussion to something relevant to the case. Perhaps we would be able to bond someday again as two girls, or as much as a girl Runa could be without sneering at the need to get regular exfoliation. 'And there's all chaos going on in the building,' I added before she could get a word in edgewise. 'There were police in the lobby, they took one guy, this really fat and ugly dork, away. And the lobby is cluttered with furniture, completely, it's insane. I almost tripped over a low stool and broke a nail. I just had a manicure done a couple of days ago.' I paused. 'Runa, could you find out anything further on the deaths in our building complex?' I asked, knowing well that Runa, with her penchant to trawl police stations ferreting nuggets of information off cops, would definitely have more on the murders than I, even if I did live right there.

'I have. I will tell you about that too in a bit if you are quite done with all you have to say,' she said petulantly. Nothing was going to dampen my spirit today, no Runa with her knickers in a twist, no Bermuda Shorts. I perched on an available vacant shelf and listened.

'Why did you ask me to check with whoever had given me the lead to Devyani, yesterday, Kay?'

'Just a hunch I had. Did you?'

'I did,' she said, and drew out a long-drawn out sigh. 'This Devyani of yours is a true piece of work. And there is no husband. She lives off this money she extracts. The husband living abroad is a myth. She divorced her husband when her son was two and since then has been in a series of relationships. With married men ...' She paused to allow the importance of what she was saying to sink right in. 'Rich married men.'

'Jaya's husband?' I asked.

'Yes,' she answered. 'He was one of them. Devyani had begun flaunting her affair with her husband to Jaya. Jaya thought he would leave her for Devyani. And then, when Jaya killed herself and Jahnavi confronted Devyani about driving Jaya to it, she threatened to go to the police about Jahnavi's illegal moneylending business and made her go underground.'

I had been expecting that, somewhat, ever since my conversation the previous morning with Devyani.

'Jahnavi panicked. Jaya's husband hired me because he suspected Jaya had learnt about his affair with Devyani and wondered if Devyani had indeed pushed Jaya to suicide. Devyani had, in fact, moved out of the neighbourhood after a rather unpleasant showdown with the society members objecting to his visits to her flat at odd hours. Bingo, Jahnavi told him the other day that Devyani was blackmailing her too, and when I called him yesterday, he told me he wanted the case closed. He's over that affair, he never realized his fling could push his wife to suicide, and now Devyani needs to find a new sugar daddy.'

I gasped. 'So Jahnavi has been found, has she?'

'Yes, she's back and she's called up all those whom she owed money to and spoken with them, and she's paying back people in bits and pieces. So that is settled.'

Quite a tangled web: a wife learning of her husband having an affair with her best friend, terrified she was going to be dumped for the best friend and then taking her own life; women being blackmailed into parting with huge sums of money or risk their nefarious affairs being revealed with proof. The head spun. It was a good thing that I was seated on a solid surface, else I would have cracked a tile on impact.

'So,' I replied, 'I guess, the kitty group will miss me.'

Runa laughed. 'Or you will miss the lunches.'

'Both, I guess,' I replied. 'So this case is closed? I can stop being friends with Devyani, since I'm not having an affair nor laundering any money she could blackmail me with?'

'Kay.' Runa chuckled, a chuckle that would have hyenas fleeing for cover in terror. 'Perhaps you should have an affair. A mindless fling. It would shake things up for you a bit. Make you live on the wild side.'

I shook my head determinedly. The only living on the wild side I was going to do was to wear animal print, and let my hair air-dry with no serum.

'You must tell me what made you tell me to ask the person who put us onto Devyani.'

'It was just something she said in a conversation last evening, and her tone. She was suddenly defensive and prickly and very reluctant to meet you. I felt there was something she was hiding, and wondered how her name had come up in the investigation and not any of the other twelve women in the group.'

'That's what you have which I don't: a something that makes people tell you things they wouldn't ever tell me. And you have an instinct about people, and a natural curiosity about things, which is the primary requirement for this business. Want to work with me on a permanent basis? As an associate?'

The heart skipped a couple of beats and then speeded up into tachycardia. 'Me? You think I could do it?'

She paused. 'You need a lot of training. And you need to stop vamoosing off on holidays without a "by your leave" in the middle of cases, but I think we will work well as a team. And I can't offer you much money. Just a percentage of what I charge the client.'

That was high praise coming from Runa. 'I must check with the spouse,' I muttered uncertainly, promising to do so when I returned home.

As it turned out, the Bermuda Shorts man had been stopped from taking possession of the flat, seeing as the flat was the location of a police investigation and his papers were not in order. The lobby had been divested of all the clutter and one could walk without fear of tripping over low boxes and smashing one's nose in.

The latest on the death of Mrs 504 and her sister, as per my driver and unconfirmed by the police, was that the wife had been pushed into the canal and the sister had been strangulated and thrown out of the refuge area to make it seem like a suicide and the crime had been committed by the husband, who wanted to get rid of both of them and then get out of town. It seemed rather easy: one would seem a suicide, and the other would be an unidentifiable decomposed body that would go under the police radar. For a murderer, though, he had been silly enough to book his flight tickets to Delhi in his own name, and use his credit cards for the transactions. The police had swept down on him when he had been having a hearty breakfast at his brother's home in Noida, and whisked him away for interrogation. I didn't blame him from wanting to get away from the craziness, though I drew the line at murder.

That night as we fastened our seat belts, the spouse gave me one of his A-grade lectures on how he soundly disapproved of all this play-acting at being a detective. His regular speech, with the sequence of the words shifted around a bit. And then the airhostess came around smiling gently and checking for fastened seat belts and upright seats and window shutters put up before take-off, and he stopped his mini lecture to smile graciously at her as she passed.

'I have a few people who made a presentation for funding to set up an experiential marketing firm the other day, and it seemed like something that would be right up your alley. All you need to do is tell the client how to improve his brand experience and this involves checking out the services and evaluating their services. Or get into image consulting. I'm sure you could rock it.'

And the phone rang, unwilling to be ignored.

'Switch the phone off, Kay,' the spouse hissed, 'we are about to take off.'

'I can't,' I said, the mommy guilt in me imagining fire and mayhem and Kabir tightrope-walking across balconies. 'It could be Kabir.'

It was Runa. I beamed.

'Kay,' said Runa, when I answered. 'Since you're off to Bali, I have a case there. A honeymooning couple. The husband just seems to have packed his bags and left the hotel room in the middle of the night. He hasn't left the country and his wife is going mad trying to track him down. I'm WhatsApping and emailing you all the details.'

'Do that,' I answered and disconnected the phone with a swift, professional air. A soft smile played on my lips and I looked at the husband. 'I have a new case,' I said, watching as the expression of horror and disbelief played out across his face, and quite revelling in it. 'In Bali.'

'For God's sake, Kay …' he began, throwing his hands up in exasperation of the order where you are allowed to express your exasperation but know in your bones that nothing will come of it. 'Don't ruin this holiday with this detective nonsense. I've had it up to here with this craziness. Surely there are better things you could do?'

Like all legitimate spousal complaints, that too would be roundly ignored.

I smiled gently at him, as he turned his face away in a huff and buried himself nose-deep into the in-flight magazine. He would come to realize I enjoyed this official poking of my rather prominent nose into everyone's business, I told myself, and that this was something I could do and do well at that. I switched off the mobile, put my eye mask on and went off to sleep.

Life was good again.

Acknowledgements

So many people. So many.

But I'll keep this short.

To Suhail Mathur at The Book Bakers who found this work a home.

To Prerna Gill at HarperCollins who patiently went through my manuscript, cutting it down to size and coherence with acuity and gentleness.

To Sanchita Jain for the absolutely lovely cover, that completely captures the mood of the book.

To my family for putting up with me. It is quite a drag to have a writer in the family, we're miserably unsocial company wanting nothing but to be left to our books and our computers in splendid isolation.

And finally, to my readers. I couldn't be without you.

About the Author

An author, TEDx speaker, columnist and mentor, Kiran Manral in previous avatars, has been a journalist, researcher, festival curator and entrepreneur. She has received multiple awards, such as the Women Achievers Award by Young Environmentalists Association and the International Women's Day Award 2018 from ICUNR and the Ministry of Women and Child Welfare, Government of India, for excellence in the field of writing.